WAIT A LONELY LIFETIME

WAIT A LONELY LIFETIME

•

Leigh Verrill-Rhys

AVALON BOOKS
NEW YORK

Published by Avalon Books,
an imprint of Thomas Bouregy & Co., Inc.
New York, NY

Library of Congress Cataloging-in-Publication Data

Verrill-Rhys, Leigh.
   Wait a lonely lifetime / Leigh Verrill-Rhys.
        p. cm.
   ISBN 978-0-8034-7402-4 (hardcover : acid-free paper)
   I. Title.
   PS3622.E765W35 2012
   813'.6—dc23

                                    2011047495

PRINTED IN THE UNITED STATES OF AMERICA
ON ACID-FREE PAPER
BY RR DONNELLEY, HARRISONBURG, VIRGINIA

*In loving memory of my father, Captain
Thomas Anthony Verrill, Sr., U.S. Army*

Acknowledgments

With gratitude to my editor, Lia Brown, of Avalon Books, the only other person to have read this book before now. DR, whose continuing support and belief makes him the rightest guy. PL, who kept the flame, and LS, who presented me with my most treasured literary prize.

Chapter One

Sylviana met her friend's steadfast stare for a long, dry moment. "So, you think he's dead."

"Sylvi, it's been fifteen years. That's what happens to lots of soldiers."

Sylviana looked over the balcony of the restaurant onto Ghirardelli Square. "How did you know? I mean, how did you find out what happened, what Eric did?"

Aggy pushed her fork around her salad plate for a few moments. "He was kind of cute, and I didn't think you were interested. Turns out he wasn't interested in me either—and not in the kind of life we were all leading then, anyway. I don't know how I heard or who from, Sylvi. Someone gave me his phone number—Steve, maybe—but I only tried calling him once. A few months later, I just heard from someone that he'd packed in his job at the insurance company and re-enlisted. So what else but dead can you expect? All these guys are just cannon fodder for one bigheaded politico or another. Didn't you know he'd gone back into the Army? Steve brought him to the parties—didn't he tell you?"

"Steven hardly mentioned his name after Eric disappeared, like he had never existed." Sylviana rubbed the side of her nose and along her cheekbone.

"And you've been carrying a torch for this guy for how long? Since your divorce was final?"

"Since I met him, Aggy. Since that first party at Frankie's show."

"Holy cow, Sylvi. That's some torch. The whole time you were married to Steven?"

"It wasn't like that, Aggy. I loved Steven—it's just that, since the divorce and dating a few guys, I can't get Eric Wasserman's face out of my mind. No one else has come close to what I felt the first time I saw him."

"You sure had a funny way of showing you were interested in him, Sylvi."

"What do you mean? I talked to him for hours. I couldn't take my eyes off him."

"Maybe, but never without a pack of baying wolves around you. Poor guy couldn't get very close."

"That's not how I remember it," Sylviana replied.

"Then you've been dreaming. Eric was about the hunkiest soldier any of us had ever seen, and the only girl he saw in the room—you—scarcely seemed to give him a glance. Once Steve Langdon came on to the scene, that was it for you."

"But that's not true. I didn't talk to Steven. I talked to Eric Wasserman—endlessly—though he barely said a word. I probably didn't give him a chance to," she moaned.

"That's not the way I saw it. But it doesn't really matter anymore, does it? If Eric's *not* dead, he's probably married with a family," Aggy told her. "Shy guys like him do that too. Don't know a good thing and can't stay out of trouble."

There was nothing else Sylviana could say to Aggy. Her best friend from kindergarten had always been radical, cut-the-corn and get on with it, anti-war, anti-nuclear, anti-fascist, anti-establishment. Sylviana ran her fingers around the base of her wineglass. Her daughters were safe at home with her parents, and she was baring her soul to the only woman she knew who wouldn't laugh in her face.

She knew her ex-husband's military record. She knew his unit members and a couple of the people he hadn't written out of his life the day his discharge came through. Eric Wasserman was the only one who'd appeared on the scene and stuck around for a few weeks, come to a few parties, captured her heart, and then disappeared forever. Steven Langdon had been quick to let her know that *he* wasn't going anywhere out of her life fast. He'd swept her off her feet with his avid courtship, and months later, marrying him had seemed like the best idea at the time. Twelve years and two little girls later, she'd asked for a divorce.

During her lunch hour, the Monday following her talk with Aggy, Sylvi pushed open the door of the Army recruiting office four blocks from her office. The soldier at the desk glanced up, gave her a quick smile, and looked back down at his paperwork. When his eyes indicated a chair in front of the desk, she positioned herself on the edge, folding her hands over her shoulder bag.

"I'm not here to enlist," she said, then wished she hadn't.

The recruitment officer didn't smile. "No, ma'am."

"I'm looking for someone."

"I'm sorry, ma'am, but we don't have that kind of information here. Classified, unless you're family."

"I'm not family. He was a friend. He *is* a friend."

"Sorry, ma'am. Can't help you."

"If I *was* family? If we just lost touch? Circumstances? Relocated?"

He studied her face for a while. "There are a couple of groups that reunite service families, ma'am." He pulled a card from a drawer and laid it on the desk in front of her. "They won't tell you anything outright, but they may be able to contact the soldier you're looking for. It's up to him then."

Sylviana drew the card toward her and couldn't conceal the trembling of her hand. "Thank you. You're very kind."

"Good luck, ma'am."

April 10
San Francisco

Dear Eric,
I know you won't remember me, but we met about fifteen years ago. My name is Sylviana Innocenti Langdon.

The letter had been on Wasserman's desk for two days, in his pocket for another, then held unopened in his hand for half an hour before the feeling that one of his unit had shoved a bayonet into his gut and was twisting it around finally subsided. Ten more minutes passed before his thumb ripped through the last fraction of glue, but his hand was still shaking so badly, the single sheet of pale blue paper refused to be taken out. He finally worked it free, crumpling a corner, and smoothed it on his thigh. As soon as it unfolded, he read her married name, and the bayonet jammed straight through to his spine.

"Captain?"

He lifted his eyes from the blur of ink. "What is it, Clee?"

"It's Martinelli, sir. Wants to know what to—"

"Tell her, I'll be right there." He shoved the letter back into the envelope, pressed it down into his pocket, and felt the barbs driving into his chest. He took it out and tossed it onto the desk. The envelope skittered across the surface and caught in the pages of the duty roster, face up. *S.I. Langdon, 81 Hill Street, San Francisco.*

Why is she doing this?

"Where's Martinelli?"

"Down by the vehicle dump."

"What's she doing there?"

"That's her assignment, Captain."

Wasserman looked at his second in command for a moment. They'd been a team for two years. He knew Lieutenant Cleonina Jones as well as he'd known any one of his lieutenants. Better. Whatever was going on, she wasn't part of it. "What does Martinelli want to know? Never mind. I'll go down. Need a walk, anyway."

Clee walked back to her desk, shuffled through papers, and watched Captain Wasserman through the open door until he was out of sight at the end of the camp before she leaned over enough to see into his office and the letter on the desk that hadn't come from his sister. "Sure is pretty handwriting."

Eric was nowhere near the dump by the time he raised his eyes. Not a word from Steve Langdon for three—almost four—years and now, this. *What kind of joke is this?* The vehicle dump was on the other side of the camp, camouflaged in trees and under nets—coolest spot in the valley, now that the winds had died down. The combat support unit captain straightened his back and headed in the direction he'd meant to go, keeping his eyes on the vineyards on the hillsides.

Martinelli wasn't in sight. He ducked under the strips of camouflage and called the second lieutenant by name. The wheeled creeper swept out from under a truck. Hard to believe anyone that small could be such a good mechanic. Of course, everyone was tiny compared to six feet four inches Captain Eric D.D. Wasserman. Even the biggest of the combat unit didn't look him straight in the eye without tilting his chin a bit.

Martinelli jumped up in front of him and dusted off her backside. Her grin broke through the fog in his brain—pure, fresh, San Francisco fog—and he grinned back. She pointed in one direction at the oily wreckage of a truck and hooked her finger at a ratchet-jockey in the other. Whatever the private had failed to fix, he wasn't owning up to it until Martinelli had raked him through the eastern European dust for a good half hour.

"Well? Who's it from?"

"Who's what from, Angel?" Clee shoved the drawer of the cabinet with her hip and pulled her CO's office door shut so that Private Angel Watts couldn't walk in.

"Don't be coy, Jones. Everyone in the unit knows he's gotten a letter, and it's not from Lodi. Scuttlebutt says he's got a sweetheart out there."

"Scuttlebutt is wrong."

"Scuttlebutt says it even smelled nice."

"Scuttlebutt wouldn't know a good smell from the latrine."

"The least you can do is tell me if he opened that envelope yet." Private Watts sidled to the door and cupped her hands to the rippled glass.

"What are you talking about? He opened it—ages ago. What do you think? He's some kind of kid?"

"What's in it?"

"How should I know? Whatever it is, it's private. Just like everybody else's mail."

"Let's have a look," Angel said, clamping her hand around the doorknob and easing the latch free. "You're going to know, anyway, sometime."

"No way," Clee hissed, yanking the door solidly against the frame. "One, I would never do that to him. Two, he'd know the second he opened the door."

"Well, how are we going to know what's going on?"

"Just like every time, everything, and everyone else, Angel. We'll find out when Captain Wasserman is good and ready to tell us."

That didn't happen before mail call put another pale blue envelope on the CO's desk, on top of company and field dispatches, requisitions and requests. Eric didn't meet Clee's gaze but felt her staring at him, drilling a hole in his neck with her cocoa brown eyes, the same color as her skin. He didn't flinch when he pushed the square aside. He didn't even look up when she sighed, folded her arms, and went back to her desk. All the clicking and clattering on her keyboard and the constant whirr of the printer didn't break through the blank in his brain, like it had been blown out. All he could do was slide documents back and forth, stare at lines of type he couldn't read, wait for something to catch him before he dropped like a grenade, that moment before the sound of the explosion hit him, when the ground just rocked.

"Are you going to take this call, sir?"

"Yeah, put 'em through. Who is it?"

"I told you, sir. It's the colonel."

"Yeah, yes, right. Afternoon, Colonel."

"How's it going down there, Eric?"

"Good, sir. No problems."

"We've got some civilians coming down from NATO this week. It'd be good if you can show them a pretty picture, something the press won't hash and trash."

"We'll do our best, sir. Not a problem."

"Good. Glad to hear it." The colonel paused, then hummed for a moment. "Eric, anything going on I should know about?"

"No, sir. Nothing I can think of."

"You'll let me know, right? Whatever it takes. Whatever you need."

"Yes, sir. We'll get the job done at this end."

He held the receiver to his ear for a few seconds, letting the dead, empty silence take over for a moment. Everyone, from his CO to his youngest rookie, knew something was going on. Captain E.D.D. Wasserman had gotten two letters from Stateside in less than two weeks. His sister wrote him letters once, at most twice, a year, sometimes with more than an eight-month gap between missives. That was it. No bank statements arrived. No demands for payment. No complaints from anyone that he didn't write. He hadn't even heard from Steve Langdon the way he usually did around his wife's birthday, not for a couple of years. His hand was steady until the moment he unfolded the first letter on his desk, and he forced his eyes to focus on the lines Steve's wife had written.

April 10
San Francisco

Dear Eric,

I know you won't remember me, but we met about fifteen years ago. My name is Sylviana Innocenti Langdon. We met at a party here in SF. I don't know if you and Steven are still in touch, and you will probably think I'm crazy, but a few events over the past few years have given me reason to think about those times.

A friend of mine, Aggy Tarkingdon, mentioned the party, and we talked a bit about you, just remembering faces, and we both wondered what you were doing now. You will think I am insane when I tell you that it became a kind of quest.

A very nice recruiting officer for the Army took pity on me. Just so you don't go gunning for him, I won't mention his name, but he gave me the name of a group to contact.

If you get this, I would be happy to hear from you, Eric. Let me know what you're doing—if you want.

Fondest regards,
Sylviana

She had olive green eyes and dark brown hair that swept across her shoulder blades like silk, thick waves of heavy silk, and she was wearing something blue, some long dress with pant-legs instead of a skirt. He had stood inches away, wondering how she'd gotten into it and how he could get her out of it. Every guy in the room had been thinking the same thing.

What could he write? She was married to his best buddy, the

guy who'd taken the bullet that had his name on it. If Steve Langdon hadn't gotten in the way of that bullet, he would not be feeling this pain now. Wasserman sucked air hard into his lungs, clenched his jaw, and slapped his hand onto the second blue square, ripped his thumb through the flap, and tore out the blasted, scented, bayonet-wielding letter.

April 15
San Francisco

Dear Eric,

I'm not sure whether you received my first letter, but I'll pretend you did so I don't go over what I've already told you, which wasn't much, I know, and, well, not very important either.

We're having a pretty typical San Francisco spring. I don't know if you were here all that long, but, if you were, you'll know it's foggy, windy, and cold—just like Mark Twain said about our summers.

I'm working for a charity, the same one I've worked for since my youngest was a baby, almost six years now. My job is pretty routine, admin and form-filling mostly. All the important stuff is done upstairs. We look after—well, support, really, no hands-on or face-to-face encounters at all—kids who have lost their parents in war zones or never knew who their parents were. I'll tell you more about that, if you want to hear it, some other time.

My job is part-time so I can fit it around the girls—my two daughters. I don't know if Steven told you anything about them. Eva is twelve, and Enid will soon be seven.

Aggy says hello, by the way.

Write whenever you can, if you want to.

Fondest regards,
Sylviana

Steve Langdon was still getting in the way. He'd gotten in the way of that bullet. He'd gotten in the way that night of the party. She'd been right there. All he, a gawky, twenty-two-year-old, Lodi pump-jockey had had to do was open his mouth, say something. She was looking right at him, guys all around, smiling, grinning, showing off like they were something because they had two years of college under their belts, crowing, spouting that stuff about art—but she was looking straight at him, the ex-GI who couldn't think of anything more profound to say than "Hi."

What's the game? All of a sudden Steve has to get his licks in and enlists his wife to help out?

Only logical explanation. Eric slumped back in the desk chair, refolded the letter, and slid it back into the envelope. When he'd let out a long, steady sigh, he dropped the letter into the top drawer with the other, way at the back, so he wouldn't see them every time he wanted a pen.

They were both there, lurking, waiting in ambush, snipers taking aim, figuring out his weak spots. He'd read the first letter twice. He'd read the second letter twice more than that. He was now a thirty-seven-year-old career Army officer, and he already knew she had two daughters. He knew their ages, when they celebrated their birthdays—as though he'd been there. Steve had kept him informed—in the loop of all that happy family time: *You'll want to hear this, Wasserboy. Sylvi's got a job. How she did it, don't ask. Seems to be doing all right. No tears yet, anyway. Just part-time, so plenty of time for me and the girls. Not that she needs to work. My bonuses are sky's-the-limit right now. Bought that house I told you she loved—right on the bay, half a block from where I first set eyes on her.*

April 20
San Francisco

Dear Eric,

Wow, I can hardly believe how fast the last few days have gone by. Is it ten whole days since I first wrote to you? Seems to have gone by in a flash.

I know you won't remember, but I ran into one of the gang from art college the other day. Frankie Jarvis. Do you remember her? She says hi. She's still at the college— teaching now. Loves it. Says the students are just the same. Pretty crazy, just like us. Full of importance and vision— just like us. Some of her new work is in the same gallery—do you remember that night? Maybe not. Anyway, they still like her work. She's sold some paintings and made a little money. Frankie says I should buy one because she'll make a lot of her friends rich when she's dead.

It's about four in the afternoon. Sunshine for a change. The sun won't set until a bit after eight, but it's usually lights-out for the girls before that. I have to work tomorrow— nothing new about that—but Eva has joined the Glee Club and has to be in school by 7:30.

Enid has walked home on her own for the last week— well, only from Aggy's place, so I don't worry too much— but she's growing up faster by the minute. Aggy says hi too.

I'd better go, or Eva will be home before I've made any plans for dinner.

Maybe when you write, you could give me your address. I have no idea how long it takes for my letters to reach you. It would be nice to know that they do and also how you are. Only if you want to write, of course.

Warmest regards,

Sylviana

That night had been the second time he was in the same room with her, and the last. And the girl said, "Hi, *again*. We met at the art gallery, remember?"

"Yeah, I guess." *Yeah, I guess.* Just the way to let a girl know you hadn't stopped thinking about her, hadn't stopped seeing her no matter what you were looking at, aching in your soul to put your arms around her.

And Steve Langdon had gotten in the way. "See that girl, Wasserboy? That is the future Mrs. Steven Langdon. She is the one—no doubt about it. First time I saw that girl, I knew. Bells and whistles. Confetti. The works."

Steve Langdon—war hero, saved his buddy's life, decorated for bravery, smooth and headed for success—had suddenly had this olive-eyed girl on his arm, and he'd already all but married her. And "Wasserboy"? Couldn't win. Choked on everything. *Yeah, I guess.* The officer she'd smiled at, chatted to, touching his arm when she spoke, looked into his eyes, and made him love her so hard, he couldn't think straight—was still not thinking straight fifteen years later.

This was not Steve Langdon's annual *What do you think I should get my wife for her birthday?* letter that blew his brains out. Then, what? What *was* this? Nothing. Old friends. Being kind to the boys in uniform. Patriotic duty. Nostalgia. He could think of a lot of reasons why she had gotten in touch. Curiosity. Pity.

Steve Langdon had never once said that Sylviana Innocenti remembered him, asked about him. Steve had said: *I am one lucky guy, Wasserboy. Sylvi isn't just the most beautiful girl created for guys like us, she's pretty smart too. Don't know what I'd do without her right here beside me. When things go wrong, she's there. Like they say, stands by her man. One hundred percent my girl. Never thinks of anyone else. How you doing over there, good buddy? War zone after war zone. Plenty of chicks in the service these days, though—must be tough.* In all the time since he'd re-enlisted, he had read, maybe, twenty-five similar, scribbled notes on smart, corporate stationery. *Steven Langdon, Sales Manager. Steven Langdon, Director of Sales. Steven A. Langdon, Executive Director, Sales and Marketing.* What was Wasserboy doing all that time, his best buddy asked but didn't want to know. Wasserman never said that the Army had paid for him to go to college. Never said he had a degree in International Law. Never said he had field commissions and stripes up his arm. Never said he commanded a combat support unit or a peacekeeping unit that cleaned up the messes, rebuilt lives and villages.

What kind of dumb cluck loves a girl he can't have for fifteen years? What kind of a hick stands next to a girl for hours, every chance he gets, and can only say, *Yeah, I guess*?

Chapter Two

The key was in the lock and the front door open before Sylviana realized the afternoon was gone. The girls were there early. Either early or late, and often enough right on time, Steven was inconsistent just to make sure she was stuck in the house. She pushed the pad of airmail-weight paper under the cookbook and went to meet her daughters in the hallway. While she took the girls' bags of dirty clothes and received their quick hugs before they ran back to the door and their father, Steven strolled into the apartment and put his hands on his hips.

"They've worn me out."

She didn't say, *They wear me out every day.* She didn't say, *You could have taken them out for dinner.* She said, "They're kids, full of energy."

"Eva has homework."

She didn't say, *You were supposed to make sure she did her homework last night.* She said, "Eva, finish your homework before dinner, okay?"

"What's on the menu tonight, Sylvi?"

"Nothing special." She didn't say, *I was counting on you to feed them. I was just going to make myself some toast and soup before they came home and I had the whole Sunday-night routine to face.*

"Can Daddy stay, Mom? We hardly had any time this weekend. At. All."

"Not too much trouble, is it, Sylvi? I'll go if you want."

"Mommy, please. *Please.* Pretty please?" Enid wrapped her arms around her mother's waist and gazed up at her with big green eyes.

"Yeah, Mom. Let him stay. We haven't had dinner with Daddy. In. Ages."

"Come on, Sylvi. I won't eat much. Promise. It'll be like old times," her ex-husband said, sliding his arm around Eva's shoulders, grinning at his ex-wife, knowing he had already won the battle in just another Daddy-will-bring-you-home episode. "We've had an exhausting few days. Be nice to relax a bit—like you did all weekend."

Sylviana didn't say, *Twice a month, I get a chance to pull myself together.* She didn't have to say anything, not after three years of going through the same act. He won. He always won because he played the game better, got the shots in sooner. She didn't say, *Why can't we be civilized about this? I asked for a divorce because you were cheating on me, not the other way around.* "I'll make an omelet."

"That's your idea of a decent meal for two growing girls?"

"You said you'd take them for burgers." She should not have said that. She should not have fallen into the trap. His triumphant scowl indicated that this was the moment he'd been waiting for, and she'd given him the advantage.

"So it's my fault they wanted to come home, do their homework, see their mother?"

"We like omelets, Dad." Eva's sweet face was pinching into the pain the twelve-year-old always felt when this happened. A fight. Tears. Recriminations. Guilt.

"You know it's not good enough, Sylviana. You're the one's always going on about their diet, nutrition, health—all the lectures I get, ad nauseum."

"You win, Steven. I'll make lasagna."

"Now, you're cooking."

Sylviana opened the doors of the girls' bedrooms and began the Tuesday-morning routine of rousting Eva out of bed for Glee Club, one eye on the front door as the mail dropped through the slot. Window envelopes. The utilities bill. All recognizable, known commodities. She knocked on Eva's open door, told her the time, got a grumbling response, and tossed the mail onto the desk in the kitchen. Nothing that couldn't wait. Nothing she wanted to read right then, before she even had her cup of coffee. She held the cup in both hands and stared at the dripping leaves in the garden. *It's up to him.* She had stopped writing; she had no idea if he'd received any of the three letters but was pretty sure that, if he had, he hadn't remembered who she was, and if he had, he probably thought she was some kind of nut—a floozy, writing to her husband's friends. *If he writes back, I'll tell him about the divorce . . . eventually. If it feels right.*

Aggy was nagging her to do so. Frankie always cocked an eyebrow when the subject came up. Her parents didn't have a clue she was writing to Eric Wasserman. Neither did anyone else. No one but Eric Wasserman—if any of the letters had reached their destination. She didn't know if he was even still alive. She didn't know how long partially addressed letters handed in to a volunteer group took to reach the addressee. She didn't know his rank or where in the world he could be. She didn't know if he was married or had a family.

Too late now. Writing to him had felt right, easy, as though she had just picked up a conversation that had been dropped a few minutes before—like talking to a friend. But Eric Wasserman wasn't a friend. He was a man—a boy she'd met twice at a couple of flamboyant, artsy parties and had never been able to forget.

He had been out of step with the rest of the guys. Hair still short-cropped, still wearing neatly creased trousers and a button-down shirt. He'd worn boots—the only thing that didn't set him apart, except his were clean and polished. His aftershave was a popular scent. Most of the art college guys weren't shaving *or* washing. His eyes were big and blue and so hangdog sincere, she'd wanted to cry.

The guys lurking around her, getting in her way, were rude, aggressive, snide, so full of their creative genius. "There are just two kinds of people, man. Those who create and those who destroy." But despite his military service, Eric Wasserman didn't look destructive. He looked like he had a whole world of wonder waiting to burst out of him. He looked like a kid waking up in a magic place, rubbing his eyes, and staring at the first girl he'd ever seen in his life. He looked like she felt, and when she touched him, there was no one else in the poky, back-alley art-supply shop calling itself a gallery but Sylviana Innocenti, dizzy artists' model, and this blond, blue-eyed, clean-shaven, quiet guy—falling in love.

"Mom! I'm going to be late!" Eva was dragging a brush through her hair, whipping a scrunchie around her sandy brown hair, and stuffing toast into her mouth.

"Don't forget to brush your teeth."

"I haven't got time. Why didn't you call me? I'll miss the bus now. Mom, where's my school jacket?"

"Right where you left it."

"Bye!"

She was out the door, down the front steps, and flying along the pavement, school bag on one shoulder and the jacket dragging off her arm, one sleeve on and the other flapping on the concrete. The Muni bus stopped at the corner. Eva waved her arm and shouted, then gasped her gratitude when the driver left the door open long enough for her to hop in as he crept away from the curb.

Where is your head? She, Eva's mother, set the coffee mug in the sink, then gathered her hair off her neck. *It could happen. He could remember.* "Come on, Enid. Rise and shine, sweetheart. It's another beautiful day."

She talked too much. She had always talked too much. "Sylviana, be still. Your father and I can't hear ourselves think." "Enough, Sylvi, I just got home from talking all day at the office. Give it a rest," Steven had complained. She had talked too much that night. Prattling on and on about anything that came into her head. Inane. How to make good coffee. What flavor of ice cream she liked best. Nicest restaurant in the neighborhood. Where she went to school. Her favorite book, movie. It had to be Chianti, or it wasn't wine.

An hour later she stepped off the bus and walked up the hill to the dilapidated house that was her workplace, the place where she had found out just how much of a liar Steven Langdon was, just how much and how often he had cheated her out of the life she'd believed she was meant to have. She had suspected that he was unfaithful, that it had started a few months before Eva was born. But what could she do, once they had a baby? He never admitted it, but he wasn't there when Enid was born either.

She hadn't known then that he was an incorrigible liar, not until her co-worker—three years ago—had handed her an application for support from yet another GI's abandoned child. "Some coincidence, huh?" A girl, fifteen years old, claimed her father was Corporal Steven Augustus Langdon.

"I know that can*not* be Steve's service number," the co-worker giggled.

It was, but Sylviana didn't say that. "That's not his middle name either," Sylviana lied.

"Phew. That was close. It's your case, Sylviana. Not urgent. She's been well looked after for the past five years."

"What about before then?"

"Usual story."

Usual story. Pregnant local girl. Promises. No letter. No American visa. Make some kind of living, die young. Relatives don't want the child. Orphanage if she's lucky, working on the street if she's not.

The girl had the names wrong, got all the American GIs mixed up. "It's like I told you, Sylvi, just before we got married. That kid is Wasserman's. He told me he was going back to take care of it. Guess he lied." This was not Steven Langdon's child. He promised her. He swore to her.

Steven was lying. He had always lied. He lied to her about Eric Wasserman. He lied to her about his own daughter. He lied to her about where he was on the night that Eva was born. When Enid was born. Sylviana had the divorce papers sent to his office downtown and took her two little girls to live with their grandparents until the final decree.

"That's the third letter you've gotten, sir."

He tossed it to the back of the drawer with the others, then shoved the drawer in hard, in no mood for chats. "Anything important, Lieutenant Jones?"

"No, sir, unless you want to talk about morale."

"What about it? I haven't noticed any change lately."

"With respect, Captain. You haven't been 'around' much these past few days."

Wasserman turned to look at the best second in command he'd had in years, ready to deny the implication but not wanting to have the conversation he saw in her face. "We're moving on soon. That gets people nervous. What kind of films are they watching?"

"Films, sir?"

"Order happier ones, Clee. Comedies. Something like that."

She had a way of laughing at him that made him smile, but there wasn't any smile to make from any of the past few days.

"Shoot me down if you want, sir, but it's my duty to tell you that this unit looks up to you, and I hate to admit, we're all disappointed."

"Why? What's happened?"

"Sir, you've gotten three letters—"

"Not your concern, Lieutenant Jones." He stood, towering over her for a moment, but she stared back, just as determined.

"Three letters, sir, and you haven't answered even one of them."

"That's my business—"

"Maybe, and I'm not saying I want any part of your business, sir. Everyone here respects that, but three letters and no response, sir, that's conduct unbecoming an officer and a gentleman, Captain Wasserman. It's not what any of us have come to expect from you—to depend on from you."

The intervals between letters were getting shorter. If she kept writing every five days, he'd have another letter and another lecture from his junior officer unless he got his head around whatever it was that Sylviana Innocenti Langdon wanted.

May 2
APO New York

Dear Sylviana,

Thank you for your letters. It's always good to hear from people Stateside.

I hope Eva is enjoying the Glee Club. Enid sounds like a great kid.

Glad to know you're doing well, and thanks for getting in touch.

Sincerely,
Eric Wasserman

He studied the typed letter—the third draft from the printer. It was *Yeah, I guess* all over again. Nothing he couldn't live with. Nothing that would let her sneak up on him and shoot him in the back. He could have said hello to Frankie or Aggy, but he couldn't remember their faces, let alone ever meeting them. He'd seen only her. He figured she was filling space on the page. He could have said something about her job—*sounds interesting, important work, fulfilling*—but he didn't want to open any channels that led down dark alleys. *Keep it light. Neutral, Wasserman. Stick to the kids. Everyone talks about their kids.*

There was a stack of mail on his desk on the fifth. Just another workday for his unit until the Cinco de Mayo barbeque at 1800 hours. Clee was the Morale Officer—she kept tabs on all the possible excuses for celebrating. Captain Wasserman flipped through the pile. Nothing square. Nothing blue. Lieutenant Jones didn't mention it. He didn't mention it. Could be hung up in the post, he reckoned. Got lost. Or April twenty-fifth hadn't happened.

There was no letter dated April thirtieth on the tenth either. Wasserman worked through the math. The earliest he could reasonably expect an answer to his letter was the twentieth—if she wanted to answer another, *Yeah, I guess.*

By then, every Joe and Jill in his unit was watching for something. Lieutenant Jones set the stack of official mail on the corner of her CO's desk where he expected it. Nothing caught his attention. Nothing was said. He pushed paper. He filed reports. Hit the gym at 1730 hours and stayed there, punching a bag. Better than being one.

This girl was like a slow poison, the kind a man puts into his veins or drags into his lungs, knowing he's killing himself but would rather that than the alternative—nothing. At least he could count on feeling dread. Dread that a letter was waiting. Dread that there wouldn't be a letter. Dread that the letter would tell him something he already knew. Dread that the next letter would disembowel him. All he had ever known for certain was that Steve Langdon loved her. That had been good enough to stop him in his tracks, good enough to get him out of the way and keep him out. He didn't need dread. He didn't need to be waiting for a letter that was likely to mean either more dread or, worse, the end of it.

Has to be a joke. Steve must have told her something, something to make her think there'd be some fun in drilling a hole into his head.

May 11
San Francisco

Dear Eric,

Thank you. I wasn't sure if you were getting my letters, so I thought I'd better leave you in peace for a while.

Eva is still enjoying the Glee Club but not the early-morning wake-up call. She says it's the worst time in the day to sing. She's also in the marching band—she plays snare drum—and they practice at 3:30 in the afternoon but not every day. Glee Club is on Tuesday and Thursday. Band is on Wednesday for two hours. I let her practice at home but only when the neighbors are out!

Enid went on a school trip last week. Aggy is her teacher this year, so she didn't want me to go with her. Felt like a brick through the window for me, though. Upside was, I didn't have to take time off from work—hard to do when you work for a small charity, and staff is thin on the ground. Her class went to a matinee performance of Peter Pan—*amazing, isn't it, that a story like that can transcend so many generations? I took Eva to see the animated film, but this was a live-theater production. Enid loved it and is still sprinkling "fairy dust" wherever she goes.*

I bought one of Frankie's paintings—just after I wrote to you about it. A small one but one I've always liked. Even if it is a good investment, there's no sense in having

something you don't like, is there? Her husband is keep-
ing a record of all the buyers, so when she's famous, he'll
know where all her work is.

Thanks for giving me your address. I was beginning to
feel you'd think I was a bit overbearing, writing to you so
often. Anyway, I know you're doing an important job and
won't have time to write very much, but I was so happy to
get this letter. My girls thought I'd flipped into another
universe when I saw the envelope.

What will you be doing for Memorial Day? We'll prob-
ably go to my brother's in the East Bay. They always have
a picnic and fireworks—any excuse for fireworks. Steve
won't be there this year either.

If your APO is in New York, does that mean you're in
Europe? What's your job? I haven't been to Europe since
Enid was a baby.

We have a lot planned for this weekend. The usual
chores—getting the girls to help around the house is a
chore in itself. I'm happy if they keep their rooms tidy, but
they live here too. I'm probably a nag. I'll take them to the
library on Saturday afternoon and maybe a movie. My par-
ents are celebrating their ruby wedding anniversary, so
most of the family is getting together for a barbeque. And
fireworks!

                              Take care of yourself, Eric.
                                    Warmest regards,
                                          Sylviana

Yeah, I guess hadn't put her off, and her hooks were sinking
deeper, finding places to latch on he'd forgotten were there. If he
wasn't careful, he'd be finding excuses to write. He was getting
too close to the *I wonder what Sylviana will think* stage, a place
he had abandoned when he heard from Steve they were married
and expecting their first baby. That hadn't killed him. Seven war
zones, friendly fire, all the usual, day-to-day routine—nothing
had killed him. This wasn't going to kill him either.

"A-OK, sir?"

"What does *ruby wedding anniversary* mean?"

Lieutenant Cleonina Jones answered the question—a fortieth anniversary—but there was another question in her eyes that Eric Wasserman denied he recognized. Telling her why he'd asked would mean telling her who was married that long. Opening that gate would lead to not holding anything back. This was nothing he wanted to talk about, to anyone.

There's this girl I met fifteen years ago. Loved her ever since. She married my best friend.

It was all true, and he didn't want anyone to know anything about it. He had made a career for himself. He had a life. He loved his job and the people he worked with. This bit of his past had nothing to do with who he was now or why they respected him, looked up to him, depended on him. Even if he was stuck with his hand out, begging this olive-eyed girl not to twist the knife again.

"All right, sir?"

"Right as clockwork, Clee. Any problems on your desk?"

"None at all, sir. Nothing I can't handle."

"Same here."

Chapter Three

Aggy looked straight at her, her arms folded. The girls were watching television in the living room, and Sylviana had made sangria for Aggy and Frankie. Frankie hadn't arrived yet and wasn't expected until after the girls' bedtime.

Sylvi sloshed the fruit around in her wide-mouthed glass, but it didn't relieve the pressure. From the drawer of the computer desk she removed the envelope with the Army insignia in the upper left corner—the first thing she had seen peeking out from the pile of bills and had leaped on as though she had won the lottery.

Aggy examined the address and the postmark. "The Army doesn't give much away, does it?"

"I guess not."

"Typical of these guys. So important. Secrets and all that jazz we're supposed to swallow." She pulled open the top Sylviana had sliced through with the silver letter opener, one fraction at a time, prolonging the agony of excitement—and anxiety. She *had* flipped into another universe when she saw it, sent the girls to school, carried the letter to work, and opened it only when Enid and Eva had gone to bed. "He hasn't wasted much ink, Sylvi."

"I know."

"Sounds polite. Not even friendly."

"I know."

"What are you going to do, hon? Are you disappointed?"

"I was, but I got over it."

"Too bad. But I did warn you. He's probably married and really embarrassed that you'd do such a thing. He's probably having to explain big-time to his wife now. Gosh, we didn't think of that, did we?"

"No. I didn't think of that."

"I know what I'd do if my husband got a letter from a ditzy woman from his past."

Sylviana finished her sangria and poured more for both of them. "What would you do, Aggy? Chop her up, boil her in oil, send in some heavies?"

"No, Sylvi. I'd make damned sure he never wanted to open another letter from any other woman ever again—and I don't mean I'd hurt him." Sylviana's puzzled expression made her closest friend laugh. "No wonder you're divorced, hon. I'd have made certain that my husband wasn't even tempted to open a letter from another woman."

"How, Aggy? How do you do that?"

"Like I said. It's no wonder you're divorced."

"I'm divorced because I married a rat-bag."

"Honey, I'm not saying Steve was a saint. Guys wander, some more than others. Nature of the beast. I think it's pretty clear that this guy's giving you the brush-off—polite, but he's not interested."

"You're right," Sylviana said, taking a big gulp from her glass. "I should have thought of that. Too late now."

"Oh, Sylvi, I'm so sorry. Me and my big mouth. Forget I said that. Forget I said anything."

"No, you're right, Aggy. I don't think. Just leap out there and believe someone will catch me."

"Someone will, sweetie. Honest. Don't break your heart about this joker. He's so not worth your time. What about that guy you were dating in February? He seemed kind of sweet. Or the one with that great laugh? What was his name, Neal? At your Christmas party—you remember him?"

May 13
APO New York

Dear Sylviana,

The salutation churned in his gut, sucking his combat boots into mud up to his knees. After that, nothing he could think of to say made sense. After *Yeah, I guess*, what did she want? All of his training in hostile negotiations and volatile combatants went AWOL. So her parents had been married for forty years—why was she telling *him*? She took her daughters to the library, made them do chores. Why did she want him to know? Wasserman unfolded the third letter and spread it open next to the first and second. Short. Not too much detail. Just enough to give him a sense of her life. Why?

Under the glare of the desk lamp, he studied every line. Each letter was a little longer than the one before, a little more about her friends, her two girls, her family of origin. What she and the girls did on weekends. He sat straight, scanning the letters, dragging his finger down the lines. She and the girls. *Her* friends. *Her* parents. Nothing, not a word, about her husband's part in their routine. *We met at a party . . .* a few events . . . and . . . *Steve won't be there this year either.*

This girl knew how to interrogate. This girl knew how to find his weakness, where she could cause pain without leaving any marks—she had inside intelligence. Her "target" hit the Delete key, picked up his cap, and found himself in the officers' mess, where he took up a chair at the poker game and ordered a beer. He lost a few hands, encouraged his fellow officers to bet higher until he got his head on straight, then concentrated on his game and started to win.

When he fell onto his bunk, he held his watch over his head, staring at the luminescent dial. Ten hours difference. 0700 hours in California. Eva was catching her bus for Glee Club.

May 20
San Francisco

Dear Eric,

You won't believe how cold it is here. And wet. The girls spend most of the weekday afternoons with their grandparents until I can pick them up after work. It's only three hours, and I guess I should be glad my parents can help out while I work full-time. I'm filling in for a colleague on maternity leave—first baby. I'll be glad when we're fully staffed again.

I'm taking a few days off at the end of the school term so I can take them on a road trip, camping, or something like that. After you get this, we'll be going to Lassen Vol-

canic National Park. *Have you ever been there? It looks like a long way, but it's straight up the I-5 and across. Even I can do that, right? We're not doing the whole pitch-a-tent-and-build-a-fire act. That's not my idea of a vacation! I booked a cabin, and there's a cafeteria—at least I hope there is, or we're going to be pretty skinny by the time we get back on July 2.*

After that, they'll spend most of the summer with my parents, go to the museums and the library when they can, but if the fog and rain threaten all the time, they are going to be stir-crazy. In August we'll spend most of the weekends shopping, getting their clothes and school supplies ready for the start of the new year. Eva is good with her clothes, but she grows so fast and goes through shoes like a boy. Enid is a real tomboy and goes through the knees of everything in no time—including her own skin.

There's not much else to say about us, I suppose. So, how are you? What sort of work are you doing over there, wherever you are? Do you still—never mind, send me a picture. Is it hot and sunny there? I'm crossing my fingers that Lassen is—I could use some sunshine.

Very warmest best wishes and take care,
Sylviana

Sylviana studied the letter she had written. The period after the first paragraph didn't show how long she had hesitated. The ink hadn't soaked into the paper while she thought about how she could word what she knew she had to tell him. *I divorced Steve . . . Being a single parent . . . Steve and I have been divorced since . . .* Nothing sounded right, and she wasn't ready to hang her heart anywhere she didn't feel it was safe. *He's a smart guy. He'll figure it out.*

The turquoise envelope went into the side pocket of her document bag. She had to have faith in someone. She had to get over the guilt and fear that it really was all her fault. She didn't tell Aggy about this fifth letter.

* * *

"Who are you seeing now, Sylvi?"

"No one special."

"That's not what your daughters tell me." Eva and Enid were *her* daughters when they snitched on her and Steve's daughters when it suited him.

"Then you already know, so why ask?"

"Any good for you?"

She didn't say, *Better than you ever were.* She didn't say, *He rocks my world.* She couldn't say either, even though they were true for her, even if they weren't true for anyone else in this one-sided relationship she had started with Eric Wasserman. She had to have faith—even if it was only that Eric Wasserman wasn't lying to her. If he was polite, unfriendly, at least he was honest.

"You know I love you, Sylvi. That's never going to change."

"I don't love you." She didn't say, *I never loved you.* That wasn't any more true than that he still loved her. She had loved him, or thought she had, for a lot longer than she should have.

"I love your smile, Sylvi. Give me a smile."

Steven's hand was on her neck, working his fingers into her hair. Familiar. Easy. So simple to fall where he wanted her to when the guy she had set her heart on didn't write. *I wish I'd never met that guy.*

She sent the fifth letter the morning after she almost lost her faith.

June 15
APO New York

Dear Sylviana,

It's hot and dry. Sunshine is overrated when you can't duck out of the way. I've been in Lassen a few times, always on training exercises. No part of the park where you'd want to be. I remember rain and the smell of sulfur.

My unit is in a village surrounded by hills and vineyards. European for the most part but primitive by any standards. The wine is good, but nothing compares to Chianti.

We've been posted here long enough to feel comfortable,

get acquainted, like the food, but no nice restaurants in this neighborhood.

I hope Lassen is sunny enough for you. I know the sun will have every reason to shine while you're there.

Regards,
Eric Wasserman

Clee had taken the letter out of Eric's hand mere moments after he sealed the flap. The mailbag was now on the truck. Even if he had walked to the truck, stuck his hand out, and demanded the Army-issue envelope back, it wouldn't have worked. There was not a single member of his unit who hadn't been waiting for him to write this letter. Although there was no audible cheer when Lieutenant Jones dropped the envelope into the mailbag, the CO *felt* a collective sigh of relief from his unit. His own sigh of relief was certain. Whatever was going on Stateside, he had staked his claim in the outcome.

That night he played poker with the Colonel and two other officers. His winnings were meager but respectable. He hadn't let rank undermine strategy. He came away from the game unscathed—not the triumphant victor but not a loser either. Ahead, with a steady hand.

July 6
San Francisco

Dear Eric,

Your letter was waiting in the hallway when we got home. My parents were taking care of the apartment while we were away. I hardly heard a word they said when I saw your handwriting.

We extended our trip to take in a bit of the coast on the way home. We had a wonderful trip, exactly what the three of us needed—some quiet, peaceful togetherness.

Lassen was stunning and sunny enough even for me. Eva has reached the age of boredom, especially when there are no boys around. Enid has a new hobby—rock collecting—but only the rocks that have a layer of quartz through them. By the time we got back to San Francisco, there were enough pebbles in the trunk to cobble our patch of sunshine in the garden.

I'm glad to know you're somewhere in Europe—doesn't seem as dangerous as the rest of the world right now. I haven't been to Europe since Enid was a baby—six years, at least. We visited relatives in Wales and Italy—on my father's side.

Where else in Europe have you been? Where else in the world have you been stationed? Unless that's a military secret!

I can hardly believe you remembered I liked Chianti. Do you know that Chianti comes from the region in Italy where my father's family lives? That's why it is my favorite. I wouldn't dare think otherwise! And that nice restaurant is still just as nice.

I think about you and hope you are keeping well.

> *Much love,*
> *Sylviana*

Much love? Steven had told him about that trip to Italy to meet his in-laws, what a great time he had had getting to know his Italian family, how *generous* they—*especially the women*—were to Americans. Wasserman had been half a world away, in a rain forest, digging out mud slide casualties. The message had come across clearly enough, even for a hick. Wasserman had let it go, gone back to work. Before his rotation back to the States came through, though, he'd asked for an extension of his tour in the jungle. By the time he emerged six months later, he hadn't forgotten that his best friend was cheating on his wife, had pretty much always cheated on her.

> *July 16*
> *APO New York*

Dear Sylviana,

I was in Italy on leave last year. Nice place. Usual tourist stuff but nowhere near Tuscany, so no chance to see any of the places you told me about years back. I won't likely get a chance to get back there—not on this tour. One of my people spent a couple days in Pisa a few weeks back—no Chianti for me on the manifest, though.

My unit is being rotated out before my next leave comes up. We've got a lot to clear up before we decamp—leave the place better than we found it. Between now and when we depart, I won't have much time to keep up correspondence— sorry. I promise to write when I can.

I figured the sun couldn't resist doing its best for you in Lassen. Your trip back along the coast sounds good to me. I haven't seen the Pacific in so many years, it's hard to imagine. Am I right in thinking Steve wasn't with you on this trip? Don't know how he could pass up spending a couple of weeks in the mountains and driving along the cliffs with you.

Best regards,
Eric

Clee wasn't in a mood to give him any slack. As far as he could tell from her tight–lipped, narrowed glare, he was falling short of expectations. She had no way of knowing he was writing to his Army buddy's wife, letting Sylviana Innocenti Langdon know he remembered small, inconsequential things she had told him fifteen years ago, monumental things he couldn't forget, edging toward the abyss. Taking the slow poison as if his life depended on it, driving the bayonet in to the hilt, begging to take the sniper's bullet—wanting to know for sure where his buddy was in the picture.

August 4
San Francisco

Dear Eric,

I know you've been busy, so I waited until now to write. Not easy. I've gotten used to writing letters to you, kind of depend on it. I hope you don't mind.

I've returned to part-time at last. None too soon. The girls have been back to a normal routine for a few days. Normal for us, anyway. They're with my parents most of the day, and my dad brings them home. Or my mother stays with them here so they can have friends over.

How's the decamping and clean-up going? Do you know where you'll be stationed next—gotten your marching orders yet?

If you're coming back to the States anytime, I would like to see you. Here's my telephone number, in case you get to San Francisco—we'll show you the sights and throw you a party—a welcome-back party, so you can see all the people you met here all those years back!

I remember the first time I saw you. It was at the opening of Frankie's gallery exhibition. She was so excited, no one could hold her down. I wasn't much help—I had my own reasons for being off the planet.

The girls are looking forward to school! Couldn't wait for summer. Eight weeks in, and they are counting the days to September. We'll start shopping this weekend.

Do you have family in California, or are they with you over there? Do they like living overseas?

You're right about Steven not being with us. He hasn't been around for a while, only sees the girls when he has a free weekend—not often these days.

All the very best,
Sylviana

The kill shot. Steve knew he'd never married. Steve knew he had no family—none to speak of Stateside except a sister who had her own life and about as much time for him when she got around to it as he had for her. He had come a little too close to getting comfortable hearing Sylviana's news, more about her life, the girls, her family. Less dread, more waiting, anticipating. He had come too close to letting her know she was still part of his life, that he wanted her with him, whatever she had to give him, whatever her reasons—until this. *He hasn't been around for a while.* He'd cheated on his wife, had no time for his girls. So this was about revenge. About using the pump-jockey hick to get back at her husband, his buddy. It was about filling the gap or making Steve Langdon jealous, nothing to do with Eric Wasserman, the dumb cluck. *Drive it home, Wasserman. Kill it.*

August 27
APO New York

Dear Sylviana,
   Just wanted you to know I've appreciated your letters and the time you've taken to write them.
   I won't make it Stateside for at least another two years. The next rotation is a long assignment, and the people in my unit will need all the family time they can get. As their CO, I'm at the bottom of the list for leave.
   Take care of yourself, and say hello to your friends for me.

Regards,
Eric

As soon as she read the scrap of a note, she blamed the invitation to visit, the questions about his family, saying anything about Steve. That or she had talked too much, had come on too fast. He didn't want her in his life—that was *her* fantasy. She had been dreaming, as Aggy said. So what if he had remembered her parochial bias for Chianti? Just a dig at the talk-talk-talk, saynothing girl she had been when they first met—and probably still was. So what if he remembered that her father's family came from Tuscany? So what if he was glad the sun did its best for her? So what if he had promised to write when he could?

And all of these things were more than she had thought possible. She was still off the planet, still ready to leap, still had faith—unreasoning, blind, and pure fantasy. She was on the precipice of the rest of her life. This was the man she knew she'd been meant to marry, to spend her life with. If he wasn't up to speed, she had a couple of years to figure it out.

Dragging him up to her level of understanding was her job. If he never got there, it was not going to be because Sylviana Bethan Innocenti gave up on Eric Wasserman. If he wanted her to know he was married, had children, he had to tell her. If he didn't want her, he had to say that—in writing, plain and simple, flat-out with no hidden meanings. Sylviana had allowed him to disappear once. She wasn't letting him get away with that again. And that meant she had to risk losing him.

September 7
San Francisco

Dear Eric,

When it took you so long to write back, I thought you'd already gone to wherever it is you're going and I'd never hear from you again. To be honest, I wouldn't blame you.

If you've been wondering since my first letter to you why I suddenly started writing after all these years, I admit I've been doing my best to avoid the issue, but maybe you know already. So, I don't know if you are still in touch with Steven. If you are, he may have already told you this. Steven and I are divorced. We separated over three years ago, and the divorce was final about two years before I first wrote in April.

I know you and Steven were close friends. If you are uncomfortable about writing to me, just say so. I will understand. It is just that I remember so many things about the first time we met and the last time I saw you. I was hoping we could be friends. I will understand if that's not how you see it.

Eva likes her teachers this year. She has a math teacher who's so eager for the kids to get a handle on Algebra that she's told them, if they have trouble, she'll give them after-school tutoring. Her name is Hughes—has to be Welsh! My dad has already claimed he knows her family. No more early-morning Glee Club, though. Can't say I'll miss getting up at 6:00 AM.

Enid isn't as happy. She's in the second grade now, with lots more homework, and she claims her teacher doesn't like her—well, Aggy was her teacher last year, so she was spoiled. Aggy has been my best friend since kindergarten. She's always looked after my daughters, even when they're a pain, and that's been pretty often these past few years.

In case you've forgotten, here's a picture of me with my girls—it's not a great shot, but that's us in Lassen in June. The sun was in our eyes, but the park ranger who took the photo said we looked fine.

If you do ever get home, let me know. The offer of the party still stands. We'd all like to meet your family too.
Keep safe and good night,
Sylviana

She walked back from the mailbox at the corner just as Steven's fancy car slid to a stop in front of the Victorian building and the girls spilled onto the sidewalk, thirty minutes early. Enid was dancing—a sure sign she wanted to be in the house, quick. Sylviana trotted toward the steps, but Steven had already taken the key from Eva. He used his shoulder to open the door and was inside before he saw her. Enid scooted past him toward the bathroom, and Eva dumped their overnight bags in the hallway. Before Sylviana reached the door, Steven was in the kitchen. She took a long breath and followed him.

"What if Eva didn't have a key? I should have one, you know."

"Eva always has a key, Steven. You know that." She kept her eyes on him, away from the computer desk. Eric's letter was there, open, on top of the pile of bills. If she didn't look, if she distracted him . . . "Have you eaten?"

"Guilt talking?"

"No. You're early, and I only went for a short walk."

"Yeah, we saw you, Sylvi. Not much exercise to the mailbox and back." He grinned at Eva when she came into the room, leaned his hips on the sideboard, and folded his arms—getting into position for a fight. "Your mom's invited me to stay for dinner, Cookie. What do you say?"

"Great, Dad! You can help me with my homework. If you want." Under her breath, she added, "Thanks, Mom."

"First, I'm going to help your mom start cooking."

"No need, Steven. You spend some time with Eva. I can handle the meal."

"Too late for that, Syl. I know what's cooking and who's stoking the fire. Sad thing is, you don't remember what a loser—"

"I don't need *you* to tell me about losers, Steven. Help Eva with her homework, or go home."

"Mom!"

"Don't worry, Cookie, she doesn't mean it. Do you, Sylvi? You know how important it is for kids that their parents agree on what's best for them. You don't want to drive a wedge, do you? Not now, right? Just when you're getting some fun, messing around with a burned-out old Army—"

"I'm making dinner. If you're staying, you'll have to help Eva first."

"Conditions? If you want to set some, I can think of plenty, Sylviana. Like you're pretty stupid to be messing with a jerk like that."

"It's none of your business, Steven."

"I'm only thinking of you."

Sylviana glanced at their elder daughter, but Eva wasn't looking at either of them. Her eyes were fixed on the computer desk. Her homework notebooks were stacked among all the bills and Eric's letter. Steven swept the letter away and hung it under Sylviana's chin. "This is what's got you all revved up, Syl? He's got you pegged for desperate. Laughing his head off. I've been protecting you from guys like Wasserboy from the day we met."

"How? How have you done that, Steven? By lying about him, telling me your story, and blaming him?"

"Sylviana, your head is full of cotton candy. Don't you get it? This is the real Wasserboy." He shook the letter in her face. "Rev 'em up and dump 'em. That's why we called him 'Pit stop.' "

"I never heard you call him that, Steven. You hardly mentioned his name."

"What was there to talk about? He's a jerk. He's one hundred percent bad news to women—pick 'em up and drop 'em cold. Never did the right thing, never could stick being a stand-up husband or father. You'd do better finding a decent guy, Syl, by hanging out at singles' bars."

Chapter Four

Not one single thing he remembered about her had changed. Still the same big, olive green eyes, staring at him and through him, down to his soul, as if she knew when the ranger took the photo that she was sending it to the gawky twenty-two-year-old hick she had sunk her hooks into. Same thick, silky brown hair. Her daughters looked more like their father—fair complexions, sandy blond, but they both had her eyes—staring back at the camera. He slipped the 6x4 photo into the edge of his monitor. Clee stared at it for a while and smiled at him when he caught her.

"Nice-looking group, sir."

"Anything else, Lieutenant Jones?"

"No, sir. Anything else with you, Captain Wasserman?"

"She's a friend."

"Yes, sir."

"Her daughters."

"Yes, sir."

"Known her a long time, years. Before I re-enlisted," he said, and he had already told her too much.

"What's her name?"

"Sylviana."

"Pretty. And the girls?"

"That's Eva, and the little one is Enid." The dark alley widened, and the sniper had Wasserman in his sights, taking aim, waiting for him to make one wrong move.

"Husband, sir?"

"My best friend. Divorced. Never really kept in touch—Christmas, that sort of thing."

"Easter, sir? That's about the time this lady started writing."

"Yeah, I guess." His hand was steady when he took the photograph and slid it back into the envelope.

September 16
APO New York

Dear Sylviana,

I am sorry to hear about your divorce. Steve never mentioned it, but I haven't heard from him in a few years. I hope you and your daughters are okay.

My unit's gotten its walking papers. We'll be leaving Europe soon. The address you have for me will work for now. I'll let you know if it changes, as soon as I know.

Sorry this is short. I know, they've all been short. Can't be helped right now.

All the best,
Eric

Yeah, I guess. Just a little more. Not too much but *yes, I will write* and *yes, I want to hear from you.* Once again a choke hold on the gawky kid straining at the chance to say more, so much more. An apology. An excuse. Cool. Keeping the doors open but not onto any alleys or into the target area of any sharpshooters. He printed the letter and scrawled his name at the bottom.

"What do you call that, sir?"

"Call what, Clee?" Stalling for time, backtracking, hedging his bets. Too scared to own up, grab handfuls while he could.

"You know what I'm talking about, Captain." His second in command was a block of solid determination when she folded her arms and refused to get out of his way. "You have been writing to this lady for five months. At least, *she's* been writing to you pretty much like clockwork even when you don't give her the time of day."

"Your point, Lieutenant Jones?"

"Sir, with respect, I don't know what's going on, but it seems to me she's been laying her cards right out there in full view, and you are still holding yours close to your chest."

"Conduct unbecoming?"

"That is my point, Captain, my point exactly. If there's a game in town, get to that table, Captain Wasserman, sir, and place your bet."

September 17
APO New York

Dear Sylviana,

I know you won't have had my last letter yet. When I wrote, I thought I'd be moving out in a few days. The switch-over has been delayed, and I have some leave. Do you have any thoughts about places I should visit in Italy? I'll only have a long weekend.

The tone seemed okay to him, neutral idea, a possibility, better than *yeah, I guess* but not flat-out *I want you so bad I'm losing it just thinking about the possibility of seeing you again.* Divorced. Two years. About the time he'd been posted to Europe. A year before that, when she left her husband, Wasserman was in Georgia and DC. If he'd known, he'd have taken the first flight west, been on her doorstep, ready to catch her when she came out.

Langdon's last note came around that time—just a quick scribble about a big promotion and bonus, taking his girls to Hawaii to celebrate, and *What's the best gift you can think of for a gorgeous woman who's stuck by her man through some tough years?*

He didn't want to know what had happened. He wanted to get his head around Sylviana Innocenti's stack of letters. He wanted to get his arms around her. He didn't want to feel like the sniper. He didn't want to be the one to shoot a friend in the back. He let the screen saver blot out what he'd written and what he was thinking. Clee knocked on his open door, stacked the mail on the corner of his desk, and looked at him with her eyebrows raised in question.

"Working on it, Lieutenant."

"Glad to hear it, sir."

He thumbed through the usual paperwork, unit logs, requisitions. Cleonina had reached the door when he hissed, "What the hell."

"Sir?"

Wasserman choked, his survival instincts blazing so white-hot, he felt he was exploding. On his desktop screen was the note

he was struggling to word just right so his best friend's wife—
ex-wife—would understand he was stepping up where he had
wanted to be half his lifetime ago. And suddenly here on his desk
was another letter, an entirely different kind of letter. Cleonina
Jones stood in the doorway of his office. He snapped a gesture
for her to close the door. When she did, he slammed his hand
on the white envelope and dragged it toward him, all the while
staring at the photograph of Sylviana and her daughters. He
nicked the skin between his thumb and index finger when he
worked the flap open, the corporate letterhead spread under his
big hands flat on the desk.

> *Sept. 8*
> *Municipal Mutual—International*
> *From the desk of Steven A. Langdon*
> *Vice President, West Coast Division*

Eric,

*How're you doing, buddy? Yeah, it's Steve—long, long
dry spell, I know. Good reasons—not good, but plenty. You
know how it is when you're ambushed, watching your buddies mown down—that's what the past couple of years have
been for me.*

*I guess you were right. I wondered why you dropped
out of the game, but I know now you saw what was coming. I swear, I must be the dumbest guy on the planet to
think that girl had an ounce of decency. I've finally faced
facts.*

*I never wanted to believe she could do that to me. Lucky
you didn't stick around, Wasserboy. You'd have been just
another notch.*

*Long and short is, I'm a free man. Only good thing
came out of twelve years—two beautiful little girls (and
they* are *my girls) who love their dad. I'll get custody of my
daughters—even if I have to drag up all the dirt.*

*Take care, Bro. I know I can count on you, always
could. Keep out of the trenches, if you can.*

> *Steve*

The typed letter with his best friend's signature at the bottom sailed across his desk in a white blaze, bounced off the computer screen, took the photograph down with it, and crackled as the crimped edges unfurled. He peered at the note he'd sweated blood to write without sounding like a screwed-up yokel. Ctrl + A. Delete.

Enid's Lassen pebbles were lined up along the brick wall of the flower bed, half-hidden by the cascade of golden poppies still curling their petals in the early-morning heat. Sylviana was counting the days until she could expect a letter from that place somewhere in Europe. She estimated he had had her confession three days ago. There were still five or six days to go before she could have any reason to watch for the mailman's shadow at the door, hear the thump of magazines and bills hit the bare floorboards, and see the one letter she hoped for. Unless Eric's unit had shipped out between the time of his brush-off letter and the day she wrote back, she still had some hope. She had filled the whole weekend with chores. The girls had left at 8:00 AM to be with their father on his new sailboat in the Bay. Chores wouldn't keep her mind off Eric's cold "Thanks but no thanks" or Steven's "I've been protecting you" or her own "I wouldn't blame you."

She should have been honest from the start. She should have told him three years ago, when she walked out on her marriage. She should never have written in the first place. Too late for any of that—plow on. If the hole is deep enough . . . She scrubbed the bathroom tile grout, punished her hands, and broke three fingernails. By the time she had washed the kitchen floor on her hands and knees, cleaned the bottom of the fridge with an old toothbrush, and filled three bins with recycling, she had done her penance and was ready for a long bath.

"Mom!"

"What's wrong?" She held her stringy hair back from her eyes, staring at Eva. Steven followed Eva up the steps carrying Enid. "What's wrong? What happened?"

"She's been sick. What did you feed them last night? She's

been sick all over my boat. As soon as we got into the Bay and had a good sail up, there she blows."

"Poor baby." Sylviana took her youngest from her father and smoothed her hair back from her forehead. "Seasick?" Enid nodded, then dropped her head onto her mother's shoulder.

"First day I've had free with a good sailing wind, and this," her ex-husband said. "Too much popcorn at the movies, Syl?"

"Maybe she was just seasick, Steven."

"That's you all over, Madonna Innocenti, never taking responsibility. You're a wreck," he said, frowning at her from head to foot. "What have you been doing?" He backed toward the front door. "Hope you feel better, En."

"But, Dad, what about me? I'm not sick."

"Too late, Cookie. Wind has dropped. Maybe in a couple weeks." He shut the front door, and they watched him jog to his car, slip his aviator sunglasses onto his nose, and drive away.

"This is all your fault," Eva accused Enid.

"She's just a little girl," Sylvi defended.

"It's you, Mom. It's always you. Always. You do it on purpose."

"It's *not* me," Sylviana said to her twelve-year-old's back.

"It's me, Mommy," Enid said just before she threw up on the bare floorboards of the hallway.

"It's not you either, sweetie. It's not any of us. Go to the bathroom and brush your teeth. Do you feel any better now?" she asked, scooping up the mess into the dustpan.

"I told Daddy I was scared, even with the life jacket on. I said I'd wait in the car," Enid said, watching from the doorway.

"You couldn't wait in the car all day, sweetie. You didn't have to go with him this morning, you know. You could have stayed with me."

"He gets mad if I don't want to do something. Then Eva says I'm a baby."

"It's hard, my darling, but we'll get through this. I promise. Everything will be better."

"Did you get another letter today, Mommy?"

"No, darling."

"You will."

Part of her was glad it was over. Part of her was still wishing that she had never met that tall, earnest, blue-eyed guy with the sweet grin. Part of her was aching to know for sure.

Eva emerged from her room just as the linguine went into the pot. Sylviana tossed a few of her secret herbs into the cream sauce and set the flat bowl on the table. While she cut the sourdough bread, the girls helped themselves and were halfway through their meals when she sat down. She dragged the bowl across the table and swirled the serving fork through the pasta but ended up taking only a tiny portion.

"I'll get it!" Eva sailed from the kitchen table at the first ring of the telephone.

"If it's your father—" After a few moments, she asked, "Is it Grandma?"

"Who is this?"

"Eva, don't be rude," Sylviana said, pushing away from the table, poised to get up, hoping it was a telemarketer. "Just hang up."

"My mother says to hang up."

"May I speak to her?" Eric studied his watch, calculating the time again. "Are you having dinner?"

"Yes. Are you the one my father says is a jerk?"

"Probably."

"Mom, you'd better take this. Some jerk guy wants to talk to you."

Sylviana covered her eyes for a moment, sighed, and met Eva's insistent gaze as the girl thrust the receiver in her direction like a knife and scrunched up her face, not taking no for an answer.

She threw her napkin onto a corner of the table, then watched it slip to the floor that wasn't as clean as it was that morning and held out her hand from the doorway. The receiver bounced when Eva slammed it into her palm, and she dove to catch it. "Hello." Sending Eva back to the table with a dismissive wave, she turned her back to the two girls and rubbed her neck. "Hello! Who is this?"

"Hi. It's . . . uh . . . Eric. Eric Wasserman."

"I didn't expect . . . I mean, I wasn't expecting . . . I'm sorry.

I thought . . . Eva didn't say who was calling. How are you? Where are you?"

"On base. I—we're pulling out soon."

"You said. I got your letter." *Why are you calling me? Why are you doing this to me?*

"Sylviana."

Her heart stopped. "What is it, Eric?"

"Are you okay?"

"Yes, fine. We're fine." She heard him shift his body; a chair creaked, and something brushed against the mouthpiece of his phone. "Where are you?" *You've asked that.* "I mean, what time is it there?"

"I have a few days leave."

Her heart shuddered, then crammed into her throat. "When?"

"It's not long, just a weekend."

"Soon?"

"End of the month. I thought, since you've been over here, you might have an idea of what I should visit before we leave Europe." The wording wasn't the way he wanted to tell her, to let her know he wanted to see her, but he figured if she wanted to hear anything even close to that, he'd said what he could after fifteen years of nothing.

"Can you get to Florence, Eric?"

"Yes, ma'am."

"How long will you have?"

"Five days, beginning that Friday, last of the month."

"That's not long." She worked out on her fingers how many days until the end of the month. "You won't have much time. A tour guide would be a good idea."

"Do you— Can you recommend one?"

"Have you booked a hotel, Eric?" *Stupid question.* "I mean, I can do that for you. I know all the good ones. I can arrange everything, if you want. If that's okay."

"That's okay. I appreciate the offer."

"Friday. That's less than two weeks. Okay. All you have to do is be at the train station, the Santa Maria Novella Station, right? Anytime between one and four in the afternoon. Okay?"

"1300 and 1600 hours. Yes, ma'am."

"Whenever you can get there, Eric. I'll make sure someone will be there to meet you."

"Thank you, ma'am."

"There's only one train station, okay? You won't get lost, will you?"

He laughed, the same laugh she had heard across the room at Frankie's show and had pushed through the bodies of her friends and fellow art students to hear again—big, generous, full of life. "That is one thing you can count on, Sylviana. I won't get lost. I promise you."

Catching a lift on a transport to Rome was not the barefoot trek across the Himalayas that wrangling leave out of the Colonel had been. For a man who had once declared that the combat support officer could have anything he needed, whenever he needed it, Eric's CO had asked a lot of questions. Thursday night, Wasserman sat back on the bench, wedged his bag between his feet, and planted his hands on his knees. The chopper ride got him to the east coast. From the supply depot, he had scored a front seat in the truck. The rest of the journey was by taxi and train. 1415 hours. He flashed his ticket at the platform and walked onto the concourse, found a seat against the wall, sometimes watching the entrance, sometimes the ground at his feet, keeping his temperature down by repeating the phrases Martinelli had crammed into his head. *Buongiorno. Buonasera.* Not much. *Grazie.* He should have made a better effort.

"Capitano Wasserman?"

Eric raised his eyes and met those of a small man. "*Sì.* Yes, sir." He unfolded his body and stood a head and a half taller than the man there to meet him.

"I am Marcello Innocenti. Sylviana's cousin. One of many, and I am your guide."

"Thank you, sir. Uh, *grazie.*"

"I will see you get to your hotel, *Capitano.* Call me Marcello. We will be friends. Good friends." On the street, a car waited at the curb, and when Marcello whistled, a young man stood erect, opening the car door. "Alessandro will take you to your hotel."

"Call me Eric." Eric offered his hand to the older man and received a hug and a clap on his back. The young man took his bag and locked it in the trunk.

"Eric. We have heard a lot about you. When Sylviana's papa phoned his cousin, Julietta, what a time! We have been busy, very busy, preparing for you. Everything is ready."

"Thank you, sir—Marcello." He settled his long body into the front seat, passing his hand over his eyes for a moment. "I appreciate it."

"Sandro will take you to the hotel, Eric. In an hour, we will start the tour. Yes?"

"*Sì, grazie.*"

The small car swept through the streets and piazzas and finally slid into a space in front of a wide, half-glazed door. When Eric took his beret from his pocket, the young man grinned at him, looked him over, and nodded his approval of the soldier's fatigues. Sandro hadn't spoken. Eric followed him into the lobby and watched his bag land on the tiled floor. The man behind the desk grinned at Sandro and then at Eric, turned the guest book toward him, and held out a pen.

"Marco will see you are comfortable, *Capitano*. My father will be back to walk you around some of the sights. We will all have dinner together."

"Thanks. *Grazie.*"

"We are happy to do this for Sylviana."

Chapter Five

On the fourth floor, Marco showed the American soldier the guests' lounge, the staircase to the roof terrace, and the corridor to his room and then opened the door and handed him the passkey. Eric dug into his pocket, but the clerk waved him away and shut the door. He hung his dress uniform in the closet, stripped, and took a shower, letting the lukewarm water run over his face until he felt some of the tension subside. When he shaved, he avoided looking himself in the eyes and changed into another set of fatigues. While he laced his boots, he saw the two bottles of Chianti on the table and smiled for the first time in weeks. *Could be worse, Wasserman, could be a lot worse.*

"The room is okay, *Capitano*?" Marco asked the moment the elevator door slid open onto the lobby.

"*Perfetto.*" If he could keep his head clear, if he didn't think about how he'd get through the next five days, if he remembered even a quarter of what Martinelli had tried to drill in, he was confident he would get back to his unit without disgracing himself. He walked into the bar and sat at square table facing the door so he could see Marcello walk in. He had been on leave so few times that he'd forgotten how it felt to be sitting alone in a bar. In uniform, he could explain the sense of separation—he could be identified. He belonged in another place. Even if he had thought about it, he didn't have civilian clothes. He was on his feet as soon as the door swung open.

"Good. This is good, *Capitano*. We have a lot to see before we meet everyone. I will show you Florence as we see it. Many of the tourists are gone. They come in the summer, but this time of year, we are alone, as alone as a beautiful city and the home of the greatest artist ever born can ever be."

Eric bowed his head when his tour guide spoke, attentive, polite. He was grateful.

"This square is a good place to begin, *Capitano*. Here, we commemorate the many men who stood and fought for the independence of Italy. Soldiers. Men who believed in their battle for freedom and died. You will understand this better than many who look at this statue and see only war and killing. You will understand this with your Fourth of July."

"The Battle of Mentana."

"You know," Marcello said. "I could see in your eyes that you would understand."

"I'm a soldier, Marcello. It's part of my job to know the history of war zones."

"I think it is more than that."

"Caught," Eric laughed. "I confess. I did some research."

"Yes, I see. But not for me. Sylviana, yes? To impress my pretty cousin. This will make Julietta like you very much."

"Know your location and the terrain," Eric replied in his defense, but Marcello wasn't buying any avoidance of the truth.

"*Capitano*, I think we will be excellent friends by the end of your visit to our city. And"— he winked—"I will tell Sylviana everything you say."

"That is guaranteed to shut me up."

"We shall see, Eric. We shall see."

They completed a circuit of the piazzas and small vias around the hotel, coming back along the Arno. The square in front of the hotel was crowded, and every head turned to watch the tall American as he appeared at the corner café with his guide. An older woman stretched her arms in his direction but didn't approach. After a moment, she clasped her hands together. "*Sì*. Very handsome. A very handsome man. All the pretty girls will be jealous."

Sandro soon held out a tall glass. "*Birra, Capitano*. You might like it better than Chianti."

Eric laughed and closed his hand around the glass. The condensation cooled his palm but did nothing to remove the pink stains on his cheeks when he drained the beer. The older woman walked toward him, nodding her head, and Eric stood up to her scrutiny, squaring his shoulders. "*Buonasera, signora*."

"Ah, I have been told all about you, Eric Wasserman—tall

American with such a big smile. Everything so far is just as I expected." She dismissed two girls from the table on the terrace at the side of the entrance and pulled him into a chair beside her. "It has been such a long time since I saw Sylviana, and that time was a mixture of so many things. Two little girls, one just a baby. So happy to be here, and then, so much difficulty. Such a hard thing, and now this!" She brought her hand down on his arm and laughed. "I am Julietta, I forgot to tell you. So delighted to meet you, tall American with the big smile."

"Glad to meet you, *signora*."

"We are family. Call me Julietta. I will call you Eric. Do not allow Sandro to call you anything but 'Capitano Wasserman.' He is too full of Alessandro Innocenti, too much of this smart, college boy. You have met my nephew, Marcello. He is also delighted with you."

"That's very kind of you. Of you all."

"You can do nothing wrong, Eric. You have already made us all very happy. Delighted. Charmed."

Another *birra* appeared by his hand. More family arrived in the piazza. The breeze across the Arno brought silk scarves from the women's bags, and the sun dropped, lowering its crown to the splendor of Il Duomo. Moments later, the family stood and began to move west along Lungarno Diaz, weaving through the tourist groups, nodding and laughing together. Julietta held his arm and laughed with her nephew.

Along the route, Marcello gave a commentary on every building and monument. As they came to a narrow via beyond the Galleria, the family slowed its pace and made room for their guest to proceed first. Marcello was saying, "Tomorrow, you will see this most famous bridge, but tonight—"

"What's this about?" Eric asked, pointing.

"Pardon, *Capitano*?"

"This plaque, the tree?"

"Yes, as you see, this is a tribute to the Firenzians who were massacred by the Mafia. One of their evil men. A terrible atrocity."

"Criminals," Julietta said, patting Eric's arm. "Do not think of them when you think of Firenze."

The doors of the *ristorante bistecca* opened the moment the family filled the via outside. The waiter took Eric's hand, examining him from head to toe before nodding in approval. "You will enjoy this meal, *Capitano* Wasserman. A man like you will have no problem."

"Sounds like a challenge," Eric replied, but the waiter had turned away to give orders to the rest of the staff. In the main room, there were only a few small tables. To one side, another room was empty, all of the tables had been pushed together, and the Innocenti family was filling the chairs. He was guided to the head of the table, where everyone could see him. The happy din increased with every bottle of Chianti and glass of *birra* that appeared from the bar. His hand was never empty, and the glasses lined up throughout the evening until he was offering them to all the family members crowding around him.

Arguments flared at the far end of the table, were settled, and moved on to the next section until they passed him with big grins and rippled back to their origins. By his watch, it was past 2300 hours when the staff marched from the kitchen carrying platters of food—all the same meal—slabs of beefsteak, sizzling, juices seeping. All of the men at the table received a platter. All of the women were served hot, empty plates for sharing. The chef entered the dining area with a platter big enough for a twenty-pound turkey and set it in front of the American.

"This *is* a challenge," Eric murmured, and he searched the length of the table for some help, but Alessandro had disappeared. When he offered a quarter of the beefsteak to a nearby girl, she declined more than a thin slice. Julietta declined even a sliver. Eric picked up the steak knife and cut into the charbroiled flesh, filling his lungs with the aroma. He put the first chunk into his mouth and nodded his approval to the chef, who smiled, shrugged, and went back to his work.

"Good. Good," Marcello cheered when Eric put the knife down and pushed the platter away. "You are going to need the energy. Tomorrow—"

"I'd better get back to the hotel, if you have a big day planned. What time do they lock up?"

"No. No. *Capitano*. Eric, everything is fine. Tonight we celebrate, get to know you. Drink and eat. Tomorrow, you will see the city—whenever you are ready."

Some of the family at the far end of the table had risen and now talked in groups, standing at the big window. Eric pushed to his feet, ready to leave with them. Julietta touched his hand, but when he looked down to speak to her, she nodded in the direction of the door. Alessandro was parking his small car, and the headwaiter wedged the door open. On the opposite side of the car, the door swished open just as Sandro reached in, a grin on his face for all his cousins. Eric took one step forward as Julietta released his hand but was immobilized when Sylviana Innocenti Langdon turned to face her waiting relatives with a smile he had seen only twice but remembered as though it had been etched into his skull. His mouth was dry.

The bayonet that had been twisted through his gut lodged in his spine. He was in the open, no cover, an easy kill. He swallowed hard but couldn't close his eyes to relieve any of the ache, couldn't drag his mind back from brain-dead, didn't have a clue. He was instantly twenty-two, a pump-jockey from Lodi who had served his country and hadn't touched a real girl since his eighteenth birthday. She was everything he'd ever thought she was— beautiful, smart, sophisticated, hotter than blazes, and ready to bring him down with one clear shot. He could not find the thirty-seven-year-old commanding officer trained in modern warfare, hostile negotiations, military strategy and hostage rescue. That guy went AWOL the moment Sylviana Innocenti came into view. She hadn't looked in his direction, hadn't noticed him, wasn't coming near him. She was surrounded by cousins—the same flocking of adoring lesser beings that had kept the pump-jockey from getting near her—until she decided she was inclined to grace him with that smile, drilling five-inch bolts into his head.

Julietta abandoned him to take her place in the crowd around Sylviana, but Eric Wasserman was a lead weight, spiked to the floor, a clump of camouflaged flesh, not one gram smarter or wiser than he had ever been. If Sylviana spoke to him in that state, he couldn't have said anything other than *Yeah, I guess.* She laughed. She smiled. She hugged and was hugged. Someone slid a glass of Chianti into her hand, and she said, "*Perfetto.*

Grazie." His guts churned. She had edged closer, close enough for him to say something, but he was a blank, staring wall.

Sylviana dredged up all her best Italian, apologized for being so late, gave news about her parents, her daughters, accepted all the commiserations about her divorce—but all the time her whole self was fixed on the man she had traveled over five thousand miles to see. All of the potential of his good looks fifteen years ago had been realized, all the sharp angles smoothed and filled, as though Michelangelo himself had sculpted the muscle covering the perfect bone structure and fashioned another David to slay all the giants of the world. He was bone-achingly beautiful, still blond, still with those big, wide, clear, earnest blue eyes. And that smile to break any loving girl's heart. All the preparations and phone calls and begging for crumbs had brought him into the vast circle of half her family, and now they were keeping her away from him, just as all those boys from art school had, just as Steven had when all she had wanted was to get close to this giant-slayer, wrap him up, and make him hers.

All her family seemed to want to do now was tell her how sorry they were that Steven wasn't the wonderful, handsome, successful husband and father they had thought. All they wanted to do was tell her how much they missed her and thought about her in this trouble, how they wanted to help her, and what a handsome, charming American they had found. All she wanted to do was fly straight across the tables and let him catch her.

"Such a pretty woman you still are."

"*Grazie*, Julietta."

"We have met your American soldier."

"Do you like him?"

"*Sì*. Very good man, but we thought the same of your husband. So charming, he was."

"Steven could be that."

"This one, well, quiet, nice, not so . . . charming."

"No? I think he's *perfetto*."

"For you, *sì*, I think so."

"I hope so," Sylviana breathed, hardly daring to believe that possibly it was true and that someone else, someone who had met him only a few hours before, saw it too. "We'll . . . maybe we'll find that out." Her sudden, overwhelming distress that it might not be true showed in her face when her aunt directed her toward her long-intended destination. "Hello, Captain Wasserman. You've met my family. Have they taken good care of you? I couldn't get the flight I wanted, or I would have been waiting at the train station for you. Did you wait long? Marcello promised—" *Too much talk.*

He bowed his head enough so she could hear him over the excitement. "Everything is fine, Sylviana. I'm glad you're here." Was that any better than *Yeah, I guess*? He touched her elbow, took a breath, crawled on his belly through his brain for something, but that was all he could find. Hostile terrain. Everything else was an IED—immediate embarrassment device. *You're just as beautiful. I can't believe you did this. Am I dreaming? What was I thinking, leaving you, working so hard to forget you? You must think I'm an idiot. You'd be right.*

Another Chianti found her hand. Another *birra* waited for him at the table. He stepped back, moved the corner of the table for her, seemed to take a long breath before he sat down again, next to her. There was no friendly hug, no peck on the cheek, not even a handshake. *Something's wrong. Something is so wrong.* Sylviana shook off the glitch and kept her radar fixed on Eric Wasserman. He drank from his glass, chatted with Sandro, listened to another tour talk from Marcello.

The table began to fill up with bottles of wine. The talking and arguing returned. Every so often a cousin would raise a glass and shout, "Happiness to you both!" in Italian.

"Do you like your room, Eric? Is it okay?" Without thinking, she squeezed his hand. *That's bad. He can't wait to get out.* She couldn't blame him. Such a crazy thing to do.

"Yes, ma'am." He stared at their hands, closed his fingers on hers, met her eyes, and felt the incendiary burn start somewhere near his jugular. Her family smiled and nodded, but once he had her hand, nothing justified letting her go; no excuse materialized to allow him a graceful escape from the adolescent blunder. Even while he engaged in debates on global politics, discussed the sins of the combustion engine, he held her hand.

He's so smart. How does he know all this stuff? Without

thinking, she clamped her other hand over his, holding on for dear life, nothing in her head worth saying. They stood up to say good night. He shook hands. Sylviana stood with him, couldn't let go. No one demanded a hug. No one wanted a private word.

One by one, members of her family started on their journeys home. The mass of them spilled onto the via, wrapped their arms around one another to stroll through the streets, dwindling to a few as they found their cars, leaving Sylviana and the American alone to walk along the Arno toward the hotel.

The silence got through the fog in his brain, and he said, "This is really nice of you, but I can find my way back to the hotel. You should go."

"You may be able to find it, but I'm completely lost. It's been years since I was here, and I never paid attention to where I was going. Even in the best of times, I can't find my way to the end of the block."

"That's one skill I did learn in training."

"Then you lead."

"Where's your family? Shouldn't Alessandro be taking you home?"

"Then who would see you to your door, Captain? Who would see you got back to the hotel safely?"

"You don't know the way."

"I can ask directions," she retorted defensively.

"Where's Marcello? How are you getting back to where you're staying?"

"Don't worry about me, Eric. That's one place I can find, once we've gotten you back to the hotel."

"How far is the hotel?"

"I don't know, Captain. It's that way." She took a few steps farther along the river, then wobbled a bit. "These shoes were fine for riding in a car, but they're killing me now."

"You'd better take them off."

Using his arm for balance, she did as he suggested. He made no move to prolong the contact. After a moment, she hooked the heels over her fingers and continued barefoot on the sidewalk.

"I guess you should let me carry you." She didn't protest when he stepped back and studied her, then picked her up like he would an injured comrade and threw her over his left shoulder.

"Unique," she laughed. After a few steps, she lifted her upper body, pressing her hands on his lower back, and said, "That's the Ponte Vecchio. We can walk across that tomorrow. There's a wonderful museum and shopping area, cafés, and a spectacular garden on the other side of the river. That will see us through lunch. Then we'll come back here to the cathedral. Il Duomo. Wonderful." *Shut up, Sylviana.* "My uncle has invited us to have dinner if you'd like that. Sunday, we can drive to Pisa."

"You've put a lot of thought into this."

"Of course! I wanted you to have a great time. This is such a beautiful part of Italy."

At the entrance of the hotel, he set her on her feet and stepped back. "Will you be all right to get home? Should I ask them to call you a taxi?"

"That's okay, Eric. Don't worry about me. Before I go, let me buy you a nightcap." Before he could decline, she said, "Marco, *due limoncello, per favore.*"

"*Sì,* Signora Innocenti."

Leading the way into the reception lounge, she took a seat in one corner of the sofa, crossing her legs as he sat in the armchair facing the low table. She watched him plant his feet squarely on the carpet and his hands on the arms of the chair, staring around the room until Marco brought the two cocktail glasses of a pale yellow liqueur and set them on the table. Sylviana lifted her glass and touched the rim of his. "I'm glad to see you again, Eric."

"Same here." He wasn't getting over the hurdle. He choked on every possible word that went beyond *Yeah, I guess.* When she asked if he liked the drink, he nodded. She smiled, sipped her drink, and was silent. "How old are your daughters again?" he asked when both their glasses were empty. He knew the answer. She knew he knew the answer. *Shoot me now.*

"Eva is twelve. You spoke to her, I think. Enid is seven, still pretty easy to handle, but Eva is becoming a teenager too fast."

Shut me up, please. "They're both Welsh names from my father's side, but Eva is both."

"I thought your father was Italian."

"He is! Welsh-Italian. His grandfather emigrated to Wales after World War I and married a Welsh girl; so did his dad before they emigrated to America. My dad married an American girl whose family was a bit of this and that."

"Sounds like my family."

"My nephews and nieces are all of mixed races too," she said, staring into her empty glass. When she leaned forward to put it on the table, she raised her eyes to look into his face, but all she saw was his profile.

"My sister and her husband have a couple of boys. One's starting college this month." Eric put his glass down on the table. "I haven't seen either of them since they were just starting middle school," he said.

"They're practically men by now," Sylviana blurted, and then bit her lip.

"Yeah, I—" *Get a new line, you dumb cluck.* "I don't get to Lodi much. By the time my plane lands, it's time to turn around and get back to my unit."

"You must like your work, if you don't get home very often."

"Not much to get home for these days," he said, and he willed a sniper to stand on the wall by the river. "Did I thank you for the invitation? And the offer of a party?" *Right between the eyes. Make it quick.*

"You did." She laughed, leaning toward him. "Make sure you find a good reason to get leave, and make it a long one this time. But first, we have a date with Michelangelo."

Eric cocked his head and returned her grin with a puzzled smile. "The painter, right?"

Sylviana could almost hear his inner groan, and she laughed again. "Is eight—sorry, 0800 hours—too early for breakfast? My family has a full day planned, but if you need some sleep, we can start later."

"0800 is sleeping in for me." He took the hint and stood, keeping his eyes on her face. "I'll ask them at the front desk to get you a taxi."

"No need." Sylviana smiled for a moment. He ushered her from the lounge, keeping his hands to himself. "See you in the morning, Captain." She waved good-bye from the desk and watched the elevator climb to the fourth floor. "*Buonanotte*, Marco."

Chapter Six

3:00 AM. Sylviana removed her makeup and stared at her bare-faced reflection in the mirror in her room, three floors below, on the other side of the hotel. With a shrug for the thirty-five-year-old divorcée staring back at her, she dialed the number for her parents' home. When she'd left her daughters there on Thursday morning, Eva had refused to come out to the airport shuttle, too busy getting ready for her grandfather to drive her to school. She didn't expect her nearly teenage daughter to have changed her mind about her mom's importance in thirty-six hours.

"Hello, Enid. It's Mommy."

"Are you there? Did you see him?"

"Yes, sweetie, and he's very handsome. Hasn't changed one tiny bit from how he looked in the photograph of him with your daddy."

"Did he kiss you, Mommy?"

"Not yet, sweetheart."

"Then you'd better."

"Why, Enid?"

"Because someone else might kiss him first."

"Is your grandma there?"

Once her mother was on the other end of the line, all her big-girl bravado cracked. "I'm not so good, Mom."

"Don't be cagey. Hit him between the eyes. If he passes out, at least you'll know where you stand, Sylviana."

"Mom, I can't just do that. I can't just blurt out that I love him. He'll think I'm even crazier than he already does. And he's so smart, Momma."

"He's there, isn't he? He showed up for the big date."

"He's here, but I don't know if he thinks of this or me like that."

"Well, just remember that you only have a few days to find

out. If what you feel is right, nothing you say is going to be wrong as long as you're true to yourself. If he's all you believe he is, be happy. If he isn't, be glad you found out before you got hurt again."

After he took another lukewarm shower, Eric set his watch alarm for 0730 and watched the minutes tick off before his dead brain gave up and let him sleep. Used to autopilot, internal time zone, his eyes opened at 0530. Throwing a beautiful woman over his shoulder *was* "unique." He laughed to himself. Better than what was really going through his head there on the sidewalk. If she had held his arm for one more second, taken any more time to get those heels off, held her arms out to him with any more of that smile, he'd have lifted her onto the waist-high wall and kissed her right then and there. All she had to do was take a step closer. Just before that happened, he'd stepped back. Because his best friend from fifteen years ago got into his head and asked him to. He was dreaming about his buddy's wife again—ex-wife. He was thinking about living with her, putting his life in her hands, making her understand that he wanted to be the guy she loved, the only guy.

He dropped his feet to the floor, looked at his watch, and turned off the alarm. Rubbing his face, he switched on the radio and found a channel but couldn't understand anything being said. He left it on low volume for noise and company when he went into the bathroom, shaved, and met himself in the mirror. All he saw was the kid he'd been fifteen years ago. Twenty-two or thirty-seven, not much change. Steve Langdon was like his older brother, looking out for him the whole of their tour. A guy like that didn't deserve to get a bullet in the back—no matter what had happened in their marriage. Okay, Eric had seen her first, but Steve had stepped up, and she'd chosen him.

The career Army officer braced his hands on the edges of the sink and stared into the mirror. He'd never told Langdon outright how he felt about the green-eyed girl. As soon as he knew how it was for Steve, he'd backed off, way off, so far off even the girl forgot him. Just a couple of parties. He'd said maybe ten words all night at the first, half that at the second. Choked up, nothing in his head but wondering if she'd go out with him and how to ask her for a date, still wondering what to say to a pretty girl who was way too smart for him.

How hard was his unit laughing? *No good, Wasserman, no way.* He hung his head low between his shoulders and closed his eyes. *Nah.* His guys were solid. His second in command would not do that to him. He was not the kind of guy who got shot in the back—except maybe fifteen years ago, when he'd done the right thing for his best friend.

The phone rang in Sylviana's room at 7:00 AM, but when she lifted the receiver, no one answered. Annoyed, she started to dial Reception until she remembered that she had booked a wake-up call. She threw off the blankets and ran into the bathroom. While she scrubbed and buffed, she thought about the clothes she had brought with her and what she could wear that would hit Captain Eric Wasserman hard enough between the eyes to wake him up. She stood in front of the mirror and assessed her equipment.

She still had a waist, mainly because her hips were wider after giving birth to two babies—two big babies. Her breasts weren't sagging—not too much, not yet—pretty good with a support bra. Some cellulite. A few stretch marks—she could get away with a lot in low lighting. Divorce had given her some stress wrinkles— really, it was the marriage that had caused them. *Thirty-five is not old.* She ran her hand over her belly and grabbed a fistful of flab. *Okay. That's bad.* Meanwhile the guy she was just thirty-five minutes away from meeting, did not have even a quarter inch of fat anywhere on his body, just skin and muscle. Big deal. *He's probably got women ten years younger, half my age, waiting for him to get back from this pathetic weekend with a nice Italian family and a flabby single mother who's doing all she can to re-write history.*

A guy like this Army officer wasn't going to be knocked unconscious by any of the clothes in her suitcase. He hadn't even batted an eye when she walked into the restaurant with a skirt up to here and shoes she couldn't walk in, and what was that carrying her over his shoulder like a sack? No way would he have treated a gorgeous, long-legged twenty-year-old like that.

Sylviana Bethan, you need your head examined. And now you're going to look even better with red eyes and blotchy cheeks. What made you think, that after fifteen years . . . If he ever liked you, he wouldn't have dumped you for second best. He probably can't wait to get away and have a good laugh. Okay. Stop. It's bad. You're in a nightmare, but you promised this guy a great time, whether he likes it or not. Make the best of a stupid whim. He doesn't have to know you're a crazy woman.

The blond waitress brought him a coffee. Eric looked at the cup—a thimble on the saucer—and shrugged. 0811 hours. The dining room was filling up. His camouflage fatigues, laced boots, and green T-shirt didn't encourage any of his fellow guests to talk to him. The waitress didn't speak that much English. Coffee was about it. As soon as he'd needed it, he'd forgotten all the Italian he'd studied to get by. Brain-dead.

"*Café Americano, per favore,*" came Sylviana's clear voice.

Almost every muscle in his body was aching to reach out and grab her. One muscle was working overtime to figure out how to let every guy in the dining room know that those beautiful long legs were off-limits, without looking like the jerk he knew he was.

"*Buongiorno, Capitano.*"

"*Buongiorno, signora.*" He was on his feet, standing by his table. The waitress had taken away the second place setting when he'd sat down alone, Sylviana noticed. He stepped forward and laid his hand at her waist. "Sit with me?" he asked, his mouth near her ear. "Are you hungry? Can I get you anything?" His hand was still on her waist, and she could feel what others in the room could see. Captain Eric Wasserman had staked his claim. The knit fabric of her top, she knew, molded to her body and showed off her curves, a preview of what she was hiding beneath, and the American Army officer had to know that he was the only man in the dining room, in all of Firenze and the rest of the world, who had an invitation to know her secrets. He slid his hand to her hip and rested his thumb on the waistband of her jeans, one finger worked into the belt loop. "Cornflakes?" Sylviana nodded.

"Sleep well?"

"Yes," she lied, "did you?"

"Same as you."

She took the empty chair at his table, dropping her purse and scarf over the back. When the waitress came from the kitchen with her coffee, Eric nodded in his guest's direction. "On my room, *sì*? *Conto mia, per favore*?"

"*Sì, signore*, four-ten, *sì*." The waitress spoke for a moment with another guest and put Sylviana's cup at her place.

"*Grazie. 146, sì*?"

"*Sì, signora*."

Eric set the bowl of cereal in front of her with a jug of milk and a bowl of fruit salad.

"*Grazie*, Eric." She looked him over for a few seconds.

"Something wrong, ma'am?"

"Nothing at all, Captain Wasserman."

"Does my uniform bother you?"

"I just thought there was only one uniform. You seem to have a variety."

"Depends on the job and the location."

"So, what's this one?"

"Forest, jungle camouflage."

"Is there— Is that where you're posted now, in a forest?"

"No, ma'am, not exactly."

Since he didn't elaborate, Sylviana asked, "Do you ever wear street clothes?"

"No reason to. Not usually."

"What about Christmas and Easter, things like that, Eric?"

"The people in my unit with families take priority. My next in command has two kids. Second lieutenant just got married. Things like that." He drove his fork into the prosciutto the waitress had brought and washed it down with juice, then filled his plate a second time with meat, cheese, and rounds of bread.

"How many are in your unit?"

"Noncombatants, about twenty, combat support, thirty, and regulars, around a hundred."

"Wow. That big?" Sylviana speared watermelon and pineapple cubes, popped both into her mouth, and touched the paper napkin to her chin. Eric reached across the table to brush a crumb of something from the corner of her mouth.

"About average for what we do."

"And what's that exactly? What do you do, Captain Wasserman?"

"Clean up messes." He finished his salami and provolone, pushed the plate aside, and dragged his coffee cup closer.

"Like post-war—" She caught the way his eyes shifted away, the way his mouth tightened around the edges. "Sorry. You probably don't want to talk shop while you're on vacation."

"There's not much to talk about, Sylviana. If it isn't classified, it's routine. We're clearing out, moving on. The assignment's over. We did a good job with what we had. I'd rather hear about you and your girls." He had stretched his hand toward her, beckoning with his index finger until she slid her hand toward him. "Do you mind? It's just stuff I don't want to think about right now. Not while I have a chance to talk everyday stuff with you." Lifting her hand from the table, he eased his thumb over her knuckles.

"Sure. I understand."

"What are the girls doing while you're here? Do they know about . . . ?"

"You? Hard to keep that a secret, Eric. I've been going nuts for weeks—Eva's threatened to have me committed." Half his face rose in a smile—not the smile she wanted, not the one she remembered so well that thinking about it made her warm—but just enough encouragement for her to smile in return. "They're staying with my folks this weekend, until Wednesday, when—" She couldn't help trembling a little, and he squeezed her fingers.

"Yeah." Eric dropped his gaze for a moment and clenched his jaw. "If you're about done, Sylviana, I'll meet you back in the lobby in ten minutes."

"Sure." Sylviana finished her fruit and cereal and reminded herself not to ask questions about his job. When she returned to the lobby, she found him waiting in the lounge, wearing a light jacket and twirling a beret in his hands, staring at the carpet. A strip of canvas weave above his pocket read *Capt. E.D.D.*

Wasserman. "Two *D*s," Sylviana commented. "What do they stand for?"

"Daniel David."

"What do people call you?"

"Captain or sir," he said as he rose to his feet. "My superior officer calls me Eric when he's winning at the poker table. Everyone else calls me Wasserman."

"Friends? What do they call you?"

He set the beret on his head and adjusted the angle. "Eric." He held the door to the street open. Looking down at her feet, he said, "No chance I'll have to carry you home today, huh?"

"I've learned my lesson," Sylviana said, staring at her solid, sensible walking shoes.

He opened the hotel door. "Was it your feet or the way I carried you that provided the lesson, ma'am?" he asked, as she passed him, ducking under his arm.

"Both."

"A few lessons in chivalry might do me good."

She draped the silk paisley scarf around her shoulders, surprised when he straightened the corner at the small of her back, disappointed when he didn't put his arm around her shoulders or his hand at her waist.

"Marcello not with us this morning?"

"He'll meet us after lunch, if that's okay. I know enough about the bridge and the museum. And he'll want to tell you his own version of the de Medici family. I wouldn't want to steal any of his best lines."

"So it's just you and me this morning, no chaperone?"

"Do you think you need one, *Capitano*?"

The officer looked into the distance for a few moments, smiling. "I think I'll be okay."

Sylviana walked ahead of him along the narrow pavement until they reached the opening of the bridge. Passing the spot where he'd wanted to lift her onto the wall, Eric let out a low whistle and followed her to join the other tourists walking across. Sylviana waited for him to catch up to begin her story about the gold shops. He listened to every word, bowing his head to hear her in the early-Saturday shopping noise as they passed scores of tiny shop windows laden with gold jewelry and ornaments. She had the sense that he was also always keenly aware of everything and everyone nearby, although he seemed at ease.

When a street vendor approached, the American raised his eyebrows but did not prevent the man from offering his wares to the *signora*. Sylviana shook her head and walked on. The vendor said something under his breath that made her glare at him, but she moved farther along, out of his territory. At the center of the bridge, she stopped near the wall. When he stood in front of her, she continued her tour recitation. Without warning, he lifted her onto the wall with a sudden grin and rested his hands on either side of her hips.

"Even in decent shoes, you need to rest sometimes," he explained, smiling for a moment longer. "Sorry. I didn't mean to interrupt." Her tiny smile wasn't much encouragement, but after a few moments he stroked her thigh with his thumb, still listening to her commentary.

"And every bridge was blown to bits when the Germans left—except the Ponte Vecchio, on Hitler's express order."

There was no question in his head about that fact, Sylviana registered, no encouragement that he heard or had any interest in her information. When he put his hands on either side of her knees, she kept them pressed together while she pointed at various objects and sights nearby on her left and right, fighting to keep her head clear when he pulled her slightly forward and her knees met the solid wall of his abdomen.

"I don't want you to think I don't appreciate all you've done to make this visit something special." He was looking into her eyes. "But I'm having a hard time working out why. This is a lot to do for a guy you hardly know, a guy you haven't seen and probably not thought much about in fifteen years."

Sylviana gritted her teeth and looked away to the other side of the river. "Kind of a shock, I guess."

"Your first letter, after all that time, when we hardly knew each other, was a shock, Sylviana. This is beyond shock. This is slam-dunk, heart-stopping, blow-a-man-to-kingdom-come. This is maybe I've died and gone to heaven or some kind of new, rip-a-guy's-guts-out interrogation method, and I'm the lab rat."

Sylviana stared at her hands, clasped white-knuckle-hard together in her lap.

"Why did you write to me?"

"Why did you answer?"

"My second in command made me," Eric replied.

"I like him already."

"Her. Clee is female."

"Really? I might like her too. How did she make you answer my letter?"

"Morale. She said morale was low and I was letting the unit down. I told her to order happier films."

Sylviana laughed. "What was her reaction?"

"Same as yours. You haven't answered my question."

"And what question was that, Captain?" She cocked her head, batting her eyelashes.

"Why did you write to me in the first place?" He lifted her down from the wall, stepping back when she was on her feet.

"My mother said you owed me at least one date."

"How does she figure that?" he asked with a laugh, folding his arms across his chest.

"That is something you will have to ask her when you meet her."

"Do you think I will?"

"Maybe. Depends on how this date goes, doesn't it?"

He laughed again and dropped his hands to his hips.

"So they all know where you are?" Sylviana said, taking the arm he offered. "Your unit?"

"Hard to keep things like this to yourself when you live in a confined space and Cleonina Jones opens your mail. Everyone had some advice to offer."

"Anything good?"

"Some of it was useful," he said, "but a lot of what the guys offered was way off base."

"I can imagine," she replied. They had reached the other end of the Ponte Vecchio. Sylviana continued on the main street. Eric stopped and looked back at the bridge. "What's wrong?" she asked him.

"Nothing," he replied, a streak of pink flaring across his cheekbones. "I saw something—in a shop."

"We have to go back that way after lunch to meet Marcello."

"Sure. I'll get back there later. It's not urgent."

When they crossed the street, he switched sides, walking next to the curb, and put his arm around her waist. Sylviana glanced at his profile but turned her attention to the shop windows when he kept his eyes on what was in front of them. At a café opposite the museum plaza, he ordered two *Americanos* and sat beside her in silence until his coffee had gone cold. Sylviana drank her coffee, leaning back in her chair, watching her "date" and the merchants setting up their stalls for the wine festival that afternoon.

"Steve saved my life," Eric said at last. "I would be dead if not for him."

"He told me."

"I owed him for that. Still do." *Fifteen years of payback.*

"No doubt he thinks the same," she replied.

"You don't?"

"I'm glad he saved your life, Eric, but I lived with him for twelve of the past fifteen years. I paid any debt I might have owed him for saving your life, but—" She glanced at Eric's profile and decided the time wasn't right to tell him his friend had betrayed him. "If you think you still have one, that's between the two of you."

"Payback for some things takes awhile, Sylviana. This, being here with you, feels like betrayal. Maybe you don't know all he did to keep me alive, not just taking that bullet."

"I know what he did *after*."

Eric dropped his hand over hers, searching her face. "I know he messed up with you. I'm sorry. If I wasn't such a—" He couldn't say he was a coward, not to her. "If I'd known—" He knew. He'd always known. There was never a sniper around when there should have been.

"Don't you dare take responsibility for him, Eric Wasserman. I don't want to hear it, from you or anyone. I've been carrying *that* burden long enough myself."

"Baby, I—" He closed his eyes for a moment. Without meeting her steady gaze, he swallowed his cold coffee. She watched the vendors until Eric pulled a handful of bills from his wallet. "Do you understand these?"

"No problem, Captain." Sylviana selected a few bills, added coins from her purse, then slid them under his saucer.

"Tip?"

"Done."

Eric stuffed the remainder into his wallet and pulled her up. "Do you mind if we skip the museum?"

"It's your weekend, *Capitano*. But the garden is worth seeing, especially this time of year."

"No garden. I wouldn't see it, anyway. Let's just walk, Sylviana."

"Okay, Eric. Whatever you want." She straightened her scarf around her shoulders. *Baby.* She was floating on the sound, the way he'd said it—way out there in the fantasy-land of *it could happen.*

"You lead the way."

"That's taking a big risk, soldier. I have no sense of direction."

"I'll get us back in time to meet your cousin," he assured her as he put on a pair of aviator sunglasses and took her hand. He checked his watch. "1130 hours, ma'am. You have one half hour to find us a good restaurant."

"Tall order, sir."

"Just do your best."

"Yes, sir." Sylviana looked in all directions and started her search along the river. "What kind of name is Clee? Is that her first name?"

"Nickname. Short for Cleonina."

"What's she like? What does she like to do?" *Jealous.*

"Push me around," he said with a quick grin.

"Is that easy to do, Captain?"

"I let her think so. Only way to get any peace."

"What does she look like?" He shrugged. "Long hair. Short? Blond, dark?"

"Short. She's combat support—has to keep her hair short. Comes up to about here on me," he added, measuring at the middle of his upper arm.

"Pretty?" *Green with it, Sylviana. Lay off.*

"Her husband thinks so."

"Is he in your unit?"

"No. Couples don't serve in the same unit. Too dangerous. If they're on a mission, if one is wounded—" He shook his head with a scowl. "Policy."

"Does that happen? Is it dangerous where you are?"

"You'd better find a place pretty soon, ma'am, or we'll have to go on rations."

"What sort?"

"When I need fuel, I'll eat anything," Eric said, wrapping his fingers around her lower arm, pulling her closer. "What's your house like? I don't know the area."

"It's an apartment. Huge front room, kitchen, dining room, study, bathroom, and three bedrooms."

"You lived there with Steve?"

"When I asked for a divorce, I wanted a clean slate. We sold our house. Steven took his half and bought another, bigger house. I bought the apartment so the girls would be close to school. It's not far from Aggy's place. She still lives in her studio apartment."

"Aggy?" he quizzed.

"A good friend. I think I've told you about her. She had a party at her place, the second time we met. Do you remember that?"

"I don't remember her or that apartment."

"It's not important. Anyway, I live just a few blocks from there."

"You were wearing some kind of blue dress," he said, a crooked smile lifting his cheeks. "I couldn't figure out how you got into it. Some kind of long dress with legs."

"A pant-dress," she said, looking at the brown surface of the river. "It was the latest fashion back then. I made it. It just zipped up the back, like any dress."

"I wasn't looking at your back."

"It's my best feature," she said, then wished she hadn't.

Eric leaned backward and glanced down the length of her spine to her bottom, sliding his hand lower on her hip. "There's a lot of competition for that title," he said, then cringed inside and left his hand where it was.

Sylviana pressed her lips together, struggling to disguise the delicious shiver coursing through her from the top of her head to her toes. "Aggy invited a lot of friends from college," she continued. "Some of them were pretty mean to you."

"I didn't notice." He looked at the board outside a café. "What about this place?"

Sylviana followed him into the small room and sat at the window where the waitress directed them. Eric sat on the wooden bench next to her and picked up the menu, folding his beret into his jacket pocket. "How could you not notice? I almost hit that one guy when he called you—"

"I was twenty-two, just barely out of the Army. I wasn't listening to any *guy*." When she cocked an eyebrow at him, Eric returned a brief grin. "I was figuring out how I could get you out of that contraption."

"You and a few others."

"I noticed *that*."

"And I noticed you were one of the first to leave."

"Not my choice," he said as he handed her the menu.

"And you had left Frankie's early too."

"That was the art exhibition in some gallery, right?"

"That's right. You seem to remember a lot more than my dress."

"I remember *you*," Eric confessed, holding the waitress off with a wave of his hand.

"How could you miss me? I talked my head off to you," she said, cursing the blush sweeping up from her chin and making her eyes smart. "My Chatty Cathy to your—I haven't changed much, have I?"

"I could have listened to you all night. Saved me having to think of any clever stuff."

"You said plenty."

He gave her a quizzical look.

"The way I remember, anyway. But maybe it was the way you listened to my every word and agreed with all my ideas." She laughed. "I don't know how I kept talking when all I wanted to do was watch you smile and hear you laugh." She hadn't taken her eyes off him at the art gallery, as though he was the only person there and everyone else had disappeared in a fog of chatter and self-importance. In the midst of it all, this tall, grinning, wide-eyed, boyish man with nothing but clean and shiny all around him, stood like a guiding beam from a lighthouse to safe harbor. After two years in art school, she'd had enough of grunge and darkness.

"Someone had to do the talking, Sylviana. My brain was mush. All I wanted to do was listen to your voice." After almost five years of bullets and grenades, hate and fear, this pretty girl in blue had been standing less than ten inches away. She seemed to have come from nowhere, all silk and softness, talking, laughing, a giggle and a gasp now and then. *"And you know what? My father comes from the same region as my favorite wine! Well, not really, he wasn't born there, but I was raised on Chianti. Not from birth! Just when I was old enough. Where are you from?"*

"Lodi."

"I've never been there. That's in the central valley, isn't it? There are hundreds of vineyards around there, right?"

"Yeah, I guess."

She had seemed to know everything, full of life and joy, like a whirlwind straight from the mountains, wrapping him up in enthusiasm, optimism, the future. And the second time he saw her, he had his words ready, had practiced in his head for most of the walk up the hill to the address Steve had given him. Halfway through the party, beer in his hand, head bowed listening to the life swirling around her, Steve Langdon had pushed in, crowing, dragging him off.

"Hey buddy. I see you've met her."

"Who?"

"Who do you think, Wasserboy? The future Mrs. Langdon."

His options had diminished as though the whirlwind had been abruptly sucked back to earth. He had taken one final look. The pretty girl with the pretty name was dancing and smiling at him—or maybe that smile was for his best friend. *"I'm the luckiest guy in the world, Er. My girl and my best buddy don't hate each other."*

The kid from Lodi had buried that beautiful future and opted for grenades and bullets.

*   *   *

"I'm going to order the *zuppa di giorno*. We'll be having a big meal tonight."

Eric stared at her for a moment, got his head back to real time, and ordered the same but added antipasto and bread to fill the corners as well as gelato to finish. "Big deal tonight?"

"They've called in all the favors. I hope you don't mind, Eric. It's partly a family thing. My fault. And partly to make you feel welcome. They like Americans—think we all have Italian blood by now. And I haven't visited since . . . for a long time."

"Since Enid was a baby. You told me, in one of your letters." His bread and antipasto arrived. While he prepared to fill the gaps, he said, "I lost touch with Steve a little while after that. Just a note a couple of times a year and something, a few years ago, about a promotion and a trip to Hawaii."

"I didn't go. He took the girls. By then, I'd found out he had a daughter he'd abandoned when he got his discharge. It was just one more wrong thing, so I left him."

"How'd you find out?"

"Did you know?" When he nodded once, she went on. "I guess I was naïve to believe anything he told me." *Just stupid, Sylviana, like Steven always said you were.* "Anyway, one of our sister organizations takes care of children abandoned in war zones. One of my co-workers thought it was funny that one of their fathers had the same name as my husband. We laughed about the 'coincidence,' but I knew he had been there, in that war zone. I made sure she was okay and she knows she has sisters, a family. When I told Steven his daughter was looking for him, he went ballistic. He knew if he acknowledged her, he'd have to own up to all the other lies he'd told me. I knew everything by then, so it hardly mattered. That finished us."

Chapter Seven

Eric took bills from his wallet and estimated what he had to put on the table to cover the meal and the tip. "Enough?" he asked.

Sylviana nodded, following him from the restaurant. When he didn't take her hand, offer his arm, or put his arm around her waist, Sylviana walked beside him as he navigated without hesitation through the busy streets to the Ponte Vecchio and back to the hotel. Marcello was arriving at the same time Eric and Sylviana crossed the road into the square. They had not spoken during the quarter-hour journey.

In the lobby, Eric spoke briefly to Marcello, collected his room key, and started up the stairs. Sylviana explained that she would change her shoes and took the elevator to the first floor. At the door of her room, she pressed her forehead to the central panel. "Mouth, Sylviana. Big mouth."

Eric sat on the edge of the double bed and picked up the phone, reading the number from the message the clerk had given to him with his room key. While he waited for the line to connect, he rubbed his head. "Hello, Clee. What's the problem?"

"No problem, sir."

"Why the call?"

"Just checking in, sir. All's quiet here on the front line. How about the R and R?"

"Great."

"Martinelli wants photos of some big church."

"Il Duomo?" he offered.

"That's the one."

"We're going there later. I'll pick up a postcard or something."

"That'll do, Captain," Clee said.

Eric recognized her effort to keep her tone cheerful, noncom-
mittal, as though she didn't want to know what the whole unit
wanted to know. "No collateral damage, Lieutenant."

"Yes, sir."

"It's all good."

"Glad to hear it, sir."

"Tell Martinelli she'll have all the photos she'll ever want."

"Yes, sir," Lieutenant C.N. Jones said as she saluted her CO.

Eric held the receiver in his hands for a moment after Clee
had hung up. When he reached the lobby, Sylviana was talking
to her cousin in front of the desk. He noticed she had changed
her blouse to something bright yellow and her shoes to sandals.
Although they were speaking in Italian, he stood a few feet
away but within sight so they could finish their conversation
privately.

"Is everything all right, *Capitano*? Marco has told us you
have received an important call from the Army. We are still
able to give you this tour, yes? You can stay?"

"No problem, Marcello. One of my unit is a bit homesick.
Lieutenant Jones thought it would help if I brought back some
photos. Do either of you have a camera?" Sylviana dug into her
bag and handed hers to him without looking at him. "Thank
you, ma'am." He studied the small camera. "Any tricks to this?"

"Point and shoot, Captain Wasserman."

"Ten-four, ma'am," he said with a quick wink.

Sylviana made a small, dismissive gesture and walked toward the front door. Marcello stared after her and glanced at
the man she had come such a distance to see for only a weekend. Marcello scowled at the tall American, but the guest in his
city was absorbed in the camera. Sylviana dove into her bag to
find her sunglasses. Once she was hiding behind them, she pulled
her paisley scarf tight and folded her arms, walking ahead of
her male companions. Eric settled the camera in the top breast
pocket of his jacket and took the beret from the other, keeping
his eyes on his best buddy's ex-wife's back as he chatted to
Marcello about the high-water mark plaques that adorned the
wall in the lobby and some of the houses.

"That high? Must have been chaos for a few months."

"*Sì, Capitano.* Some people never recovered from that flood—lost everything. Only the jewelers on Ponte Vecchio were warned. Another sad November for our city."

When they reached Piazza del Duomo, Marcello insisted he would take a photo of his guest and his cousin in front of the marble-tiled cathedral. Eric put his arm around her shoulders. He said it was for his unit's morale, so she smiled. For the remainder of the afternoon they visited Piazza della Repubblica and the Foundling Children's Orphanage. Toward the end of the day, they stood in the Galleria dell'Accademia to stare at the *David.* Eric watched Sylviana's face as she studied the artist's most exquisite accolade to the boy-warrior.

Except for polite responses to his questions and her willingness to be photographed with him, she seemed to be miles away. He had not recognized the man she'd described, the man who was his friend. He'd known that Steve Langdon had a daughter other than Sylviana's—one he claimed he was supporting even though the girl's mother hadn't wanted anything to do with him. Eric had had no reason to think Langdon had lied about that, but neither could he believe that Sylviana was lying to him now.

He had better reason to believe his buddy had lied about how his marriage broke down. Looking at Sylviana Innocenti, transfixed by the beauty of a piece of marble, he could not believe she was the woman Steve Langdon had described. All the American soldier's reasons for fifteen years in exile had stopped making any sense—not the sense they had made when he'd walked away from the only woman he'd known, even then, he would ever love like that, not the sense he needed them to make now. He was making up his mind how to handle all that at the same time as he had to deal with not being the friend Steve had always counted on—not anymore, not ever again.

"I hope you don't mind, Marcello, but there's something I have to do." He glanced at his watch, then lifted his eyes to find Sylviana in the gallery, still deep in her adoration of the giant-slayer. "I'll find my way back to the hotel."

"Don't forget, Eric, our aunt has planned something special for you tonight."

"What time?" Marcello confirmed the time, and Eric promised he would be ready. He nodded back toward Sylviana. "She really loves this stuff, doesn't she?"

"It's in her blood, *Capitano*."

Syviana stared hard at Eric Wasserman's back as he dodged through the field of tourists blocking his escape. When the tourists settled back into their positions and there was no other sign of him, Sylviana let her eyes return to the disproportionate hand of the boy-warrior in white marble.

It was what she had said about Steven's daughter, about Steven, she was sure. Of course Eric knew. They were close friends. She had thought too much about her disappointment in Steven, not enough about the real world of war and men. She had depended too much on what she felt for Eric Wasserman and had not considered the possibility that he felt something different, if anything at all, for her. She had thought too much about the future she wanted and nothing about Eric's loyalty to a man who had cheated them both or their long friendship. *How can I tell him that?*

"Is your *Capitano* all right, Sylviana?"

"What did he say?" She slipped her hand into the crook of Marcello's arm as they walked from the Galleria toward the center of the city.

"He had something he had to do and then will go back to the hotel."

"Maybe one of his soldiers asked him for a souvenir or a picture of a particular building," Sylviana offered. "Maybe it was something from the phone call he got earlier." She kept her eyes on Il Duomo and the lines of tourists waiting to enter. "I would like to have a coffee before we return to the hotel. You and I have not had much opportunity to talk."

The café on the Piazza della Repubblica churned with Saturday shoppers, bargain hunters, and the moveable vendors of fake designer products. Sylviana waved them away before they were close enough to make an offer. Pouring her heart out to her older, male cousin seemed less attractive as the long shadows of the post office reached out and forced her deeper into her paisley scarf. So when Marcello gave her some news about his children, she responded in kind. They were both looking in the direction of the river, hidden behind the taller buildings. When their eyes met, they smiled, acknowledging with shrugs that they were both concerned for the American visitor.

"He's a big boy, Marcello. He's done all right without us for fifteen years."

Her cousin's laugh was as brief as her smile. They shrugged again, and she walked back to the hotel alone.

When Marcello arrived with Alessandro to collect their guest, he greeted Eric in the lobby with a sad smile. "I apologize if I offended you in some way this afternoon, Capitano Wasserman."

"Why would you think that?" Eric asked, handing his key to the night clerk.

"We have not seen Sylviana for many years. This trouble with her husband has been sad for all of us. We were so happy to have an opportunity to help, to make her a little happy, that I am afraid we have made you uncomfortable. Embarrassed. We have not meant to offend you."

"I don't understand, Marcello. This has been, *is*, a fantastic gift. I'm just a bit overwhelmed, and," he said, positioning his beret on his head, "it has been a long time since I last saw . . . Mrs. Langdon."

Marcello nodded his head a few times. "As long as you are happy, *Capitano*. This is all Sylviana, all any of us, wanted. Tonight, you will have plenty of time to relax and enjoy yourself. This is a gathering of relatives. A family meal to welcome you among us. There will be no reason for you to be under any strain."

At the home of Julietta and Cesario, Marcello introduced him to his youngest daughter, a girl of about twenty-three, who also had olive green eyes and dark brown hair. "At my wife's insistence, her name is Marcella."

"Pleased to meet you, Marcella."

"And I am very pleased to meet you, Captain Wasserman. We have heard so much about you by now, I feel we are well acquainted."

"I'm at a disadvantage, I'm afraid. Are you in college?"

"No, Captain. I am a teacher—English at the high school. You are somewhere close by, in the Balkans, yes?"

"Not for much longer. How did you know?"

"It is no secret here that NATO troops are there, and you all wear this insignia." She pointed to the symbol above his breast pocket. "And you all come to Italy to enjoy."

"Very observant."

"I work with teenagers, Captain Wasserman." She laughed.

"Scary. I'll watch my step."

When someone else came to the door, the American turned away from her, but the person he waited to see hadn't arrived, and he scanned the rest of the faces in the two lower rooms, recognizing some from the *ristorante bistecca*. He acknowledged them with a smile and continued scanning. Someone placed a tall glass in his hand. Someone else offered him antipasto.

"Is Sylviana here?"

"No, Captain," Julietta answered. "She felt it would be better if she did not come. She stayed at the hotel."

He felt the twisting blade cut through him, slashing through to his spine. "Where is she staying? My hotel?"

"*Sì*, she did not feel well when I spoke to her," Julietta told him, "so she stayed there."

After a while, his distraction must have annoyed Marcella. She moved to another group and was replaced by two younger boys who wanted to know more about the American Army. For the remainder of the evening he talked to them and the older relatives who chatted about houses, cars, and movies.

Julietta came to sit with him at the table, pushing another glass of *birra* near his hand. "It is too bad that my niece cannot be here. Her papa was happy that she would see his family after so many years. Sylviana was so happy when she told us she was able to come, but illness is difficult so far from home."

"Yes, ma'am. If I had known she was staying at the hotel, I would have—" He stopped. He thought better of telling her aunt what he would have done if he'd known she was so close. He wouldn't have left her there alone. He wouldn't have let her out of his sight. If he could negotiate with enemy combatants, he could negotiate a settlement with Sylviana Innocenti.

"You smile, *Capitano*. Of course you would want to make sure that Sylviana was all right. She chose to stay near you so she could make arrangements easily, if there was something special you wanted."

"You have all been very kind, very generous."

"You would do the same for us, yes?"

"If I could. If that was possible."

"You are a good man. We all saw that last night. No one knew that Sylviana had kept her arrival a surprise for you, *Capitano*. We thought you knew she was coming, but when we realized you did not think you would see her, we understood at once how hard it must have been to hide your disappointment. When you long to see a loved one, no amount of kindness can fill such an empty place. But"—she laid a hand on his arm—"the happiness in your eyes when she came through the door—ah, that was worth all of our small efforts to make you welcome in Firenze. She is a good girl. She deserves a good man like you. The two of you will be happy together. I can see that in the way your eyes caress each other when the other is not looking. I will make you a beautiful cake for your wedding."

"Thank you, *signora*."

"Have you told her what is in your heart?"

"No, *signora*. It's not as simple as that."

"Do you think she is here only to see her relatives? No. She is here because of you, *Capitano*. Are you here to see Firenze? No. You are here because of her. Very simple."

"*Signora*—"

"Be honest, Eric Wasserman. That is not such a bad thing. That is a very good thing between two hearts that have been broken." She rose from the chair and patted his cheek. "Now I think it is time you went back to the hotel, Eric. You have been too long apart from my niece, and she will be very lonely by now."

Eric sat in the front seat with Alessandro, watching the ancient buildings disappear as they sped back into the city. *Honest*. If he was honest, he had to tell Sylviana that he had deserted her, half knowing that Steve Langdon was not and had never been the right man for a girl whose heart was that open, that trusting. He had abandoned her to a guy who'd once saved his life because he'd needed to pay that debt.

"Tomorrow, you will see the palace Cosimo de Medici built for his wife."

"*Grazie*, Sandro. I'll look forward to seeing that with Sylviana."

At the desk, he checked the number of Sylviana's room and collected his key. In his room, he shaved again, staring at his face in the mirror, meeting the eyes of a man he had always thought he could trust, a man his friends, the people in his unit, could trust. He hadn't been that man for Sylviana Innocenti. He had swallowed every word Steve had told him about their happy family because he'd needed to be absolved, needed to believe he had done the right thing for her. All the time his gut had told him that Steve was grinding her down. He'd known, but he'd let it happen. One debt was paid while he built up another, bigger one.

Before he walked down the three flights to her room, Captain Eric Wasserman dug deep to find the gawky pump-jockey and the man she could trust, that honest man Julietta wanted him to be. He stood outside her door for a few minutes, put his beret into position, and tapped on the middle panel. After a few moments he tapped again a little louder and heard movement. He tapped once more and stood straight.

"Captain Wasserman, ma'am. May I come in?" He listened as the bolt and security hook were released, and he took a half step back, standing at attention, gradually lowering his gaze until his eyes met hers. "Please excuse the intrusion. I know it's late and you aren't well, but I wanted to be the first to wish you a Happy Birthday, Sylviana."

She hid behind the door, holding her robe together at the neck, her hair disheveled and no makeup. "How did you know my birthday is tomorrow? Did Julietta tell you?"

"Steven Langdon told me. A long time ago. While we were still in touch, he mentioned your birthday and always asked me what I thought you might like."

"Did you tell him?"

"No."

"Why not?

"Salt in the wound, ma'am," he answered, frowning.

One of the doors in the corridor flew open, and a large man shook a fist at Captain Wasserman. Behind him, a thin woman pinched all the muscles of her face together and shook her head at the American soldier and the half-dressed woman. Sylviana beckoned the officer into her room.

Before she closed the door, Eric turned to the couple, giving them a solemn salute. "Good evening, sir. Ma'am."

Eric stood inside the room, listening as the couple settled into their room again. "Come on, we can't stay here."

"Where are we going?" she whispered in return.

"There has to be a club or a bar open at this time of night."

"But I'm not dressed."

"You look fine to me."

Sylviana ran a hand through the tangles of her hair. "It won't take long," she promised, all her instincts urging her to take her time, make him wait, make the wait worthwhile. "Sit down, Eric. I won't be long," she assured him again.

Before she did anything else, Sylviana chose the dress to wear, the shoes—the less suitable for walking, the better. Once she had determined her physical armor, she locked the door to the bathroom and assembled her psychological weaponry. She showered, shampooed, conditioned, exfoliated, buffed, lotioned, and creamed, until she presented the new and improved Sylviana Innocenti to the thirty-five-year-old woman in the full-length mirror. Announcing her arrival to the American soldier with a click of the bathroom lock, she stood for a moment at the closed door, then let her hand turn the knob and open the door and commanded her body to stand where Eric Wasserman could see her.

He stood by the window, his beret clasped in his hands, his shoulders square and his back as straight as a wire tightened to the breaking point, but his eyes were not on her.

"I'm sorry. Did I take too long?"

"No, it's okay. Are you ready?" he asked, turning away from the window.

"Yes."

"Maybe you don't want—if you're not feeling well—"

"Eric, it's practically my birthday."

"How do you feel?"

"Don't mention it."

He took a few steps toward her. "I didn't want to make you unhappy, Sylviana."

"Then stop talking, and take me out for my birthday." She danced a few steps and smiled at him, a whirlwind. The dress wasn't blue, but it swirled around her, engulfing him in possibilities.

"Yes, ma'am," he laughed, a smile sparkling in his eyes.

At the desk, she handed in both their keys, tugged her silk shawl around her upper arms, and waited for Eric to settle his beret on his head. "You are very handsome, soldier." When his only response was a shake of his head, she slipped her hand through his arm and walked with him along the river to the Piazza della Signoria. There was music and laughter all around them.

As they walked, Captain Wasserman laid his hand over hers and smiled at the woman on his arm. "Have you eaten?" He peered into her face. "Can we get a late meal for you?"

"I don't really need anything to eat, but a glass of wine would be good."

He held her hand as they approached an outdoor bar, conscious that heads turned to follow them. As they reached the bar, he eased her closer to him and dropped his arm around her back, finding a position he could defend if necessary or escape easily if defense was unworkable. "*Un bicchiere di vino*—Chianti," he ordered, "*un bicchiere di birra, per favore.*"

"I'm impressed," Sylviana murmured, leaning close to him, her lips brushing his jaw.

"Don't be." His smile was crooked. "It took me all the time you were dressing to get that much stuck in my head."

"You did it—that's impressive."

"Hey, Americano."

Eric glanced in the direction of the speaker, a young man

among friends going for the title of big man of the night at the American soldier's expense.

"Ignore him," Sylviana whispered, sliding her arm around his lean waist.

"American soldier. I am talking to you."

Eric glanced down at the pretty face just under his chin, aching to kiss her, so she knew he was waiting for her to ask for the moon, ready to offer anything she wanted.

"Hey, soldier. I am talking. You hear me?"

"I hear you," Eric said, just above a whisper.

"Why have you come here? There is no war here for you."

"What do you want me to do?" Eric whispered against her temple.

"He's not worth it, Eric. Let's go."

"Mind if we finish our conversation and these drinks?" he asked the group of young men.

"Yes. Yes, I do. We do. Take your war someplace else, you—"

"Not in front of the lady," Eric said. He gave the young man a casual salute and turned back to his conversation with Sylviana.

Sylviana tilted her chin, opened her mouth to speak. The temptation to taste her drilled a spike into his body, and he lowered his head, just enough to touch his lips to her mouth.

"What did you call me?" she hissed at the young man, swinging away from her almost-lover, lunging in the puppy's direction, still in Eric's arms but ready to fight.

"You heard. You are worse than dirt."

Several of the patrons laughed. Sylviana straightened her shoulders and bit her index finger with a sharp flick of her hand. The young man stabbed at his throat with his whole hand, and Sylviana doubled her fist. Eric finished his *birra* and extended his hand to her opponent.

"Name's Eric." The puppy bit his thumb at the American. The drinkers closest to the couple moved away. "I have a guy in my unit named Giulio. Do you have family in Boston?" Giulio stared at the American. "What about Philadelphia? A gal in my unit has family in Firenze, last name Martinelli. Maybe you know them?"

"This is a big city," Giulio replied.

"You're right," the American said with a big smile, wrapping his arm around his date. "Nice to meet you, Giulio. If you ever get to San Francisco, give me a call, right?" He saluted the puppy and his friends, guiding Sylviana past them through a gap in the tables back to the square. "Have you eaten tonight? You didn't have much lunch."

"How did you know his name?"

"Another thing I learned in training. I listen hard." He straightened her scarf, running his hand down the center of her spine to her hip. "I don't suppose Julietta would be too happy, but I could eat again."

"She wouldn't like to hear that," Sylviana agreed.

Chapter Eight

He took her hand to lead her across the piazza to a small restaurant and asked for a table indoors. While they waited to be seated, he said, "Tell me about all your relatives here."

"You've met them—almost all of them."

"Then tell me about your relatives in Wales."

"I have nine aunts and uncles, so many cousins I can't keep track, and they all live in the southwest."

"Start with your first uncle," he said, tracing his finger along the edge of her hairline toward her earlobe and was rewarded when she leaned into the caress. "Tell me anything."

"You'll be sorry," she laughed. "There's this thing called the Welsh pedigree—either you have one, or you don't."

"How does it work?"

"Relations. Family. Who you know and who knows you." The waiter beckoned them through a gap between tables, offering seats in a corner and gold-bordered menus. Eric read his menu through before he ordered a pasta dish. "What about you?"

"*Zuppa.*"

"You had that for lunch."

"I like it."

"You won't have much energy for your birthday," he said.

"I'll eat a big breakfast."

"I'll see that you do. How much of a pedigree does your family have?"

"Not much, just four generations, but lots of cousins and second cousins. We don't keep in touch all the time, but as soon as something goes wrong, they're there—all over the place. It's annoying sometimes, but it's a good thing. Funny, though," she said, watching his face. He was listening just as he had fifteen years ago, but there was another dimension of concentration going on. She looked around the restaurant but saw nothing out of the ordinary.

"What's funny?" Eric asked

"How similar the Welsh and Italian sides of my family are. Maybe that's why so many left here and ended up there. And in America too."

He was close to saying, *Yeah, I guess*—all he had to offer in a conversation about family. Eric put his money on the table, and they returned to the public square to listen to the street musicians. He found a place for her to sit and put his uniform jacket around her shoulders when she shivered, keeping her close to him, watching her face while they listened to the music. Sylviana dropped her head to his shoulder, but when he made no response, she sat erect again and focused on the string quartet. "What's on for tomorrow?" he asked when the musicians took a break.

"Anything you want . . . until my birthday party."

"What time will that be?"

"Seven or so."

"1900 hours."

"Yes, sir."

"That gives us most of the day."

She shrugged her agreement.

"We'd better go back to the hotel."

"Okay."

When he pulled her to her feet, he buttoned his jacket around her, smoothing the shoulders, and met her eyes for a moment. "I have a birthday present for you, Sylviana. I want to give it to you now, so if you don't like it, we'll have time to exchange it tomorrow."

She pushed her arms through the sleeves of the jacket and accepted the small box he took from the lower pocket and placed in her hand. "You didn't have to do this, Eric. I didn't expect anything from you."

"You should have. I figure I owe you at least fifteen years' worth of birthday and Christmas presents, Valentine's, Columbus Day—"

"You don't owe me anything. No debts, okay?"

"Open it, Sylviana, please."

"Yes, sir. Whatever you say, sir." She saluted with a giggle.

"If you don't like it . . ." he began as she pried the velvet lid open. The meager illumination from a lamppost cast a white glow over them. Sylviana tilted the small flat box to catch the light and lifted her eyes to peer at Eric, her eyes shining as brightly as his. He grinned, pressed his lips together, and raised his eyes to stare over her head.

"It's beautiful."

"It . . . uh . . . I thought when I saw it, you should have it. I would have given it to you at your aunt and uncle's, earlier—"

"This is better," she said, pressing two fingers over his mouth. "Will you help me put it on?" She worked the chain free and turned her back. Holding the two interlocking hearts tightly against her palm, she trembled when he fumbled with the clasp and took a deep breath.

"I've never been very good at these things."

"You're doing fine, Captain Wasserman." She swung around to show him. "Does it look all right?"

"On you, perfect." He reached to straighten the gold chain over her collarbone, and his hand shook. "Good thing this isn't a combat zone."

"Why do you say that?"

He lifted his eyes to her face again and shrugged away the comment. "Do you like to dance, Sylviana?"

"Yes."

He clasped her hand and slid his arm around her back, taking a few dance steps in time with the violins, out of the circle of light and into the shadow of the Palazzo Vecchio, keeping a distance of the width of his hand between them, and he didn't stop dancing when the music ended. "Can you walk back to the hotel, or do I need to carry you?"

"I can walk. These shoes are not as silly as the others," Sylviana answered, displaying the shiny black sandal on her left foot.

Eric studied her foot and ankle, following the length of her calf to her knee and the hem of her purple dress swirling in the moonlight. "I need to carry you."

"I can walk, honestly." She laughed and swayed out of his arms to begin the journey.

"No," he said, catching her hand. "I *want* to carry you."

"Okay." She took off the sandals, hooking the straps over her fingers, lifting her arms, ready to be hoisted over his shoulder. He grinned at her for a moment before taking off his beret, setting it cockeyed on her head, and sweeping her up. "You can't carry me all the way like this. I'm too heavy. Your arms will drop off."

"You are heavy," he said, laughing, after a few strides, dropping her legs but still holding her with one arm. "That's better."

"Not from where I am."

He stopped in midstride, wrapping both arms around her, and leaned his hips against the wall of the embankment, lifting her so that her eyes were level with his. "I don't want to get this wrong, Sylviana. I never thought I would see you again. I thought I could live with that." She searched his eyes, but there wasn't enough moonlight to see what he could possibly mean. "When I got your first letter, I felt like one of my own unit had rammed a knife into my gut and was slashing around."

"That bad, huh?"

"That bad. I got over it, like I got over every letter I had from Steve telling me what a great life he had. I figured you were getting your kicks too."

"Why? Why would you think that?"

"Why wouldn't I? I had no reason to believe you even remembered me. Why would you, unless Steve had told you something, and you wanted some fun, or revenge?"

"If you thought I was capable of that, why didn't you just send my letters back or tell me you weren't interested?" She pushed against him to be released, but his arms locked tighter.

"As bad as it was, I couldn't do that. I'd thought about you every day of my life since we met. Raising your girls, being happy, going places. When Steve stopped writing, I just wanted to know you were okay, happy. I could live with that. But then I got your letters, and I read them over and over, looking for anything that might tell me you weren't laughing your head off at the dumb cluck who couldn't take his eyes off you fifteen years ago and still can't. I love you, Sylviana. I've loved you all these years—how dumb is that?"

"Not as dumb as an airhead who knows she's marrying the wrong guy but plows on like she can make him right."

He took her shoes from her hand and slipped them onto her feet, clasped her hand, and strolled back to the hotel, his free hand in his trousers pocket. Dimitri, the night clerk, handed the keys to their rooms to the American soldier, smiling at Sylviana while nodding approvingly at the beret and the uniform jacket she now wore. Eric pressed the call button and, in the elevator, punched the button for her floor.

"You don't have to walk me home," she murmured when the elevator door opened on her floor. She unbuttoned the jacket and removed it while he held the door open. "See you in the morning, Eric." She put the beret on top of his jacket.

"I'll order your breakfast," he said, punching the button for his floor. Sylviana turned to step into the corridor. "Does this place have room service?" he asked.

"Yes," she said, still in the elevator, pressing her lips together and staring at his hand holding the door open.

"If you're feeling better, will you have a drink with me? There's a lounge on my floor. We could sit there for a while."

"Okay."

He released the door. When they reached the floor, the lounge was dark, and they stood at the top of the steps, staring at the empty furniture. "Scratch that," he murmured, glancing at her and, as quickly, staring at the floor.

"We could go to my room." A nervous giggle waited for its chance to humiliate her.

"Yeah." His tone was not an affirmation. "There's a terrace. On the roof." Her whole body shivered in that state of tension that refuses to acknowledge age or sophistication. Eric turned on his heel and led her along the carpeted corridor to the stairs. "It looked okay when I did some recon. It's glassed in," he said, opening the door and standing back, "shouldn't be too cold." Sylviana walked through, seeing nothing but the shining glass wall overlooking the river. While she stood there, with her back to him, she heard him shut the door and take a step onto the tiled floor. When she turned to face him, she saw a tall, handsome man—not gawky, not silent—but still smiling as though he had woken up in a world of magic. She hoped he was seeing the girl in the complicated dress she had been fifteen years ago.

He hadn't been in uniform then, but, watching him loosen his tie, she knew he would never be comfortable in street clothes. She walked across the terrace to him. "Here, let me help you." Though her hands were shaking, she made less of a hash of the job than he had been. "There." She smoothed the two ends while he worked the collar button free.

"Do you want a drink, Sylviana?"

She lifted her gaze to his face and met the eyes that couldn't stop looking at her. "No." She had only breathed the word when she felt his body sway, as though he had been hit by a tsunami, hissing once to fight it and giving in with a groan when he kissed her. *Please, don't let me get this wrong*, she prayed as she laid her hands on his chest, then slid her arms around his neck. He kissed her lips, warm and long and hungry, so hungry that her throat ached to cry out in rage at all the years she had loved him and he hadn't known.

"Slow," he whispered against her mouth. "Nice and slow, baby."

She dropped her arms to her sides, following his lead, letting him take his own time.

He took long breaths, tracing his hands down her arms to the tips of her fingers. She laid her head on his shoulder, fighting to hold back the tears, her throat cracking like glass. "Eric—"

"Shh. Don't say a word."

"But—"

He pressed a finger over her lips, still taking deep, slow breaths, until his heartbeat decelerated, one beat after another, until he was no longer agitated, no longer frantic.

"Maybe we should go downstairs, to the lobby," she said, glancing around the rooftop at all the windows overlooking them.

"Why?" he asked, folding his arms tightly around her waist.

"You'll get a bad name."

"I'm an American soldier. I already have a bad name."

"That's not true. It's just publicity, not getting the right angle at first. Take that kid tonight. Once you talked to him, he was in your pocket."

"Training, Sylviana," he said. "We defuse first, if we can."

"You're good at it. Maybe you should go into PR."

"I like what I do." He moved away to sit on the edge of one of the sofas. "Not many get that. The Army is a career choice. Our profession. Just like PR men, doctors, lawyers."

"I know that," she replied, turning away from him. "I wasn't suggesting anything otherwise, Eric. It's not my place."

"After I re-enlisted, I did a lot of thinking. Soul-searching. I didn't give Stateside much of a chance."

"Do you regret that?"

"Honest answer is no." He watched her as she walked back to the glass wall, pressing her hands on the surface. "I went into the Army the second day I was out of high school. There were no jobs in Lodi—still aren't many—but then it was pump-jockey or ranch hand. A few of us enlisted together. A couple of guys went into the Navy, another few into the Air Force."

"Why the Army, Eric?"

"I liked tanks better than boats and planes."

"Sounds like the same logic my brother would use," she said, laying her forehead on the cold glass, staring at the silver slash of the Arno. "So why did you leave the Army back then?"

"After almost five years and as many war zones, I thought I wanted something else. Steve painted a rosy picture. But the only real difference was that no one was shooting at me. I took the job, but my boss was a bigger jerk than my sergeant. At least I knew my sergeant was doing his best to keep me from getting killed. Steve's description was pretty overblown—his job was the same jazz, but it turned out he was better at dealing with the other working stiffs. The only good thing was the chance to meet civilian girls. But that didn't work out either . . ." he said, standing to lean against the bar. "Sure you're feeling okay?"

"I'm okay. Fine." She shivered. "I can't figure out why you hardly said a word to me."

"Long story." He dragged his tie from around his neck and folded it onto the bar.

"And you're not ready to tell me."

"No. Give me a chance to dazzle you with my good qualities before I admit any flaws."

"So, there you were, a brilliant guy who'd just met a girl and . . . ?"

"And I . . . when that went south, I knew where I had to go."

"Back to the Army."

"I knew I could make something of myself there. Be useful. Serve my country. I didn't have to be target practice. I made a few phone calls and went into officers' training. Took me a while to get started—had to get a college degree."

"What in?"

"International Law."

"Wow, pretty heavy for a pump-jockey."

He was silent for a few minutes, fascinated by the tap of her lacquered fingernails on the glass. "I received all my commissions in the field, and then they put me behind a desk for a while."

"Where are you now?"

He changed the subject. "What about you, Sylviana? You were in art school."

"Me and half the kids in my graduating class." She noticed he hadn't answered her question. "I didn't have a clue what I really wanted to do. But modeling for the life-drawing classes was a great way to make some money and my dad really mad. Gave me lots of time to think, and I realized I didn't really have the same kind of artistic inspiration my classmates had. I was just the girl who could sit still for hours. I went to all the parties and gallery openings and book launches, keeping my options open for a big white light of inspiration to get me on the right track."

"Did you find out what you wanted to do?"

"No white light. Artists need an audience, right? I've always kept up my interest and . . . well, I met this guy."

He clenched his jaw, not sure he wanted to hear the next chapter.

"He was just there one night," she continued softly, "and I couldn't get close enough, fast enough. By the time I was in the same corner, he was itching to leave but I kept talking. A few weeks later, I saw him again, and that time I didn't waste any time getting up close. I was so excited, I talked the whole time, never gave him a chance to say a word, but I got to be close to him, look into his eyes, touch him, and that was it. I knew he was the right guy. After that, I pestered all my friends to have parties so I could see him again. I knew his friend from a party three or four months back, and I even asked him to bring this guy the next time, but the guy never came back."

Eric clasped his hands together, concentrating hard on the glazed tiles.

"Steven told me he'd gone off to marry a girl and take care of his kid, somewhere they'd been when they were in the Army." She turned her head to look at his quiet face, at the pale veins on his eyelids. "So eventually I married Steven. He must have guessed he was second best," she mused aloud. Then she shrugged. "After the divorce, I dated a few men, nice guys, but I kept thinking about this one, sweet guy from fifteen years ago, and I thought, if Steven had lied about one thing, maybe he had lied about other things."

"Had he?"

"Did you marry that girl?"

"There wasn't any girl. No kid either."

"I didn't think so, not after I found out that *Steven* had left a daughter behind. I *knew* you'd be the kind of guy who *would* go back, marry the girl, and raise your kid. But at the time I believed Steven, even though he wasn't that kind of guy."

"Sylviana, I'd be dead if not for Steve Langdon. He got me through some rough times. He saved my life. I still owe him for that."

"He has the medal to prove it. Got all the prizes." She stretched her arm to the edge of the glass panel and wrapped her fingers around the edge.

"He was a brave guy—never asked for anything in return. Never."

"That didn't stop him from stealing it. He never had to ask, Eric. He just took what he wanted. You gave it willingly. He lied to me. He knew exactly what he was doing, and he lied. I hadn't been dating him. He was just another guy, back from serving his country. Some kind of hero but no one special, not to me. I had already met the man I wanted to marry. Two weeks later, that man was gone before I even had a chance to catch his eye."

"You must have thought he was a jerk."

"I thought what I thought from the moment I saw him at the art gallery and the way he smiled at me at Aggy's party—the last time I saw him."

"What was that? What did you think?"

"That he was the right guy who'd always do the right thing, but I was the wrong girl. When he didn't come back, I figured he didn't feel the same, so I did the best I could with what I had left."

"You can't think that guy was worth much when you found out he didn't do the right thing after all. That he'd been run off, blindsided by his best friend."

"I didn't know that. He didn't know how I felt, and, even if he did feel the same about me, he was the kind of guy who'd rather choke himself to death than stab a friend in the back. It's just too bad he didn't know that Steven didn't have the same sense of loyalty."

"Maybe this guy wasn't the brightest penny in the roll."

Chapter Nine

P robably not," she said, laughing, turning so that the moonlight silhouetted her against the sky, "but he's cute, and I love him."

"That's a big leap, when you haven't seen him in fifteen years."

"On the contrary, Captain Wasserman. He's been there for me in my heart when it mattered, when I could never count on Steven."

"How do you know, Sylviana? Maybe he's just a jerk, like Eva said."

"She didn't know who you were when you called." She took a step forward. He glanced toward her but steadied his gaze on the city lights behind her. "Actually, Eva was the first time it mattered, Eric. I knew if I had married the right guy, he'd have been there when his baby was born. For Steven, it had all been about getting me away from you. Then the fun was over. No competition, no challenge." When he didn't reply, after a long silence Sylviana strolled back to the window wall and watched the slashes of silver across the water.

"I let you down, Sylviana." When she opened her mouth to protest, he shook his head. "If I hadn't been such a coward, I would have stayed near you and known that you needed me. I can never make that up to you. I believed Steve would love you the way I wanted to love you. I thought he would be the kind of husband and father that I wanted to be. But I didn't stick around to find out, to make sure. If I had, I can't say for sure that anything would have been any better. We'll never know, Sylviana. I left you. You married him. We can't change that."

Sylviana stared into his eyes, then searched his face. "What are you saying?" Her throat was so tight, it hurt to speak. "What does that mean?"

"We're not the same people we were back then. There's nothing I want more than to turn back time, be that kid who loved you so much that he kept loving you without seeing you for fifteen years."

"I loved you too."

"You didn't know anything about me."

"I knew enough. I just knew, Eric, and I let you go. So, we're even. Where do we go from here?"

"You were obviously meant to be a mom, Sylviana. I'm not sure I would have been a good dad back then. I don't know that even now."

She didn't say, *You didn't get a chance to find out.* "Nobody knows for sure."

"You're a great mom."

"Did you think your parents were great, Eric?" When he didn't answer, she said, "I think they must have been the best."

He shrugged, shook his head and moved to face her, laying his hand on her cheek. "I wouldn't be here if I was anything like them." He bowed his head. She tilted her chin up and touched his lips. "Neither of them saw what was on the other side of the hills or went down to the valley," he murmured, his fingers following the contour of her cheek until his hand came to rest and his fingers convulsed. "They always said, 'We don't have to go there to know we won't like it.' Drove me nuts." His lips traveled the route his hand had taken. His hand clenched, inches from plunder. *Cool off, Wasserman.* He relaxed his hand, then met her eyes. This was not how he wanted their few hours together to be. He didn't want furtive. He didn't want groping, grabbing whatever he could get.

"I think they were wonderful, then," Sylviana breathed, laying her hand on the back of his close-shorn head, arching her neck. "Where would we be if they'd taken you to all the places you've been, and you never wanted to leave Lodi again?"

Eric didn't answer. He pressed a kiss into the center of her palm, traced his fingertips along the edge of the dress. No snares. No concealed weapons. Nothing to stop him. Teenage stuff. Backseat-of-his-dad's-car territory. *Shut it down, GI. Save it.* He wanted full on, lights on.

She didn't ask, *Where are we going?* when he clasped her

hand, leading her off the terrace and down the stairs. She didn't ask, *What's wrong?*

He took the room key from her and pushed her door open, making a visual check of the room before he put the key on the dressing table. "What time is Marcello showing up?"

"It's not Marcello tomorrow. Sandro is driving us to the Etruscan village, Fiesole, and into the countryside. We'll have lunch in Pisa."

He reached out, drawing her into his arms. "I want you to know how much all this has meant—means—to me, Sylviana. You have all been so generous. Thank you for sharing your family with me."

For a moment, she thought she knew what to say, but the words dissolved as though they were seeping out of her and into some empty chasm. The abyss was terrible. She nodded her head, pressing her brow to his shoulder.

"I wish I could live on your smile," he said, cupping her chin, brushing his thumb over her lips. "I'll meet you in the dining room. 0800 hours?"

"Okay."

He was gone before the pressure of his hand faded from her cheek. When he left her, with just a whisper to wish her a good night's sleep, Sylviana watched him from the doorway until the elevator shuddered closed and the light for the number of his floor went dark. *Why can you never shut up, Sylviana?* Her mother had told her to hit him between the eyes. She hadn't said anything about talking him to death.

Sylviana stared into her own eyes in the mirror in the bathroom. "What happened? You were there tonight. What did you miss?"

Her wake-up call hadn't shifted the lethargy she'd let bully her into staring at the wall of the house across the piazza. Sylviana didn't want to know what that look in Eric's ocean-deep eyes had meant. She didn't want to think about what she had said to put that look there. She knew she'd messed up. She always messed up with Eric Daniel David Wasserman. Talked too much. Said all the wrong, empty-headed things. Showed him how dumb she was. Proved she was what he thought, what they all thought. Ditz. Loud. Empty. Why else would she travel half a world away to be with him for a few days? Had to be desperate. He had probably been thinking, *Steven doesn't want her, so, hey, why not?* And then had come that look. That *There's a reason Steve didn't want her* look.

"*Pronto.*"

"Oh. Hmm. Hi. Is Captain Wasserman there?"

"*Como?*"

"Captain Wasserman?"

"*Sì.*"

"May I speak to him?"

"*Sì.* English? Is *importante*?" Sylviana heard the woman on the other end of the line cover the mouthpiece, but she could still hear some murmuring. Another voice interrupted, and the first woman came back.

"Tell Captain Wasserman, *il Capitano*, that Lieutenant Jones called. Lieutenant Jones. Do you understand?"

"*Sì. Capisco.* Lieutenant Jones. *Sì.*"

"*Importante, capisce*?"

"*Sì.* Lieutenant Jones."

"We'll have to call again to be sure," she heard Lieutenant Jones tell her companion as she lowered the receiver. "That couldn't have been her, anyway." The line went dead.

Sylviana bit her lip. *How did that happen? That was stupid. But, hey, Sylviana, what can you expect from a ditz?* She dialed the number for Reception, too unnerved to search her brain for the Italian words she needed. "That call you put through to my room—"

"*Sì, signora.*"

"That was for another room—for four-ten. *Capisce?* Captain Wasserman. Room four-ten. Call him and let him know he missed a call from Lieutenant Jones, *per favore?*"

"*Sì, signora.* Is there a problem?"

"No. Someone put the call through to room one-four-six. Captain Wasserman isn't here."

"Ah, *sì*. There was no answer in four-one-oh. Dimitri was mistaken. Many apologies."

"No problem," Sylviana replied, breathing again. "Just let Captain Wasserman know, *per favore*, that he should call Lieutenant Jones. *Sì?*"

Once downstairs and at the door of the dining room, Sylviana took a deep breath and located her American soldier at a table with two place settings. She had chosen jeans and a white shirt, folding back the cuffs and turning up the collar. She wore only a little makeup—no mascara, just a touch of lipstick. On one side of him, the couple from the room next to hers were leaning in his direction, now smiling and nodding instead of grumbling and shaking fists at him. At another table, two young women also smiled and listened.

When Eric saw her, he broke off his conversations and rose to his feet. Sylviana hung her bag over the back of the chair.

"*Americano, signora?*"

"*Sì, grazie.*"

"Good morning," the woman, also American, said to her.

"The Captain was telling us how kind your family has been to him. Very good of you all to look after our boys," the man said.

"It is a small thing to be kind. It costs very little, *signori*." Sylviana grasped at their assumption of her nationality, hid behind it, concealing her dismay that—in the light of day—there was a distance between her and Eric so profound, they were like strangers. The call from his Lieutenant Jones was just another reminder of that. *He has another life, one he doesn't want me in, doesn't need me to interfere in.*

"Captain Wasserman has told us all about how your husband saved his life. You must be very proud."

"My *ex*-husband did one good thing, *signora*. He followed it by doing many bad things."

"Oh, but Captain Wasserman said—"

"*Il capitano* is too kind to see the truth," Sylviana said as Eric set a plate of cheese, Parma ham, and bread in front of her. "If my ex-husband had known the future, he would have pushed Capitano Wasserman toward the bullet—so that I would never know him."

"Surely, Mrs.—uh . . . your husband—"

"Stefano knew that I had fallen in love with his friend, but he did not do the right thing for me. He lied and stole from me the love of my life. Stefano replaced that with his triumph over this man." Sylviana thrust her hand in Eric's direction. "I have loved and longed for this man from the day I met him. If Stefano were here, he would rejoice that somehow he has triumphed again."

The American couple quickly returned to eating their breakfast. The two young women stopped staring at her and began talking fast about their plans for the day. Sylviana fixed her attention on her breakfast. The waitress set her *Americano* at the side of her plate. "*Grazie, signorina.*"

She did not look up to witness what her outburst had wrought, but she heard the American woman murmur, "Very emotional, all of them." Sylviana felt Eric staring at her, but she riveted her attention on her breakfast.

"Sandro is here."

Sylviana glanced at the door and motioned to her cousin's son and the young woman with him, making room for them around the table.

"I hope you do not mind, Capitano Wasserman, that I have brought Claudia. She speaks no English, but I thought . . . well, four is better than three, *sì*?"

"*Sì*, Alessandro. *Perfetto.*"

Sylviana planted her elbows on the table, holding her coffee cup in both hands, and began a conversation with the young woman. Sandro was already involved in his explanations of the day's excursion with Eric. Sylviana listened only for the tone of her almost-lover's voice and was relieved that he seemed relaxed, enthusiastic about the journey.

"I'm going up to the room for a bit. Phone call." Eric pushed his chair back to stand. "When you're ready, Sylviana, we'll be in the piazza."

She nodded but didn't look at him.

"Your family has planned a lovely day," the American woman said. "I hope you enjoy it . . . and Happy Birthday."

Sylviana covered her eyes with one hand as the couple left their table.

"Yeah, Happy Birthday," the two young women murmured, pushing past her.

Sylviana excused herself and ran up the stairs to her room. As she left, could hear Sandro and Claudia talking and laughing. *Too late for that in my story.* She brushed her teeth, reapplied the lipstick she had in her purse, and met her eyes in the mirror. "Definitely too late after that hysterical moment. If Steven ever needed your help to ruin your chances, you've handed it to him. Triumph on a silver platter." *Steven, 15. Sylviana, 0. As always.*

As she left her room, she promised that the few hours she had left with Eric Daniel David Wasserman would be free of desperation and hysteria. "I will be happy. It's my birthday, and I have more than I ever thought possible," she said in a whisper as she dropped her key into the slot at the front desk and strode through the wide door into the sunlit piazza. Eric and her young relatives were waiting for her at the car—an ancient American convertible with whitewall tires. "Where did you find this?"

"Papa," Sandro bragged. "His baby. He said it was the only way to see Tuscany. A surprise, for your birthday, Sylviana, and in honor of Capitano Wasserman's visit to our country."

Sylviana kissed her cousin's son and slid into the backseat, surprised when Eric joined her there, dropping his arm around her shoulders.

"No seat belts. More like a combat vehicle than a luxury ride," he quipped. His aftershave smelled of lime, and his jaw was smooth, as though he had shaved twice that morning.

"I'm sorry if I embarrassed you in front of those people," she said softly to him.

He looked away, across the river valley, over the terra-cotta roofs, and remained silent for so long, Sylviana gave up waiting for a response or forgiveness.

"*Capitano?*"

"*Sì*, Sandro?"

"Do you know the Etruscans?"

"Not personally," he replied, grinning at their driver in the rearview mirror.

Sandro grinned back. "I am your guide, but my cousin can

tell you information while I concentrate on this winding road past all these grand villas."

After a few moments of Sylviana's own silence, Eric leaned closer. "Are you going to keep the travelogue a secret, Sylviana?"

She caught her breath and began rattling off the guidebook notes. "The Etruscans were an ancient civilization. Fiesole was one of their towns in this region until the Florentines conquered them in the twelfth century. Virtually nothing remains of them— maybe a little in the Tuscan dialect, some mosaics."

"Some part of their fierce independence in the hearts of their descendents?" He stretched his hand toward her hair, confining a wisp that was whipping across her face.

Remember you are happy today. "I don't know if they were fierce, Eric, but they withstood the invasions of the Celts and the Visigoths and resisted Rome—as Firenze has always done," she declared, to which Alessandro responded with a fist in the air. Claudia laughed and did the same when her boyfriend translated for her.

"Rebels?"

"Ah, *Capitano* Eric," Sylviana said, turning her upper body toward him, "you must understand. What you call Italy has only existed for a matter of decades—minutes in the hearts of the citizens of its city-states. We like to fight. If we cannot fight Rome or Padua, we fight between families, between generations, brothers, sisters. North. South. Very emotional," Sylviana ended with a smile. "You see? We are not blind to our nature."

"Did you mean what you said at breakfast?" he asked quietly, finally broaching the delicate topic. "Do you love me, Sylviana?"

She turned into his embrace. She met his eyes and searched, praying she wasn't wrong this time. At least she was quiet.

"Yes? Is that yes?" He stared into her olive green eyes.

"Yes. That's yes."

"That's good. Makes it simple. You love me. I love you. No complications. What's the first thing you do in the morning?"

The abruptness of the question startled her into answering it. "Start trying to wake the girls." She settled into the crook of his arm, resting her head on his shoulder. *Simple. So simple. No fatal mistake—yet.*

"What time do you get up, Eric?"

"0530 hours."

"Yuck. What do you do first?"

"Think about you," he whispered, taking the opportunity to kiss her ear, tracing his fingers through her hair.

"Next?" She resisted the urge to succumb to the caress, exposed in the backseat of the American convertible for all of Italy to witness how much she longed for him.

"Shave, shower, breakfast."

"As much as you eat here?"

"Twice as much. Never know when you'll eat again."

"Where are you posted, Eric? What's your job?" When he again was silent, turning his attention to passing stone walls and trailing vines, she said, "If you don't want me to know—"

"It's not important for you to know. I don't want you to worry about where I am or what I do. Remember? It's just my job, Sylviana."

"Sandro, *per favore*. Stop the car. *Il capitano* and I will walk for a while. Maybe you two can go have some coffee?" *Mistake. Why can't you leave his life alone? He doesn't want you there.*

"Sure. Sure."

Too late, stupid. She watched Eric unfold his long legs and offer his hand. When the big red and white convertible drove off, Sylviana turned to face the tall American, folding her arms. "If you don't want me in your life, just say so." *Why are you doing this? Please make me shut up.* She was in full Italian-Welsh-American-emotional unfurl, and nothing she screamed at herself in her rational mind could stop her from picking this fight.

"Where is this coming from?"

"Me. It's coming from me." *This is me. This is me. I hate this.* "You think you can come back and—"

"Wait a minute. You came after me." *What did you say? You're dead, Wasserman. Brain-dead.* "I—"

"Yes, I did, but that doesn't give you the right to take what you want and go. Maybe you think I'm just a ditz or—"

"Who said I was going anywhere?"

"Isn't that easier? You don't tell me where you are or what you do, so I'll never know where to look for you—"

"You found me before, Sylviana."

"Only because you weren't hiding. And someone took pity on me, and your Lieutenant Jones thought you were unprofessional or something—"

"Behavior unbecoming an officer and a gentleman." Hard to avoid when he all wanted to do was love her, kiss her, enfold her into his life. *What kind of life? God, help me.*

"What if there is no Lieutenant Jones next time? What if you decide you don't want to be found? What if no one cares that a crazy woman loves you?"

"Marry me." *Whoa there, soldier. You can't do this.*

"What?"

"Marry me." *You're off track. It's no.* "You'll always know how to find me. The Army likes wives; they'll make sure you know. Unless it's classified, but they'll keep you in the loop." *Nothing to offer, no kind of life for her.*

"Are you serious?"

"Yes. Dead serious." *Crazy jerk, she's saying no. Listen.* "Will you marry me, Sylviana Innocenti?"

"Really?"

"Will you? We can do it here, tomorrow." *Where is your brain, GI?*

"You are serious."

"The second I found out you were divorced, that's all I've thought about."

"I love you, Eric, but you don't know me. I hardly know you. What if—?" *Be quiet, Sylviana. For once, just be quiet.*

"So what? It's got to be better than the last fifteen years—at least for me. I love you. You love me. Too soon? Is it selfish to ask?" *You know it is, jerk. You know what it will be like for her—and what about you? How're you going to do this?*

"You won't shut me out?" *Just say yes.*

"Never." *You're brain-dead, Wasserman. It's not going to be good enough for her.* "I'll make it right for you. I promise, Sylviana. I'll do my best."

"I have two little girls." *Yes, please just say yes, you dumb bimbo.* He didn't need any more reasons not to want her. She kept giving him all the reasons he shouldn't, all the reasons he'd walked away years ago.

"I know. Eva already thinks I'm a jerk. Enid sounds a little more open-minded but might change her mind when she finds out I might be her stepdad." *Good reasons. They already read you like a book.*

"She won't. She thinks you're cool."

"That's one for my side." *Leave it alone, you selfish jerk.*

"I'm on your side, Eric." *Something. That's something, Sylviana. That's good.* She watched his smile, that world-of-wonder-in-a-magic-place smile.

"That's two," he said, dropping his arms from around her waist. *Too late. Committed to the mission.* "Will you marry me?"

"Stupid question." *Is that your idea of yes, ditz?* "That's yes, Eric. Forty-two million times yes." She locked her arms around his neck, molded her body to him, and kissed his face and lips until he held her still, looking straight into her eyes.

"This is right," he said and kissed her, fifteen years' worth.

Sandro blew the horn of the flashy car, and Claudia clapped her hands. "My cousin," Sandro told the crowd of onlookers at the vista point, "and her new fiancé . . . probably."

"Audrey, come and look at this. Didn't I tell you there was something special about those folks? They're getting married."

"That explains everything," the American woman from the hotel said, joining in the applause as the American soldier and the Italian woman kissed on the footpath below the Fiesole fortress wall. A few of the young men began to whistle, but Sylviana heard only the repetition of her name and Eric Wasserman's promise to love her forever, as hard and true as he had always loved her.

"Can we really be married tomorrow?" she asked when they began the rest of the journey to the top of the hill.

"I checked, just in case I got up the nerve to ask you. All it takes is a bit of paperwork and a chaplain."

"Can you come home soon, if we're married? You'd be like the people in your unit—you'd have family, Eric."

"When I get leave. I can't promise when that will be, Sylviana. The unit's had its re-deployment orders."

"That's why Lieutenant Jones called?"

"That and to keep tabs on me. She was mighty disappointed she'd talked to you and didn't know you were *her*. She had a few things to say—thought you should know."

"What did you tell her?"

"The truth. For unit morale."

"I wasn't sure you wanted them to know."

"Know what, Sylviana? Better they think I wasn't with the woman I love?" he murmured, cupping her face in both hands. "Better for them to think you had dumped me for someone else or—?"

"Or what?"

"I don't want to make any mistakes, not this time."

Sylviana studied his face for a moment and decided she didn't need any further confession. She didn't need to know precisely what he was thinking. She didn't need to know what Lieutenant Jones might have wanted to tell her. She could find out whatever she needed in his eyes. She could be quiet. Eric crouched and motioned her onto his back, pulling her legs around his waist.

"You like doing this, don't you?"

"At your pace, we'll never get lunch," he teased.

After they had passed the last turn and waved to Claudia and Alessandro, Sylviana pressed against his back. "Do you want children, Eric?"

He stopped in midstride and turned his head to look at her. "Do you want more?"

"I asked you first."

"If it's in the cards."

"It's just that I'm thirty-five and have, maybe, three or four years of baby-making left." He set her feet on the ground again and put his hands on her waist. "At this rate, you'll never get any fuel," she pointed out.

"Fuel can wait. Here's the deal, Sylviana. I have another seven years before I can retire on any kind of pension."

"And that means?"

"That means, I'm not going to be around much. I don't want to drag you and your daughters around to live in military housing. Some people in my unit live like that. My CO's wife and kids live on base in Germany so he can see them when he gets two days together. I don't want that for you."

"What do you want?"

"You have a life in San Francisco. Let me become a part of that."

"And if I want something else?" *Can you never be quiet?*

"We'll talk about it."

"When?" *You're badgering him.*

"Not now."

"When?" *What does he have to do, you ditz, to prove he loves you?* "I'm sorry. I can't help it. I'm so scared that this isn't really real."

"Look," he said. "This is real. We're real. It's right. It's okay. I want to be your husband, look after you, be a family, have a baby with you, but it's complicated. I'm also career Army. I have a job to do, and I plan to do it while I can, while I can still make a difference. And that means I want to know you're safe. I want to think about you and your daughters—"

"They'll be your daughters too."

"I want to think about you all doing what you do—"

"What if I want a baby with you?"

"Great. I'll be happy knowing you'll get the best help there, with your own doctor, not in a base unit geared for soldiers. But I won't be around every day to help."

"Would you be happy with that, Eric? If we had children and you only saw them a few times—or less—a year?" *More reasons not to want you, Sylviana?*

Eric lifted his head and glanced at the American couple. "Anything that makes you happy, Sylviana, is what I want. That doesn't mean I can do it all. I'll want to be with you. I'll do my best, but—"

"I'm glad we settled that. I don't want to drag the girls around—they've been through enough."

"Why didn't you just say that?"

"Too risky," she said, wrapping her arms around his and returning to the climb.

"We've got a long way to go."

"About forty miles," Sylviana said happily, "but it'll be worth it. The food at my cousins' restaurant is to die for."

"*Another* cousin?"

"You've got a huge family now, Captain Wasserman." She wasn't sure if the sound he made then was a laugh or a groan.

Chapter Ten

Alessandro watched the couple, amazed that two old people could act so goofy and juvenile, but Claudia was enthralled and gave her boyfriend's "sophistication" the cold shoulder. She sat next to him on the ride back with her arms folded across her chest.

When they reached the hotel, Eric bent his head close to his intended's ear and said, "I'd like you to move to my room, Sylviana."

"Now? Everything?"

"If that's okay with you. Indulge me."

"Okay, but you've already asked me to marry you. I'm not letting you off the hook." She packed her bags and asked the desk clerk to transfer all her calls and messages to Eric's room. She stuffed tubes and bottles into her vanity case, a book into her purse, and made a visual sweep of the room she hoped she wouldn't see again. She sank onto the made-up bed and covered her eyes. *This has got to be right, Sylviana Innocenti.*

Eric picked up the receiver, twice, and each time set it back on the hook. He changed his mind a third time. What had stopped him last night from asking Sylviana to sleep with him was still his gut feeling. He was marrying the woman he'd loved all his adult life. Asking his fiancée to sleep with him on the eve of their wedding was a mistake; it proved he was a jerk, proved there was nothing special about the ceremony, proved he was no different from any of the other guys trying to figure out how to get her out of that blue contraption, proved he hadn't meant what he'd said about not making mistakes. He finished his shower and grasped the receiver. As soon as he lifted it, he heard a voice. *"Pronto?"*

"Mommy?"

Eric bolted to his feet from the bed, rubbing his short-cropped hair. "Hi, Enid, right? Your mom's not here." He wondered where the pit of his stomach had gone. His heart had stopped.

The seven-year-old whispered, "Are you having fun?"

"Yes, thank you. Wonderful. Your mom will be back soon."

"That's okay. I just wanted to say happy birthday."

"I'll tell her. She'll call you back. Okay?"

"We're at Daddy's."

Eric covered the mouthpiece before he swore. In the background, he heard Steven's voice and Eva's demand to be allowed to talk.

"I'm talking," Enid growled back. "Daddy said I could go first." When she spoke again, she shielded the receiver with a cupped hand. "I'm glad you're there. Grandma's been real worried, and Daddy's—"

"You've had your turn, Enid," Steven said, taking the receiver. Eric heard the seven-year-old's scream. "Sylvi, you know you shouldn't play favorites. What are you thinking?"

"Sylviana isn't here, Steve. It's Eric."

"Wasserman? What the hell? What the hell are you doing in my wife's room? What the hell are you doing in Italy?"

"This is my room. The call came through here." *Cop-out, Wasserman. Take the shot.* He'd put himself in the dark alley. He deserved the bullet. "Sylviana will be back in a second."

"What are you doing there? You . . . jerk," Langdon sputtered. "Couldn't wait, could you? Were you two—? How long have you been with my wife?"

In the distance, Eric heard Eva's shouting. "Steve, let me explain," Eric said, but what could he say? Not one day had passed in fifteen years that he hadn't thought about her. Not ten minutes had passed before he'd decided what he was going to do when he found out they were divorced. Not a moment had passed since she arrived in Firenze that he didn't think about making love to her, his best friend's ex-wife.

"You— How could you do this to me, after all I've done for you? After all the years we've been friends? You deserve that lying cheat. I hope she takes all you've got and—I thought you were a brother, Eric."

Eric opened his mouth, but before he said a word, Steve said, "Eva, come here, sweetheart. Your turn."

"Steve, that's not—" *A good idea.*

"Nice talking to you. I hope you're a better liar than you ever were a friend, Wasserboy."

"Happy Birthday, Mommy! I miss you. Enid's such a baby. Are you having a good time? Can we come next time?"

Eric stared into Sylviana's eyes as she slipped her hand over the mouthpiece and dropped onto the edge of the bed. "I miss you too, Eva." She still held her suitcase. "I'll be home soon, and I've got presents for you two."

"Like what?"

"Like you'll just have to wait and see."

"Enid woke everybody up because it's your birthday. We're not even dressed, and Daddy said we could call. What are you doing today? Daddy's going to take us on his boat again. Enid promised she wouldn't be sick this time. Do you want to talk to Daddy again?"

"No," Sylviana murmured, meeting Eric's worried eyes. "Tell Enid I miss her too, and be nice. She's only little. I'll see you before you go to sleep on Wednesday night. Tell your grandma that I did what she told me."

"Happy Birthday, Mommy."

"*Buonasera*, my darling."

Eric took the receiver and laid it on the hook as though it was made of sugar glass. "How did that happen?"

"My fault," she said with a grimace. "Bad timing. Sorry."

"Enid was on the phone. No warning. Nothing I could do."

"Don't worry, Eric. She already likes you."

"She won't after what Steven will have to say."

"I'd love to be there when he finds out I spoke to Eva. I wonder what he'll say."

"I don't," Eric said, falling back on the bed and dropping his arm over his eyes. "He thinks I betrayed him."

"That's rich," Sylviana whispered, lying on her side and resting her head on his shoulder.

"You're not worried?"

"What can I do about it? My mother will take care of any

fallout until I get home. Steven will do what he always does: have a tantrum."

He rolled away and sat on the side of the bed. "Can't say I'd blame him."

"You think he's right?" She told herself to drop it. She told herself she understood. "I do *not* want to have this conversation again, Eric."

"Maybe we should."

"Go ahead, but don't expect me to participate. I'm going to have a shower, maybe a nap, and then I'm going to get ready for my party."

"He thinks I had something to do with what happened between you two."

"There is no reason for him to think that. He's just looking for excuses so he doesn't have to take any responsibility." She pushed off the bed. "If the only reason you wanted me here was to defend Steven to me, I'll go back to my room."

"I just— Okay. I've been taking sniper bullets from him for years. I don't get it, Sylviana. He won the toss, so what's eating him?"

"You're a convenient target. Even if he'd never met you, he'd find a way of blaming you so he didn't have to blame himself."

"Wait a minute," he said, catching her by a belt loop before she escaped. "Don't you want to know why I asked you to be here?"

"I want to know a lot of things, Eric, but I can guess." She laid her hand over his, drifting closer to him, touching his face.

"I want," he said, kissing the palm of her hand, "to live with you—even for a few hours. I want to know what it's like watching you dress and put on your makeup."

"That's top-level security clearance, Captain. Need-to-know basis."

"It's Major to you, civvie, and I need to know."

"When did it get to be Major?"

"The other reason Clee phoned this morning. It didn't seem important at the time."

"But it is now?"

"Yeah, I guess," he laughed, "if it gets me security clearance."

"I'm still not convinced you merit that level of intelligence." She pushed his arms down and held herself away, threatening to run.

"I'll prove it," he murmured, pulling her back again.

"I'll trade. One of my secrets for one of yours."

"No negotiation on that?"

"None." Sylviana pushed her hands down on his shoulders and told herself to be quiet. "Where are you going when you leave here?" *That's not being quiet, ditz. That's a shout.*

"I know you don't mean tonight," he said. "My unit is in the Balkans. Peacekeeping. We've got another week to transfer operations over to the next NATO unit. What's the last thing you take off at night?"

"It depends where I've been, but usually my jewelry. Then I put on my pajamas."

"Show me those later," he said.

"What's your next job?"

"UN liaison in eastern Africa."

"What will your unit be doing?"

"Standing our ground to protect some folks. Hey, you owe me half a dozen answers. What do you like most about your job, Sylviana?" He kissed her fingers, eased her down to the bed, lying on his side with her spine against his chest, and kissed the back of her head.

"Making a difference. Just like you."

"I must have been crazy to walk away from you."

"Shh. I don't want to think about it."

He rolled onto his back. When he rolled against her again, he held a red box in front of her eyes.

"What's this?" she asked.

"Just open it."

"Another trip to Ponte Vecchio?" she asked as he pressed the gold catch to spring the lid wide. "You've been a busy boy."

"Good enough, Sylviana?"

"Good enough," she breathed.

He closed the lid on the wedding bands and put the box on the nightstand. "I hope Julietta's got enough time to make the cake." He yawned, settling his body to fit all her curves.

"Maybe you should warn her."

But he was already asleep and Sylviana gazed at the box until she drifted off to sleep with him.

"Too much to ask," Eric murmured into the back of Sylviana's head as he lifted the receiver on the first ring. He listened for a moment, then put the receiver to Sylviana's ear.

"Sylviana? Honey, why aren't you answering? Sylviana!"

"Hi, Mom. Sorry, I didn't hear the phone."

"Are you sleeping? In the afternoon? What time is it there?"

"I don't know. I can't see the clock." Eric thrust his wrist in front of her eyes. "It's almost five. 1700 hours, Mom. What time is it there?"

"Just gone eight. Its Sunday morning. Steven has brought the girls back. He was supposed to have them all weekend. He said he was too upset and if I wanted to know why, I should talk to you."

"Did you talk to Eva or Enid? Maybe they know." Sylviana turned onto her back, gazing up at Eric.

His head rested on one elbow. He tugged the tail of her shirt down over her waistband and wondered how he had been able to sleep for an hour—take a nap like a kid—with all this territory waiting for him to discover. *Look, don't touch. Save it.*

"I'm not that insensitive, Sylviana. They were too upset when he dumped them like that. Enid is like a rabbit caught in headlights, and Eva is spitting mad. She said Steven was yelling at you, but she didn't hear what he said."

"I'm sorry, Mom. Steven wasn't yelling at me. I didn't talk to him, and I don't know what he said. He was yelling at Eric." Major Wasserman dropped his head back onto the pillow with a soft groan.

"Why would Steven talk to him?"

"Because Eric answered the phone when Enid called."

"He was in your room? Enid never said a word about that. How did that happen?"

"Mom—"

Eric took the receiver from her. "Hello, Mrs. Innocenti. I'm sorry about earlier. The phone rang. I didn't think before I answered. Is Enid all right?"

"She hasn't said anything at all. What did you say to Eva?"

"I didn't speak to her, ma'am. By then, Sylviana was here."

"I see."

"I hope you'll be okay with this. I've asked Sylviana to marry me, and she's accepted. Can't say why she'd do that, but the wedding's tomorrow. I'm sorry you can't be here."

"Papa! Come quick. He wants to marry her," Mrs. Innocenti shouted.

"Tell him it's okay by me, but I'm not taking her back if it doesn't work out."

"That won't be necessary, sir."

"What should I say to the girls?" Mrs. Innocenti asked.

"You'd better talk to Sylviana about that."

While she spoke to her parents, Eric caught her bright eyes laughing at him. The urge to kiss her again was so strong, he sucked in his breath.

"Whatever you think is best, Mom." Sylviana put her fingers over the mouthpiece. "She wants me to tell the girls now. Stay with me, okay?" Eric nodded and dragged his gaze off her lips, folding his arms under his head. Sylviana switched the phone to speaker. When she heard her mother do the same, she said, "Hello, my darlings."

"Hi, Mommy."

"Mommy, what's happening? Daddy's so mad. We didn't do anything. We didn't fight or anything."

"Dad's not mad at you, Eva. Either of you."

"I know that," the twelve-year-old grumbled. "We just have to be extra good. All. The. Time. Because you made him mad."

"Eva. Enid. I've got something to tell you."

"What?" Eva's voice was like a razor.

"You know I'm in Florence, and I came here to see a friend."

"Eric," Enid said with a triumphant giggle.

"That's right, darling."

"That jerk! How could you?"

"Eva, Eric is right here, listening."

"I. Don't. Care. Daddy said he's a jerk, and he's ruined everything. You and Daddy were happy until he came along."

"That's not true, Eva. Eric had nothing to do with that."

"Hi, Eric," Enid whispered hard at the phone. "Hey, Mommy, Eva says you've bought us presents."

"You are such a baby! Everything is ruined. Everything!" Eva shouted at her younger sister.

"Eva, that's enough. You don't know him, and you're being rude."

"I. Don't. Care. You don't love Daddy, and now he doesn't love us."

"That's not true, Eva. Your father will always love you, and Eric will be . . . he'll look after us all." She took a deep breath, meeting Eric's eyes for a moment. "Eric and I are getting married tomorrow."

"Mommy, don't. Daddy's different now. He'll change. He'll be nice to you."

"Eva, sweetheart. I love Eric. I want to be married to him. I know it's hard for you, but I can't help that. When you meet Eric, you'll see."

"Eva, I love your mother. She'll be home Wednesday. Say good-bye now, because we have to get ready for her birthday party."

"Don't eat too much cake, Mommy," Enid squeaked, spilling over with giggles.

"Mommy?"

"Yes, Eva?"

"Happy Birthday."

"They'll be fine, Sylviana," her mother said once the girls had left the room.

"Thanks, Mom. Give Papa a hug for me."

"I'm right here, sweetie."

"Isn't there a game on TV, Papa?"

"Sure, but I wanted to see what my new son-in-law's got in his noggin."

"All right, Mr. Innocenti?"

"Hey, *paisano.*"

"He's from Lodi, Papa. Good with languages."

"Let's hope that's not all. Lots of pictures for your mama, right?"

Sylviana slid the receiver onto the cradle. "You did good, Major Wasserman."

"Eva was making me a little crazy."

"It's her age. She'll love you once she's over being mad at Steven and me. Then she'll dump you for some gorgeous teenage jock."

"I can live with that." His voice had dropped to a murmur.

Sylviana watched the sparkle fade from his eyes. "Time for you to enter the inner sanctum, Wasserman. You said you wanted to live with me so you need to know some of the rules."

"Right. I'm listening." He lowered his chin to the top of her head and closed his eyes, wondering what it would be like to wake up with her again, without the phone ringing. Natural and quiet, warm. *Restricted territory, Wasserman. Still classified.*

"Never qualify a compliment."

"In what sense?"

"If you say, 'You look good *tonight*,' I will assume you mean I looked awful last night. If you say, 'That color suits you,' I'm going to know you mean other colors I wear don't."

"Minefield."

"And there is no way to dig yourself out."

"If I tell you you're beautiful, is that okay?"

"You'll know you're in trouble if I ask, 'How beautiful?' "

"What happens then?"

"Nothing. You are already blown out of the water, and you're sleeping on the sofa."

"No way, lady. That's one of my rules. If we are in the same time zone, we are in the same bed."

"Even if we're fighting?"

"We won't be fighting."

"Even if we're not talking?"

"We won't need to talk. There are no 'ifs,' Sylviana. Any possibility we can be together, there's no way I'm letting you sleep alone, not after tomorrow."

"I might snore."

"If I can sleep through rifle fire and bomb blasts, I can sleep through a little purring from you." As soon as the casual remark hit the open air between them, he regretted it.

"Does that happen often?" she asked quietly.

"Depends where we are."

"Will you tell me, Eric?" She had turned to face him and now sat up, searching his so-deep blue eyes. When he lifted his hand to touch her cheek, she caught it, holding his hand in her lap, staring at his fingers. "If something happens, how will I find out?"

"How do you want to find out?"

"How could I possibly know that? How do you . . . tell families when someone in your unit dies?"

"There's a special unit that lets them know. Then I write a letter, enclose whatever the soldier has asked me to send. Sometimes I talk to them, by phone, if the soldier has requested that in his or her file."

"What's in your file, Eric?"

He closed his fingers on her lacquered nails and lifted them to his lips. "Nothing yet. That's up to you, Sylviana."

Every word Aggy had said at Ghirardelli Square screamed in her mind. He *could* have been dead for years, buried somewhere, and she'd never have known. Her letters could have ended up in some box. She *might* have received notice from his CO in response, impersonal, *sorry to inform you of the death* . . . "I think I'd rather know right away. I'd rather hear immediately."

"Phone call." He lifted his watch over his head, staring at it as if he couldn't make sense of the four dials. Sylviana lay down to face him, stretching her thigh across his. He dropped his hand to her knee for a moment, knowing they had to have this conversation. Nothing he could do about it. "Baby, it's a job. If I was a policeman or a carpenter, there's no guarantee I'd make it home from work either."

"I'm kind of old-fashioned," she whispered.

He could hear she was worried about something more. "What makes you think I'm not?"

"I know you'll be away for a long time, but . . . some things are important to me."

"Fidelity?"

"Yes. Is that too much to ask? Because if it is—"

"Maybe I'm more old-fashioned than you think."

"Don't laugh at me."

"I'm not—don't you know that?" He watched her face. "I'm not that guy, baby." She slid her arms around his neck, not completely happy but a little less worried. The phone rang again. "I swear, if I could, I'd rip that thing out of the wall." He dropped his hand onto the receiver again, then took a deep breath. "*Pronto?*"

Chapter Eleven

*C*apitano!"

"*Sì, buonasera*, Marcello."

"Is Sylviana there? We want to know when you will be ready to join us."

"Are we late?"

"No, no, of course not. The party begins when you arrive. Sandro will come to the hotel whenever you say."

After he had exchanged a silent communication with Sylviana, he said, "One hour, 1930 hours, okay?"

"*Sì, perfetto*."

Before Sylviana moved, he scooped her from the bed and set her on her feet on the floor in the bathroom. "I've got a lot to learn and not a lot of time."

"Me too."

"I'm not complicated," he laughed, searching through the travel cases that had proliferated all around the sink and the shelf over the shower stall. "Fuel is about all I need to function."

"Then you don't need to know anything about my procedures."

"Nothing doing, Innocenti. You are mine for the next hour, woman. Need-to-know situation. What is all this stuff? What's first?"

"My facial cleanser. That stuff in the pale pink bottle. Then the toner. And that, the moisturizer." When he turned toward her with his hands full, she laughed. "And that turquoise razor."

"You'd never survive in the Army."

"Wanna bet? Ten bucks says all your female personnel have this stuff. Just pay me now, Wasserman. You know I'm right."

"What's first?"

"See? Face. Facial cleanser. About half a teaspoonful." She withstood his lathering and buffeting her face, but when it came to shaving, his hands were so unsteady, she refused to let him touch her. "Just watch, okay?"

"Pleasure." He ran the razor over his chin but couldn't feel any drag. "It's dull."

"It's not for stubble like yours."

"Rough?" he asked, rubbing his chin against her cheek. When she pulled away, he caught her around the waist. "Shave me." He put his steel double-edge into her hand.

"Okay, but you'd better be prepared for the sight of blood."

"Mine or yours?"

"You won't mind a scar or two in the wedding photos, I guess."

"Haven't you ever done this before?" He studied her scrubbed face, then pressed his lips to her hairline.

"No. Have you?"

"No, ma'am. No better time than now. Are you going to take my name?"

"If I keep my own, there'd be three names above our doorbell. The girls', yours, and mine." She patted foam over his cheeks and jaw, then eased the razor over his chin. "In one of your first letters, you told me you weren't going to be home for at least two years." She rinsed the razor and wiped his face with the washcloth, examining her effort, proving the result on her cheek.

"Not bad for a first attempt." He ran a hand over his face, looking into her eyes reflected back at him in the mirror. "I might get be able to get leave in six months."

"We'll have Christmas, New Year's, Easter, *and* Thanksgiving in six months."

"What happens next?"

"In the get-Sylviana-into-decent-shape protocol?"

"Is there something about that question I need to understand before I answer?"

"You're a quick study, Major. I'll have to be clever to catch you. What do you know about pedicures?" His crooked smirk was answer enough. "Oh, boy. We'll be late for my party for sure."

At the first vibration of the phone, Eric yanked the receiver off the hook, then held it at arm's length until he could think, preparing for a bullet or a bayonet. He met his almost-wife's eyes and felt less adolescent the longer she smiled at him. "*Sì?*"

"*Capitano.*"

"Sandro. Sylviana is almost ready. Five, ten minutes."

Sylviana took the receiver and put it back, wrapping her arms around his neck, cuffed his ear for blaming her.

"So that was a pedicure?" he asked her.

"Well, my beautician never took that much interest in my baby toes."

Eric straightened his arms and sat up, tightening his tie and smoothing the front of his dress shirt. Sylviana wriggled her red-tipped toes into her black sandals. Eric fastened the straps over her heels and pulled her to her feet. "Are you okay about this, getting married tomorrow?"

"Scared, soldier?"

"Quaking in my size elevens."

"My relatives won't hurt you—not while I'm there, anyway."

He turned toward the dressing table and ran his hands over his face while she handed him his hat. He set it on his head and met her eyes in the mirror. "If I didn't know better, I'd swear I was some gawky kid headed for boot camp."

"Anything but. You've got great potential as my body servant."

Eric gave Sandro a casual salute when the elevator door opened. The young man sat in the red and white car, staring at the front door of the hotel, straight through the lobby as Eric dropped the room key in Marco's hand. When Sylviana walked toward him, Sandro was tapping his fingers on the steering wheel in time to the music on the radio, shook his head and grinned. He leapt from the car to the door of the hotel, and trotted back to the car to open the door of the backseat.

"*Buonasera*, Sylviana, and Happy Birthday. *Buonasera*, Eric."

They responded with smiles and nods but had no words. Sandro winked at Marco who was leaning over the Reception desk and drove out of Piazza Mentana toward the north. He glanced at his passengers from time to time, but they were sitting close together in the back, with their eyes lowered, looking at their joined hands. When the car reached his uncle's winery, he drove to the front entrance beneath a flower-festooned canopy. He leapt out again and pulled open their door. Eric stepped out and extended his hand to Sylviana. Still neither of them seemed to notice anything about their surroundings, only each other. Even when the glass doors were flung open, they walked through as though they had not even seen the doors move. The first time they began to come out of their dream was when the whole of the company of guests began to applaud.

Major Wasserman lifted his eyes to take in the eager faces crowded around them. Surprised, he pulled Sylviana within the circle of his arm and presented her to her family—the guest of honor. Sylviana looked into the crowd, perplexed to see so many faces she did not recognize. She smiled at those who smiled at her but sought the comforting face of Julietta. "I thought this was going to be a small party, just family."

"We are all family here," Julietta said, patting her cheeks. "I see your cold is better. You are very healthy. I am never recovered—two weeks sometimes."

"I apologize for that. I . . . I was a coward."

"No matter. Your friend was fine with us, but it was so sad to see how the pain he felt was hidden."

"We have talked."

"So your papa has said. Now, my little chick. You will need a drink. Your friend is already whisked away, so you can tell me what you should."

"What is that, Julietta?"

"Do not be difficult, child. I will tell your papa to take you over his knee as he did when you—"

"When she what?"

"Ah, *Capitano!* How handsome you look."

"Thank you, ma'am." Eric bowed his head but didn't take his eyes off Sylviana's blushing face. "What crime did you commit? I think I should know."

"Nothing anywhere near as bad as you . . . probably."

"Sylviana, this man is an angel. You said yourself he is *perfetto.*"

"I did not."

"Children," Julietta laughed, "no fighting. This is a happy night. A joyous night. Smile. Kiss. Make up." She pushed Sylviana into Eric's arms, and as their heads tilted toward each other and their lips met, the banquet room was flooded by flashing lights and the snaps, clicks, and whirrs of cameras, cell phones, and video recorders. One of her cousins took Eric's uniform hat so he had both hands free. By the time Marcello rescued them, Sylviana was wiping her eyes from laughing, and Eric was wiping lipstick from wherever she pointed.

"You'd think they had never seen people kiss before."

"They see that every day," Marcello told Eric. "What they do not see is Sylviana on her birthday being kissed by her American fiancé."

"All this flattery will go to his head," Sylviana said, rubbing his short hair with her palms. She accepted the glass of Chianti and took a deep breath of happiness.

"Do you want to dance?" Eric asked.

Sylviana set their glasses on the bar and opened her arms. Eric unbuttoned his jacket, peeled it off, and saw it disappear with another pretty cousin. When he turned back to take Sylviana into his arms, she was already dancing with a man in a suit.

"You are as beautiful as you were when we first met, Signora Langdon."

"I don't use that name anymore, *signore*. Forgive me. I don't remember when we met."

"Why should you?" He laughed, holding her a fraction closer. "You were a very busy mama then. How old is your daughter?"

"I have two daughters, Signore . . . ?"

"Natale. My name is Natale, Sylviana. A friend of the family."

"I don't remember meeting you, *signore*." The first three things she had noticed about him were his cologne, his silk tie, and the gold signet ring on his right hand. In the following moment, she noticed they were on the other side of the room, and the distance between their bodies was not the width of his hand. "Excuse me, *signore*, but I was about to dance with my fiancé," she said with an apologetic smile, backing away.

"These are not the words of the Sylviana I remember. *Sì*, a

Madonna. But also, also this wild creature—this model for students at the Accademia. *Sì*. Now, you remember."

"Who are you?" Her first thought was that Steven had put an idea into this man's head, a way to embarrass her, a way to make Eric mad.

"This is not important. My work is important. When my brother—he is married to your cousin, Ana—told me you were here with your American soldier, I had to see you to give you a gift, as you gave me. Such a sweet gift, bestowed with such kindness. You have been my Madonna since that morning."

Sylviana searched the opposite side of the room, but Eric was not at the bar. She looked for him among the young women who had taken his jacket, but he wasn't there either.

"Now you remember Natale, *sì*?"

"I remember the Accademia, *signore*, but I do not remember you."

"This is also not important. I had hoped you would remember the moment of inspiration that has driven me these past years, but a Madonna does not look upon her admirers to see them, only to bestow her gift."

Sylviana withdrew her hand from his and dropped the other from his shoulder, resisting his continuing embrace, but he ignored her.

"As a wedding gift, Madonna Innocentina," Natale began, smiling into her eyes, "I would like to give you—no, return to you—something that you left with me that morning and that I have kept, ready, always ready for your return to Firenze."

"*Signore*, thank you, *grazie*, but—"

"There is no need to thank me. Your American husband will perhaps not understand what this means—that will be our secret, *sì*?"

"I don't know what you're talking about," she said, dragging herself out of his embrace.

"Madonna, my Innocentina," Natale called after her, "I am talking about this."

There was a sudden silence, as if a breath was drawn by everyone in the room. Sylviana found Eric among the cousins and

crossed the room toward him. Everyone she passed was looking toward Natale. She pushed through them all until she stood
in front of the tall American soldier. He looked once in the same
direction as the others and then into her eyes.

"What is it?" he asked as she wrapped her arms around his
waist and hid her face in his neck. "What's wrong, Sylviana?"

"*Signore e signori*," Natale announced in the silence.

"Let's go." Sylviana tugged at Eric's sleeve.

"We've just arrived. What's happened?"

"I want to go outside." She tugged at his waist.

"I am Natale." A patter of applause followed the introduction.

"Weren't you just dancing with him?"

"A few years ago, I was a student at the Accademia," the artist began. "Lost. Confused, uninspired. Like so many, my aim
was to become another Michelangelo. Instead, I was given the
greatest gift. I became—myself. In gratitude, allow me to present to you, in honor of these two people who have found love in
our beautiful city, the first public showing of *Madonna Innocentina*."

The crescendo of applause filled the room. Sylviana bowed
her head against Eric's chest, preparing for his reaction. She
heard a few voices whispering, exclamations, and felt a surge
forward.

"Don't you want to see this?"

Sylviana shook her head, staring at the insignia of his regiment on his tie.

"He's waiting for you to say something."

"You say something."

"Like what? You don't remember what a blank I was at those
parties, but I do. I don't think this guy wants to hear, 'Nice colors' or 'How did you get that look in her eyes?' Sylviana, I think
you need to see this."

"Are you mad?"

Eric put his hands on her shoulders and turned her to face
Natale and his work of art. The first thing that Sylviana saw
were the faces of her relatives staring at her. She felt the blood
rushing to her neck and cheeks. If not for Eric's hands on her
shoulders, she would have run. She remembered the morning

she had posed at the Accademia for a roomful of students, that same morning that she had discovered that Steven was involved with another woman—and not the first. The same morning that she had sworn revenge, she had taken her daughters with her to sit for the life-drawing class.

Eric pressed his jaw against her temple. "I don't blame him for being in awe of you. If you don't like his work, he'll probably choke to death on the spot. Put him out of his misery, baby, so we can eat."

"Eric, I can explain. . . ."

"Just look, Sylviana. I wouldn't understand anything you said about artistic merit anyway."

With an inward grimace, she lifted her eyes to the far end of the banquet room and saw a painting of herself with her daughters as they were on that morning. She and her children—they, unknowingly—forlorn and abandoned but also liberated. Sylviana pressed her fingers to her mouth to contain the cry that had been in her heart that morning, but the devilment in her eyes in the painting made her smile. Natale had captured all she was at that moment: her love for her children as she comforted Eva and nursed the infant, Enid. Her outrage at Steven's betrayal and her freedom from ever again having to pretend that she loved him. Six years had passed since she had allowed anyone to see her that weak or that triumphant. She had no idea what anyone else saw, but she knew what was there, and she said, "*Grazie. Bene grazie*, Natale."

She took Eric's hand and drew his arm around her waist, leaning back against him as he handed her the glass of Chianti she had abandoned to dance with the painter.

"That may be worth a fortune one day."

"It already is," Eric replied. "Marcello told me he's built his reputation on the mysterious Madonna."

"What do you think of it—the painting?"

"I don't know anything except that I prefer the original," Eric said, wrapping his free hand around the tall glass of *birra* one of her cousins pushed at him.

"Do you want to dance, Sylviana?" Eric asked her again after they'd taken a few sips of their drinks. When they had been on the dance floor for a few moments, he said, "I wonder when they'll let us eat."

"Who told you there'd be food, Major?" She laughed when his face became the embodiment of shock and pain.

"I need fuel, woman. I've only had two meals today. Civilian portions at that."

Once more the band was silenced, and Marcello was standing in Natale's place. Major Wasserman had begun his mission to requisition food and towed his bride-to-be after him in the direction of the kitchen. As soon as his back was pressed to the door, a spotlight found the couple and pinned them to the wall.

"*Signore e signori* and the happy ones, Sylviana and Eric, soon to be husband and wife."

Glasses rose, and arms were wrapped around them. Eric resigned himself to starvation—slow and excruciating. When a man took his hand and pulled him away from Sylviana, he watched her disappear among unfamiliar faces.

"*Signore. Capitano.* Marcello has told me that you plan to be married tomorrow in the Castell di pubblica—the civic hall?"

"Yes, but how did he know?"

"Marcello, he knows everyone and, thus, everything. Unimportant. At any other time. Another day—no problem. But tomorrow, no."

Eric stared in the direction in which Sylviana had disappeared. "Is there a problem because we're Americans or something else?"

"*Sì, signore.* Something else. A visit—someone from the European Union—members of the Senate. *Sì.* You understand?"

"I understand. Don't tell Sylviana. I'll explain later."

"*Sì, signore.* I understand. I thought you should know."

"Thanks . . . *signore. Grazie.*" As he made his way toward his fiancée, he settled his agitation and tried to resolve his disappointment. *Fifteen years, what's another six months?*

Chapter Twelve

His CO would approve his change of beneficiary, no problem; he didn't have to be married to her to make sure she was all right if something happened to him.

"Where did you disappear to?"

"Well-wishers, same as you." He laid a hand on the small of her back. "I'm going to take a walk, see if I can find some grub."

"I'll come with you."

"No, stay here. I'm the one with the sense of direction."

"Eric?" He kissed her forehead and strode away toward the foyer, disappearing again. "Just make sure you come back," Sylviana said under her breath, and she forced herself to smile at Julietta and all the other aunts, uncles, and cousins who knew she was getting married in the morning. She smiled and laughed and stood by the painting of herself and her daughters, with Natale blocking any and all attempts to photograph the portrait.

"When you buy it, you can let anyone you want take a photo," the artist told her father's third cousin on his grandmother's side.

Sylviana wiggled her toes in the sandals. She glanced at the door to the foyer as often as she fingered the gold hearts around her neck and bit her lip. No one asked where Eric had gone, but she recognized the worry in Julietta's eyes when some of the family began taking seats at tables and looking at their watches. She told herself everything was okay, that he hadn't changed his mind when Natale revealed the portrait of the three of them, nude in the studio, surrounded by students. *He must think I'm a tramp. He must have been mortified, shocked that I would expose my children to that. . . . No, if he is, I am not to blame. There is nothing wrong with that painting or the circumstances. Evil minds corrupt . . . Where is he? Why did he go?*

A young woman, dressed in Army fatigues in the same pattern that Eric had worn that morning, was crossing the room through

the relatives who stopped her and talked. Still in the crowd before the painting, Sylviana could only watch the soldier's progress toward the young cousins who had taken Eric's hat and
jacket. After a brief exchange, the female soldier took the clothes
and turned to leave the party. Sylviana was frozen in place.

"Mrs. Langdon?"

She turned, only to see the soldier come up behind her. "Yes?"

"Major Wasserman has requested that you come with me. He
would like to speak with you in private."

Sylviana put down her Chianti and followed the lieutenant.
In the foyer, a group of soldiers stood by the outside door, but
she didn't see her American among them.

"Where is he?" she demanded. An Army jeep drove up to
the door, and two men in dress uniform climbed out. "What is
going on? Where is Eric?" She couldn't keep the panic from her
voice. The two officers saluted the soldiers already gathered.

"Wasserman?"

"Here, sir," Eric said, coming from the men's room, flashing
a grin in her direction before he spoke to the latest arrivals.

"What's going on? You went to find fuel, and you've been
gone forever." Anger replaced her panic. He began pulling her
after him to a corner. "Are you going to tell me what's going on,
or do I have to guess?"

"I didn't know if I could pull it all together."

"Just tell me what all these people are doing here, Eric, or
I'm leaving!"

"Whoa there," he said with a quiet laugh, catching her hand
before she marched away. "They're here because I made a few
calls, told my CO I was jammed up, and he called in some favors for me."

"What are you talking about?"

"Some guy told me we couldn't get married tomorrow,
Sylviana."

"Why not?"

"Long story. So I begged my CO to get us a chaplain here,
tonight. I didn't have time to ask you."

"You were gone for over an hour. That wasn't enough time
away from my birthday party for you?"

"It took me that long to make the calls to get to the right people." When she folded her arms and turned away from him, Eric watched her profile and the tapping of her recently pedicured foot. "I was cracking up. I figured if I couldn't fix it, there was no point in both of us—"

"That *is* the point, Major," she said as she swung on him and poked her finger into his chest. "*Both* of us. For the last hour, I've been trying to think how I was going to keep myself together when my whole family found out you were gone."

"We've got a long way to go, Sylviana Innocenti," he said, clasping her hand and lifting her fingers to his lips. "Okay, I should have told you what I was trying to do, and next time I will, but do you mind if we have the wedding ceremony now? Here?"

"All you had to do was ask me," she grumbled.

"Is that a yes?"

"What do you think?"

He lifted a hand, beckoning to the two officers. "Sylviana, Doug Allan and Wes Tyler. Another long story, but Doug's going to work some magic, and Wes is helping out. They've brought all they need. Katie over there," he said, nodding toward the female soldier, "is liaison, and this crew are the honor guard. Once they've set up, we'll be in the hands of the chaplain, Felix. He's a rabbi, but he knows the service."

Sylviana looked from one to another of the people forming a semicircle behind her shy guy from Lodi. "Hi," she said before turning her attention back to Eric. "Where have they all come from?"

"Like I said, my CO called in some favors. It's all the Army way, baby. Hope that's okay with you."

"Is it legal?"

"We'll be married, if that's what you mean."

"You won't be up on charges for misappropriating equipment or personnel?"

"No, ma'am," Doug Allan said. "We're just doing our job. Major Wasserman is helping us out."

"How?"

"Can they explain later, Sylviana? I want to be married to you before midnight."

"I'm not Cinderella," she replied.

"But I'm a coachman. Let's do this. Now."

"Yes, sir," Sylviana said. "I wish my mother was here."

"Why?"

"She'd tell me to be quiet."

"Be quiet, baby. I love you. I want to be your husband. I want to take care of you and your daughters as best I can. If that's okay with you, can we have the ceremony now and work the rest out over the next sixty years?"

In under five minutes, Doug and Wes took over the banquet room of the winery with cameras and microphones, and within an hour Sylviana Bethan Innocenti declared that she took Eric Daniel David Wasserman as her husband.

"I can't believe this," he whispered into her ear as he slipped her ring onto her finger.

"Do you want me to pinch you to make sure you're not dreaming?"

He felt the weight of his own, wider band and helped her push it over his knuckle, kissing her hand. "Don't wake me, Sylviana. I'm the happiest I've ever been."

Lifting her arms around his neck to the applause and shouts of "Bravo," she said, "Eric?"

"Hmm?"

"Did I tell you I love you?"

"I'm pretty sure you did say that once or twice."

"If I don't say it often enough, let me know."

"I will, but I'll know."

"How?"

"Too hard to keep that a secret, Sylviana."

Eva and Enid stared at the computer screen in their grandparents' living room, sitting on the sofa between Sylviana's parents, watching their mother, by video call, marry a man they did not know in a country they hadn't visited for six years.

"Dad's going to go ballistic," Eva told her grandmother. "She looks so happy, Grandma," the twelve-year-old said, pressing her face into her grandmother's chest. "Didn't she love Daddy like that?"

"There are all kinds of love, Eva."

"What if they have a new baby?"

"A mother's heart is so big, my darling, the more she loves, the more she can love. And this new husband, he has a big heart too. He will love you and your sister as much as you need him to love you."

"How do you know that, Grandma?" Enid asked, peering hard at the screen as her mother and Eric began their first dance as husband and wife.

"He loves your mother. How can he not love you?"

"Daddy doesn't love any of us anymore."

"He doesn't love *you* because you like that jerk! He stole Mommy from us," Eva burst out.

"Eva, keep an open mind and an open heart."

"You're on his side. You. Are. All. On. His. Side."

"Leave her be," her grandfather said as Eva bolted from the room. "She will find her way back."

Sylviana peeled off her sandals as soon as she was in the car, curled her legs under her, and snuggled close to Eric as the cool night breeze whipped around them on the country road back to the city. Eric held her against him, kissing the top of her head whenever the urge seized him, responding to her requests for kisses on her lips. At the hotel, when she reached for her shoes, he said, "I'll carry you," and he did, all the way through the lobby. Marco held the door of the elevator and led the way to the room, opening that door for them as well.

"*Buonanotte, Signore e Signora* Wasserman."

"*Buonanotte*," Sylviana replied, tightening her grip around her husband's neck when Marco closed the door behind them. "I can't believe this."

"I can't believe *this*." He dropped her feet to the floor and led her across the room to the small table by the balcony door, wrapping his arms around her shoulders and kissing the back of her head as they both took in the efforts that had been made to turn the plain room into a bridal suite, complete with arrays of flowers, silk banners, and an elaborate meal.

"This is nice." Sylviana dropped her chin onto his forearm,

clasping his wrist. For a moment she gazed at the wedding rings on their fingers, forcing her tears to retreat.

"Where are these famous pajamas of yours?"

"You really know how to sweet-talk a girl, don't you?" she teased, pressing her temple against his jaw.

"I've been thinking about them all night."

"Nothing else?"

"Not much. I'm a hick, Sylviana. Basic. If you want me to say something knowledgeable or witty about the arts, you'll be disappointed."

"What is it about my pajamas that intrigues you?" She had turned in his arms, aware that he was defensive, expecting ridicule.

"I want to be able to *see* you—any time I look at my watch or wake up at night on the other side of the world—and know where you are, how you're dressed, what you'll be doing. Basic."

"What do you wear to bed, Eric?"

"In my quarters, away from the field, out of the fire zone, nothing."

"Otherwise?"

"Otherwise, enough so I don't get caught with nothing—undershirt, boxers, socks."

She was playing with his tie, studying the knot, running her fingers along the edges as he spoke. "What's on the walls of your quarters?"

"Nothing. Bare. We're never anywhere long enough to decorate." He laughed, running his hands to the tips of her fingers.

"Do you wear your watch to bed?"

"Yeah. Handy. What about your place, your bedroom? Double bed? Victorian, oak?" Sylviana nodded. "Firm mattress, chenille bedspread?"

"How do you know all that?"

"Neutral colors. Touch of green."

"Nope. Wrong. Touch of turquoise."

"Same thing."

"Right," she laughed. "Green. Turquoise—no difference. What do you have for breakfast?"

"Eggs, scrambled—easiest way there is in camp. Sausage.

Hash browns. Stack of pancakes with maple syrup, if I'm lucky. Coffee. Tomato juice. Toast. What do you eat?"

"Muesli with semi-skimmed. Grapefruit juice."

When the layers of lace and silk, cotton and wool were peeled away and they were standing together, hands clasped, in the dim glow of the moon on the Arno, Eric said, "I can't figure out if I'm still dreaming."

"If you are, so am I," she said softly, walking her fingers across his shoulders.

"We can't both be, Sylviana." He tilted her chin with his thumbs.

"Do you want a wake-up call?"

"No thanks. I don't plan on sleeping much tonight," he murmured, spreading his hands over her shoulder blades, tracing his fingers along her spine.

"We haven't seen the Palazzo Vecchio."

"Maybe next time, baby."

"What about all the photos for that guy in your unit?"

"That guy is a gal. I'll buy some postcards."

"How many women are in your unit?" She hadn't meant to ask, didn't want to know.

"About twenty. I love you, Sylviana," he said, staring into her eyes. "I can't be anyone else but I swear I'll be a good husband even half a world away."

She locked her arms around his neck and hid her face in his neck. *Twenty is a lot of temptation half a world away.* She memorized every line and indentation, every undulation of muscle beneath his bronzed skin, still thinking about the women in his unit.

"I love you, Eric. I'll be a good wife. Whatever you need from me. I promise," she whispered.

"I know, baby. Let's go back to dreaming for awhile," he answered. The tension in his face disintegrated like ice on a skillet, cracking and sizzling into the smile of a boy with a world full of wonder in his soul.

Voices came and went beneath the balcony, shadows of the late season tourists staggered along the wall above the dresser and descended into the silver shimmer of the moon on the river. On the other side of the Ponte Vecchio, the street cleaners started their work. Eric watched the mist from the hoses drift down to the surface of the Arno.

When Sylviana joined him on the balcony, wrapped in a sheet, he asked, "Are you done crying?" She nodded and he said, "Me too." He opened his arms and they watched the dawn chase the stars away. "Let's eat."

"Are you always hungry?"

"Pretty much. There's a lot of energy required here."

"We'd better fuel you up for the trip."

"What trip is that, Sylviana?"

"The two-week-honeymoon-in-two-nights trip."

Eric wrapped a bath sheet around his waist and pulled his wife into his lap at the table, surveyed the meal before he worked the stopper from the first bottle of *prosecco*. "There's not a lot here to keep me going. Might make an hour or two."

"You are joking. There's enough food here for an army."

"Not my army, Innocenti. Clee's tiny but she'd eat this and want more, wonder what was for chow."

"Are you going to drink that or just make it warm?"

Eric tipped the bottle to his lips for a moment then pulled her closer to kiss her. Sylviana took the *prosecco* and held it to let him have the first taste before she drank. While he poured the wine into glasses, she made him a sandwich of salami and pro-volone. "Feed me," he said, touching her skin with the tips of his fingers. Sylviana held the bread to his lips, jumping back when he snapped a bite, kissing his face and neck while he ate, offering sips of the sparkling wine from her glass.

"It's not going to be enough, is it?"

"I can last 'til breakfast," he said, laying a few slices of pro-sciutto on his tongue and washing them down with more *prosecco* straight from the bottle.

"I'm not talking about fuel."

"I know, Sylviana. I'm not as dumb as I look."

Sylviana wrapped her arms around his neck, pressed a kiss on his forehead.

"Baby, you're spending so much energy on what may be that you aren't giving what *is* even half a chance."

"I can't help it, Eric. I keep thinking—"

"Don't think, Sylviana. Just stay here, with me. We're in the same time zone. You know my rule." Eric put more fuel in his body, finished the last drops in the first bottle of wine. "Do you still model for art classes?" he asked.

"No."

"You should."

"Why do you think that, Eric?"

He tilted his head back on the chair, grinning at her. "You don't want to give Natale an exclusive, do you? You're too beautiful for just one painter."

"Modeling isn't much fun, you know. I thought it was, or would be, when I was eighteen and made my father mad enough to scream, but it's just tedious."

"You weren't bored when you sat for the Accademia," Eric observed as he finished the provolone and bread.

"No, I was hurt."

"Steve has a lot to answer for." Eric relaxed back in the chair, resting his hands on her knees. "Did he get it?"

"No. He wouldn't have cared, anyway. Hey. I'm not supposed to dwell on the future, so you can't have the past. Deal?"

"Deal." He straightened his back and closed his arms around her waist. "What do you say to a hot bath?"

As they lay back in the scented water, he reminded himself, *Past, Wasserman. Done and gone.* He lifted his fingers and pushed a curl of her damp hair from her forehead. She had taken off all her makeup and let him watch her do it, explaining all the lotions, tubes, and jars as if the effort she made was shameful. "You shouldn't use soap on your face, you know."

"Why not?"

"You've got delicate skin," Sylviana said.

He laughed. "I'm about as delicate as a cactus."

"You wouldn't be a cactus if you took better care of yourself," she said in a huff, rinsing her hands.

"Where are you going?"

As soon as he spoke, she raised herself to her knees, shivering a little as the air in the steamy room cooled her skin. He stood, wrapped her in the bathrobe and sent her back to the bed. When he joined her in a few minutes, she was groggy but awake enough to smile, tracing her fingertips along the bridge of his nose.

"So, these are your pajamas?"

"That's right, soldier. These are the real me. Not what you expected or not what you—"

"I like 'em just fine, Mrs. Wasserman." He fingered the plaid flannel collar for moment and examined the red piping on the front placket. "Nice. They remind me of my dad's but they look a lot better on you."

"If I had anything even remotely alluring, I would have brought it. So now you know. I wear flannel jammies and fluffy slippers."

"I wear socks and my watch. I think we're even, but even in pajamas, you are undeniably the most beautiful woman—"

"Maybe you should just quit while you're ahead, Mr. Wasserman."

"Right, gotcha," he said.

"Where do you get all this energy?"

"Same as chow. Never know when I'm going to get another chance. And this is a whole lot better than sleep. Or fuel. Something I've been dreaming about for a long time."

Sylviana caressed his face, searching his eyes but not looking for anything other than the kid behind the man he'd become—the man she knew she was going to love for the rest of her life. "More tears, baby?"

"Sorry, it's another part of the real me," she said, wiping her face with her fingers. "I'm just happy. So happy. Are you happy, Eric?"

"I'm more than happy. Get some sleep, Sylviana."

"What are you going to do?"

"I'm going to sleep with you. No tricks. I'm a light sleeper." Eric held her arm across his chest. She was asleep in moments and he stared at the watery shadows on the ceiling, pressed his cheek against her temple, taking slow breaths to quell his agitation. She was happy. He was happy. And scared he'd never measure up. When he closed his eyes and blanked his mind long enough, he slept.

Chapter Thirteen

As soon as he heard the phone, he dropped his hand onto the receiver, cursing himself that he hadn't thought to take it off the hook so she—his wife—could sleep. Sylviana was awake at the first buzz, though, sliding her fingers under his and holding the receiver to her ear. "*Pronto?*"

"You. What do you think you're doing, running off to Italy for a dirty weekend with that scumbag? Leaving our little girls on their own. I'm going to make sure you regret this, Sylviana. You'll never see them again after this. You've ruined their lives. You know that, don't you? Spending all the money I give you for them on a trip halfway around the world for a guy you don't even know, haven't got a clue about. What kind of mother are you?"

"Are you finished?"

"I haven't even started."

"Rant all you want, Steven. It won't change anything." She wasn't sure what he knew or whom he had spoken to, but Sylviana was leaning back in the crook of her husband's arm, resting her head on his shoulder, quiet and secure—as secure as a few hours old marriage allowed her to be.

"How could you do this to me?"

Sylviana turned her eyes away from Eric's steady gaze and demanded, "Why are you calling here, Steven? I haven't done anything to you."

"Were you sleeping, Sylvi?"

"Yes, I was. So, if you haven't any better reason to phone than to tell me how awful I am, I'm going back to sleep."

"Already tired of your boyfriend, right? He's no good for you. Never was. I'm taking my girls away from you. That's it, Sylvi. I've had enough."

"No, you're not doing that, Steven." She dropped the receiver onto the hook and retrieved her pajamas from the bottom of the bed. When she met Eric's eyes, she said, "Nothing special. More of the usual."

"He's not taking it too well, I guess," Eric said, following her with his eyes as she went toward the bathroom.

"No, you're right. He's not."

"I'll talk to him." The phoné sat like a sphinx on the night-stand, as though it hummed, waiting to catch his eye, force his hand—Steven Langdon on the other side of the world, willing him to break.

"No, you won't." She closed and locked the door, staring at herself in the mirror. *What's going on with you, Sylviana? You never barked at Steven like this. Never crossed that line.*

Eric folded his arms under his head and stared across the room at the square vase of white flowers, expecting the phone to ring and bring him face-to-face with the sniper shot *he* had taken at his best friend. When the bathroom door opened, he watched his wife cross the room, stand by the bed, and stare at the phone. When she lifted the receiver again, she covered the mouthpiece with her hand, listening for a moment until she was certain her ex-husband wasn't there.

"Anything you want to tell me?" her new husband asked.

"Welcome to my world, Eric."

"Whatever it is, baby, we'll get through it—together."

"Brave words." Sylviana stood at the balcony window.

"I heard what he said, Sylviana, and that isn't going to happen."

"I'm glad you're so sure."

"He's all talk. He'll calm down once he gets it through his head that we're married and the girls are staying with you."

"With *us*, Eric. They're part of *us* now."

"They're part of Steve too."

"That's one thing he'll never let me forget," Sylviana said, lying on the bed.

Eric dropped his arm around her shoulders. "Go back to sleep, baby. There'll be plenty of time for us to talk tomorrow."

"It is tomorrow," she said, curling up against him.

"Not in your time zone, Sylviana." *Duck and dive, backing*

off. That was something he was good at, negotiating for time, keeping his troops out of the firestorm.

"We're in the same time zone, Eric, or have *you* forgotten that already?"

"Not on any level," he said, turning to face her, "but what you're scared of isn't. I've known Steve longer than you. He's all talk, Sylviana. As soon as he's sure he's got you scared and where he wants you, he'll drop it."

"If you knew that, why did you let him run you off?"

"I said I've known him longer, baby. I didn't say I was quick." *Dodge.* He couldn't answer, couldn't say the words that were right at the front of his skull, had been there from the second he'd caught sight of her on the other side of the gallery, the words that Steve had read in his eyes, a big grin on his buddy's face as soon as he knew. *I wasn't the one who paid that debt. Free lunch the whole time I let this happen.*

Sylviana tilted her head to stare at her new husband's face. "Quick enough, Major. And a whole lot quicker than your wife."

By the time the aromas of coffee and toasted *panettone* reached the fourth floor, Eric held his wife's cleansing lotion in one hand while she whisked away the remaining swath of stubble from his jaw. She wiped his chin and cheeks with the towel and nodded when he squirted a half teaspoon of the lotion into his palm and began massaging it over her forehead and nose. They faced the mirror in the bathroom, watching each other's eyes until Eric washed the lotion from her face and folded his arms around her waist, resting his chin on the top of her head, meeting her gaze with a slow smile.

They dressed as they had on the day they first ventured into the city—fatigues and jeans. This time, in the breakfast room, there was no hesitation and no doubt that the woman on Eric Wasserman's arm was his. When they sat at the table, as close to each other as they could get without being in the same chair, the waitress brought their coffee without asking their preferences and joined Marco in offering her congratulations.

"What's all that about?" Audrey asked her husband, as the newlyweds were applauded by several of the other guests.

"Appears those two weren't married like I thought, Aud. They got married last night."

Audrey leaned toward Sylviana. "I hope you'll be happy this time."

Before they finished breakfast, Sandro, Claudia, and Marcello entered the dining room. "We didn't expect you to be here," Marcello said, "but we came all the same, in case you wanted to finish your tour of our city, *Capitano*." He looked on with a smile as Eric and Sylviana exchanged a silent communication, something they were getting good at.

"As soon as we finish our breakfast, we'll be all yours, Marcello, but we can't promise one hundred percent attendance. There are a few details we have to work through."

"Sure. Sure. We will understand."

The walking tour began in the Piazza di Angeli at the door of the house in which Michelangelo was born. Eric held Sylviana's hand, bringing it up to look at her wedding ring as if he was making sure they were married, at the same time listening to Marcello's commentary on the life of the city's famous son. When they walked through the streets back toward the Palazzo Vecchio, Marcello was saying, "You must understand this man Cosimo. He had so much wealth, and the Church was dependent on these men to—"

Eric drew Sylviana aside. "I'll need your bank account details."

"What for?" she asked in surprise.

"So I can arrange for part of my pay to be transferred into it."

"You don't have to do that. I have a job. I get paid. Steve—"

"I'm your husband. You and the girls are my responsibility now."

"That's sweet, Eric, but you don't have to do that."

"I want to do that. Write down the numbers, address, all that stuff." He gave her a notebook and pen from his fatigue jacket. "Will it help?"

"Of course it will help, but I didn't marry you for this."

"I didn't marry you just to sleep with you, but it goes with the territory. I can't spend my pay, and you need it. Done. I'll give you my e-mail address."

"Okay."

He scribbled on the next sheet and gave it to her. "Do you read your e-mails?"

"I will now," Sylviana promised. "There's a computer in the kitchen. That has e-mail, I think."

"Don't expect something every day."

"I won't, Eric. You don't have to do anything. Can I reach you by phone?"

"Let me know you want to talk, and I'll set it up."

"Eric, but what if I need to talk right then, at that moment?"

"We can't have that, Sylviana."

"What can we have?" *Another fight, Sylviana. Can't you just be happy?*

"Just this. I'll be there for you in every way I can, but it won't be instant or even close for a while. If that's not good enough, there's nothing I can do about it, baby. I love you, but this is me right now."

"I'll get used to it, Eric." *I'd better.* Sylviana slipped her hand into his. "I love you. This is good. This is as good as I can have, and I want you in any and all ways it is possible."

"We won't have a problem, Sylviana. We'll be fine." He nodded toward their tour guide with a smile.

". . . fund their great works of charity. And also," Marcello continued with a wink at his cousin, "to subsidize their great love of art. The Medici had their own monuments of indulgence to their wealth. The monks ensured that some of that wealth was in the hands of the Church—so that art, great art, was not locked behind doors closed against the rest of us. For their own reasons, of course."

At the end of the day, they shared a meal at the *ristorante bistecca* with her cousins and walked back to the hotel along the Arno in silence. In the hotel room, they prepared to go to bed as though they had done so together every night for years. They talked about Eva and Enid and wrapped their arms around each other, not thinking about the inevitable, not thinking about the words that couldn't be but had to be said.

Sylviana's relatives came to the train station to say good-bye to Major Wasserman, but before the train could start, they left the couple alone on the platform. Eric and Sylviana stood together with their arms around each other, kissed, and held on to each other until they had no choice. Walking with him to the door of the train to Rome, Sylviana held his hand and clung to his arm. Eric tossed his duffle bag on board, gave her one last kiss, and jumped on as the conductor slammed the door. He stayed by the open window, gesturing that he would call soon. Sylviana blew kisses until the last car disappeared.

An hour later, she arrived at the airport with Julietta, dark glasses covering her swollen eyes, her lips and fingers trembling at the thought of how long their separation was to be or, worse, that she might never see him again, all the words that couldn't be said but had been there from the moment she had handed her first letter to the volunteer group.

"Live on your happiness, Sylviana, not your misery." Julietta held out a mirror for the younger woman to dry her eyes and touch up her lipstick.

Sylviana saw a wreck, an unkempt, miserable fright queen who had been laughing mere hours ago when they had breakfast one final morning with their arms around each other—when the prosciutto would not be stuffed into her hungry husband's mouth because he wanted to kiss her again, and the waitress, the tiny bleach-blond waitress, was taking another photo for them. Sylviana Innocenti—Sylviana Wasserman—dipped her hand into her shoulder bag and retrieved the camera with all the photos of her trip and her honeymoon and her reunion with the love of her life on a roll of film.

She pressed the camera to her lips and sent her husband of less than two days a big kiss, estimating that he was within an hour of arriving in Rome, where he'd catch a taxi to the airport and wait for a standby flight back to his unit in eastern Europe. She knew approximately where he was and where he was going. She knew how long she had to wait before even the possibility of leave came up for him. She knew there was a chance, always had been a chance, that he might be killed. A few months ago Aggy Tarkington had pronounced him dead. *But he wasn't. He isn't.*

And she had a job to do. Martinelli wanted copies of the photos of Il Duomo. Clee was tapping her fingers on her keyboard waiting for her CO's wife to send the wedding pictures for the unit to see. His second in command was waiting for a phone call from him to tell her when his transport was due. Sylviana already knew his unit was planning a party of their own, but she drew a firm line against any thoughts of the twenty women in his unit who were going to kiss him with impunity.

"You're right, Julietta. I may not be quick, but I can be smart enough."

San Francisco International glittered at the side of the black pool of the Bay. The string of runway lights led straight up the channel, and once the wheels touched the ground, Sylviana heard the clicks of seat belts as travelers ignored the warnings of the cabin crew. She was just as impatient, but she kept her eyes on the white lines and the blinking red and yellow lights until the pilot abdicated his responsibility for the aircraft and released the passengers from their constraints. She was just as eager to get out of the plane and onto the gangway. She was just as tired of the confinement. But she watched the backs of all the people who had crossed the Atlantic with her from Frankfurt until there was no one waiting in the aisle or lifting purchased treasures in their duty-free bags from the overhead bays. Before she ended her journey, she took a deep breath and checked the time on her watch. *He's asleep. Single bed, undershirt, boxers, socks, and his watch.*

She glimpsed her parents and the girls standing at the railing beyond the frosted glass door of the customs lobby when it opened for someone else. She waved at them, but their faces were turned toward another section. By the time they looked toward her, the door had swung closed and didn't open again until Sylviana pushed against it with her trolley and saw her mother's hands pressed against her lips and her father wiping something from the corner of his eye. No railing could contain Eva, whose whole body slammed into Sylviana's side, full of accusation, rage, and relief.

"What took you so long?" Her mother spoke for all of them, pulling her daughter's head down to kiss her forehead and passing her on to her father. The question didn't demand an answer, just a sigh and sinking into the pudgy embrace of the four people who had been with her for nearly every step of her adventure.

"We saw you, Mommy! We saw you marry Eric."

"Did you, sweetie?"

"Yeah. That. Jerk."

The old sedan was parked three moving walkways, two elevators, a tramway, and a zigzag walk through echoing caverns away from the arrivals area. Beyond the parking lot, she could see the lights of the 280 weaving across the top of San Bruno and the 101 Bayshore shooting through South City. *Eric won't know this place. This is all new, all different.* Her mother sat with her in the back of the car, relinquishing her customary seat to her granddaughters, and patted her own little girl's hand.

The apartment was dark, chilly, and abandoned. Her father set her suitcase in the front hall and turned on the lamp at the living room window. Sylviana opened the case and dug out the gifts she and Eric had chosen for her daughters. She didn't expect Eva to be enthusiastic and wasn't disappointed in the twelve-year-old girl's tolerant expression for the Italian leather purse, and Enid's happy acceptance of the pink cashmere gloves and scarf relieved her guilt long enough for her to send her children to bed without any of the tears she'd expected to be shed in retribution for her misdeeds.

Before her parents wished her a good night's sleep to drive across town to their stucco house in the fog belt, she told them only what they needed to know about her new husband—he loved her and intended to take care of her and his stepdaughters. She didn't say, *I'm scared.* She didn't wonder that they had no misgivings or doubts about him—they hadn't expressed any when she married Steven Langdon either. Their trust in her was solid, but it shook her a little to realize that they, like Eric, seemed to have more faith in her than she had in herself.

Unpacking her case, sorting through souvenirs and dirty clothes, soothed and consoled her through the few hours she was alone until she took a shower and wore one of Eric's dark green tank undershirts to bed. She curled in the middle of the double bed to dwell on all the reasons she had to be happy.

When the phone rang, she automatically reached for the receiver. Just as automatically, she pulled her hand back, letting the sound reverberate, afraid her happiness would shatter the moment she heard Steven's voice. *Eric said he'd call.* She clutched the phone and held the receiver to her ear.

"Were you asleep, baby?"

"Not yet. Where are you?" She looked at the alarm clock and added nine hours. *0800. An Army wife already.*

"Still in camp. We're deploying today, soon. I don't know when we'll be set up or when I'll be able to get a call through again."

"That's okay. I'll be here. Enid liked the scarf and gloves. I'll let you know what Eva thinks of her purse as soon as she gets over feeling disloyal to Steven, but she didn't throw it down and stomp on it." She had said the right thing for once. He was laughing.

"Some progress there, anyway. How was your trip home?"

"Long and lonesome, but I'm okay. What about you?"

"Embarrassing."

"Why?" She held her breath, waiting for Natale or that painting or something Steven had said to hit her, knock her fragile, tenacious hold on living on happiness too far out of reach.

"I kept breaking out in a stupid grin, thinking about you in my T-shirt." He'd said the right thing too.

"I'm wearing it now."

"That will keep me going for a while," he murmured. "Are you working tomorrow?"

"Not until Monday. What time are you leaving there?"

"0900. About an hour from now."

"How long before you get to your new base?"

"Should be on shore by Saturday."

"By boat?"

"Carrier, once we fly to the naval base. After that it's over land."

"Will you be in danger?"

"No more than usual, Sylviana. We're not a combat unit. I've got to get to work, baby. I'll be with you every hour of the day and night. As soon as I can, I'll get leave."

She could hear the catch in his voice. "We're okay, Eric. I'm thinking of you, every minute."

"I'll call or something—whatever is possible when we're set up. Till then, just know . . ."

"Me too." In the distance, she heard big engines firing up and the growl of voices. "Get to work, Major, so I can get some shut-eye." When the line went dead, Sylviana held the receiver to her heart and fell asleep. Her alarm woke her at 6:00 AM. She hung up the receiver, peeled off the T–shirt, and dressed in her jeans before waking her daughters, beginning all the usual daily routines, knowing that Eric would glance at his watch and have a good idea of her what, where, and why so she could send him a kiss or a happy thought. That morning she sent him both, poured muesli into a bowl, and was taking a second spoonful when the phone rang.

"What did you think you were doing, talking on the phone all night?"

"I wasn't, Steven. The receiver was off the hook. Why did you call?"

"I wanted to be sure you got home all right and the girls were okay."

"They're fine," she said, smiling at Enid in her new scarf. "I got home at seven." *1900 hours.* "Mom and Dad picked me up at the airport."

"Why was the receiver off the hook? Trying to avoid me and your responsibilities to your daughters?"

"Neither of those things even crossed my mind." She didn't say, *I was talking to my new, loving, thoughtful, and ever so wonderful husband.* "What do you want, Steven?" She touched the two gold hearts resting on her breastbone. "When are you going to let me get on with my life?" Her wedding ring clinked against the cereal bowl she handed to her youngest daughter.

"You wanted to divorce me, remember? I still love you, Sylvi. You can't expect me to just give up what we had because you had some crazy notion about a jerk who didn't stick around long enough for you to realize what a waste of space he truly was. And is."

"That's your opinion, Steven. Not mine." She hung up.

When the phone rang again, she let it go to the answering machine and was sorry when her ex-husband's voice recorded,

"Eric Wasserman was and is a lamebrain coward, Sylvi, and the biggest joke in our unit for being a hick who never got—"

She ripped the receiver off the hook. "Your daughters are listening to this, Steven."

"Good. They should know the kind of loser their mother runs after since she dumped their father."

"Mom, we're going to be late for school."

"If you keep doing this, Steven, I'll get a restraining order against you."

"You wouldn't do that to me."

"Push it, Steven, and you'll find out." She hung up again and took the receiver to the fridge. "Cool off in there," she said after she shut the door.

"Don't forget it's in there, Mommy."

"Remind me later, Enid. Brush your teeth with Eva, and let's go."

Two days later, the phone rang again in the middle of the night. Sylviana dragged the receiver to her ear and mumbled something.

"Sorry I woke you, Sylviana. Just wanted you to know where I am."

"Hi, sweetheart. I miss you so much!" She yawned, scrunching up the pillow to get comfortable. "Where are you?"

"We got here about forty minutes ago, standard-issue desert base near the Equator."

"Hot?"

"Like a grill. How is it there?"

"Foggy and cold."

"Heaven, right?"

"Pretty much. Eva is using her purse. Took it to school to show her friends this morning."

"That's good."

"That's very good, Eric. Tell me about your journey."

"Long and lonely, like yours. I couldn't sleep most of the way, even on the carrier. Can't get used to being on my own."

She couldn't say that she'd had the same trouble; true, she was asleep when he called, but she had fallen asleep with her arms around a pillow, pretending she was holding him. "Maybe I should have given you one of my T-shirts."

"You can send one to my APO, but make sure you've worn it first."

"Any particular color, sweetheart?"

"Your choice."

Chapter Fourteen

Dearest, beloved Eric,

Gosh, I didn't think I'd be doing this again! That doesn't mean I don't want to. You know that, don't you? Anyway, here we are, back where we started—in a way. I love you so much, I still can't believe we are married. Maybe that has something to do with all this distance and the short time we had to be together. Do you think that's it?

Here are all the pictures taken while we were in Firenze— quite a haul. I don't remember Marcello taking so many, and what exactly were you doing all that time, taking pictures when I wasn't looking? You know you broke all the rules when you took that one of me looking at Michelangelo's David. *You're lucky you didn't get caught and didn't get much of the* David, *or you'd have been put in the Accademia's bad-boys book for sure.*

I can't even begin to tell you how much I miss you . . . so I won't.

Speaking of bad books. I'm in one—you can guess whose. No big deal and nothing I can't handle. The girls are being so good, Eric. I feel sorry for them. They're working so hard to stay on the right side of this mess. I shouldn't be writing about this. Sorry. Well, yes, I should, but I don't want to, not right now.

Happier news: The girls are settled back into their school routine after my jaunt to hunt you down. Enid is blossoming into acting. She has a speaking part in the Halloween production, but she won't tell me anything about it. That's in two weeks, and after that, she has a

Thanksgiving performance. For a long time she's been in Eva's musical shadow but has come into her own with these school plays.

Eva still enjoys band. They are practicing for all the football games. She hasn't said a word, but I think she has a boyfriend—someone in the band who plays trombone. He's phoned here a few times, and they talk about practice. She laughs a lot. I'm not making a big deal of this— the last thing I want is for her to feel pushed into or out of a friendship.

I've got to go so I can get this to the post office before it closes. Everyone is just fine. I miss you and I love you. Let me know if you need anything else. I hope you like the T-shirt I picked.

Love & kisses,
xxxooo[1000]
Sylviana

P.S.: Aggy and Frankie say hi!

"A-OK, sir?" Clee asked from the doorway of the half-canvas, half-wooden hut, keeping the screen door shut tight.

"Sylviana's sent the photos for Martinelli. Do you want to hand them over?"

"You do it, sir. They'll mean more that way, since she asked you for them."

"Right." He folded the two sheets of blue paper back into their envelope and slid it into his breast pocket, smoothing his hand over the flap. "Here are the shots from the wedding. You've seen most of the show—from the video."

"Never get enough of that, Major. Real morale-booster film— first-class."

"Comedy, Lieutenant Jones?"

"Not in anyone here's book, sir."

After he handed his second in command the packet of photos, he laid his hand on the other envelope that had arrived with the mailbag, addressed to E.D.D. Wasserman, no rank, just his APO, no return address. Tempted to crush the corporate envelope and missile it through the screened window, Eric slid his thumb under the flap, ripped through the top edge, and yanked the single sheet from its hiding place.

I never thought you'd do this to me. We were friends, closer than brothers. I saved your life so you could do this to me? I wish that bullet had killed me. I would never wish it had killed you, Er. Never. Now I just hope you can live with yourself.

No greeting. No signature. Typed hard and fast, folded with precision like a machine, edges sharp enough to slice through gristle and bone. Bayonet through to the backbone. *Had to know that was coming, Wasserman. Can't have thought you'd get away with it, not after all these years.*

You stole the only thing that meant anything to me. Did you ever think about how I'd feel, knowing that was how you were paying me back for saving your miserable life—taking my wife away from me, just when I needed her most?

Nope, Eric hadn't thought that. Not after he knew the truth. Hadn't thought it. Hadn't cared.

We were in a bad patch, I admit that. We'd started to turn things around, but then you answered her letter. Why did you do that?

He'd *had* to do that. There was more to Steve's miserable letter, but Eric folded the page on the creases and laid it on the desk.

"Martinelli is in the motor pool, sir."

"Thanks, Clee. Enjoy those. Took a while to get there, but those four and a half days were worth every second of the journey."

"Yes, sir. I can see that, sir," Jones said, grinning up at him as he walked by her desk. "Your wife looks real happy, sir."

"She was. She is."

From: EDD Wasserman   Sent: Sun 10/24 16:54
To: Sylviana Innocenti
Cc:
Subject: T-shirts
Attachments: base1.JPG (54KB); base2.JPG (91KB); majorw.JPG (159KB)

Hello, baby,
Did it have to be pink? Got the photos. Clee is over the moon. Martinelli too. They're forcing me to attach a few of the base, so you can see the state of things. Clee says she's looking after me for you, so you're not to worry. She insisted I stand in the frame; I think it's just to show the scale.

I've requested leave, as promised. Nothing doing there until March, earliest possible. Too much work here fixing up a lot of broken toys. You know what I mean. First we have to make things a lot more friendly. Happier films won't cut much of that ice.

Anytime you need to talk, send me an e-mail, and I'll phone you. There's a ten-hour difference, but Eva can show you how to set up the Webcam.

Thank Eva for me, for setting up your new e-mail account.

I love you, Sylviana,
EDD

As soon as Eva opened the photos, Sylviana leaned close to the screen, studying her shy guy's face. All she could see was his mouth and nose beneath the aviator sunglasses and the camouflage hat. She recognized Clee Jones from Eric's description and guessed who among the women was Martinelli from the wrench in her fist. Another woman stood next to her husband, right up against him with her hand on his shoulder. "How do I send a picture back to him?"

"Gee, Mom. Didn't they teach you anything in school? Or work?"

"I don't use this stuff at work. I mostly use the phone and have to fill out forms. And you know we didn't even have paper, pencils, or books when I went to school. We were lucky to have clay tablets and a stylus."

"Okay. Okay," her twelve-year-old said. "I'll show you once, but after that—"

"Eva, don't put conditions on me. Okay? I don't want to mess this up."

"It's easy, Mommy," Enid said. "We do it all the time in school."

"I'll show her, Enid."

Before a fight broke out for technical supremacy, Sylviana sent Enid to dish up the ice cream with a promise she could help next time. "Your mom is going to need a lot of help unless you two want the Army, Navy, and Air Force to come down on us like a ton of bricks for giving away military secrets."

She chose another picture of the three of them at Lassen National Park but lost track of the steps that Eva made, talking her through each one, to get the 4x6 photo from the envelope into the scanner and onto the computer screen to be grafted to an e-mail message.

"Okay, you can do the rest, Mom."

"What do I do now?"

"Boy, this is going to be a long night."

From: Sylviana   Sent: Mon 10/25 17:25
To: EDD
Cc:
Subject: Hi, it's me
Attachment: lassen2.jpg

_____

Hi. Eva is showing me how to do this. Don't blame me if everything goes wrong and this ends up at the Pentagon or

"Mom! Why did you do that?"

"What? What did I do? You told me I shouldn't say *Pentagon,* so I got rid of the message."

"You. Sent. It." Eva checked the Sent folder and double-clicked on *Hi, it's me.* "See? It's sent, and you were the one scared of us getting you into trouble."

"Letters and forms. Like I told you. I'll write him a note and mail the photo."

"Don't bother, Mom. Unless you're on some watch list, they won't be looking at your e-mails right now. But they might be looking at Eric's, so you'd better be careful what you send."

"I'm not going to try anything fancy again, so you can stop worrying. And what dangerous things would I ever say? And what's a watch list? And how do you know about things like that?"

Eva looked at her mother for thirty seconds, obviously counting each one of them in her head until she said, "Everyone knows about things like that."

"I don't." Sylviana left the kitchen and closed the door of her bedroom. Feeling stupid was all part of the daily routine with a teenager in the house. Being good at her job didn't matter. Being the best mother she could be was irrelevant. Steven had spotted her weaknesses right away, and Eva was now echoing his complaint of, "*Sylviana,* everybody *knows that. Where have you been for the last twenty years?*" Once he got over the awe and mystery of how they had reunited, Eric wouldn't be fooled for long; he'd detect all her weaknesses too.

Don't start feeling sorry for yourself, she told herself firmly, swiping the sudden tears from her cheeks. It was way past time to start being happy.

She slammed a few drawers while she changed from her work clothes into shirt and jeans and combed her hair into a ponytail. *Maybe it's better he's not here—he won't find out so quickly what a doofus I can be.* 5:30 PM. *1730 hours.* The girls were home from school. She should be in the kitchen, making their dinner.

Rebellion wasn't so difficult. She didn't *have* to follow any rigid routine. She didn't *have* to be the perfect wife and mother. She could be that wild creature, that miscreant who'd dragged her little girls to an art school in defiance of her creep of a husband.

This time, though, she did care. This time was different. Eric hadn't done anything but be smart and wonderful and thoughtful. He didn't deserve this rage.

From: Sylviana   Sent: Mon 10/25 22:45
To: EDD
Cc:
Subject: Hi, it's me again.

Sorry. I panicked. I'll get used to this. Eva thinks I'm a dinosaur, but I *like* to use pen and paper. It helps me think.

The girls are both in bed, asleep. We had dinner at 6:30 (I know, 1830 hours!) as usual. They did their homework, and Eva got me started on doing this correctly. All I have to do is click on the Send button when I'm done writing, and this message will practically be in your in-box. Amazing, isn't it? Too bad it only works for words and not people, or *I'd* be there in an instant. I don't want to hit Send instead of Delete again, so I'm crossing my fingers and keeping away from that mouse.

Thank you for the photos of your base and some of the people you work with. I hope I'll get to know them all someday. I recognized Clee and Martinelli from your descriptions—did Martinelli like the pictures of Il Duomo?

I wish I could hear your voice or at least hold a letter from you in my hands, but this will have to do for now, won't it?

Good night, Eric. I hope you are sleeping better now that you're settled. Let Clee take really good care of you, please.

With all my love,
Sylviana xxx

The attached photo to *Hi, it's me* was the only explanation for the truncated message. Something told him that his new wife wasn't comfortable with electronic communication. He replied to the message, saying he'd received the picture of the three of them and had put it on his desktop, then realized she might think he meant on the top of his desk. That made him laugh, and he wondered what could have been in Steve Langdon's mind to take all that innocence and mash it up. *Hi, it's me again* explained everything.

From: EDD Wasserman   Sent: Tue 10/26 18:06
To: Sylviana Innocenti
Cc:
Subject: RE: Hi, it's me again.

Write to me. Long letters. On paper if you want to. Sleep well, baby. I love you too. Eric xxx

The desert outside his tent-cabin sizzled in the midafternoon. The electricity from the generators had been off for an hour. The only good thing about that was the quiet. Clee fanned herself with a few sheets of paper. Eric pulled his tank shirt away from his chest just to feel the cool clamminess of the ribbed cloth when it settled again. Across the compound, along the perimeter wall, some of his unit on duty were playing cards in any patch of shade they could find. Not much of that on the Horn, even at that time of year. All-year-round heat and humidity. Lodi was bad enough in the summer. This was hotter than Arizona and four times as wet as Georgia. The sun went down to a chorus of mosquitoes and every gal and guy in his unit blasting out some profanity, slapping some exposed part of their bodies.

Their CO kept his thoughts focused on that undulation of white mist crawling over Twin Peaks, lapping at the door of Sylviana's apartment. He pulled away from the damp seat back and set his main watch dial to his wife's time zone and its morning alarm to his. Three-point-five weeks had slinked by since his weekend in Florence. On his desk were a stack of cards from his relatives-in-law, and he couldn't remember how they had found out his APO. Alessandro had sent his e-mail address. Eric sent off a quick few words of appreciation to the young man and hoped the cousins didn't all reply—with luck they were as techno-shy as their beautiful cousin. He closed the program and relaxed again, meeting Sylviana's olive-eyed stare from three different faces.

"Nice-looking family, sir." Angel Watts leaned against the door of his quarters and swept the square room with a glance. "You haven't had much time to get to know your wife, have you, sir?"

"Not a lot. What can I do for you, Private?"

"Must be hard on her too, especially with two children who've never met their stepfather."

"Yeah, I guess." He grinned at the faces on his desktop. Sometimes *Yeah, I guess* was the only appropriate response. "Was there something else, Watts?" He looked past her to the outer office. At some point, Cleonina Jones had abandoned him.

"I just thought maybe, since you're new to this family-separation gig, you might appreciate someone to talk through any, you know, stuff."

"Thanks. I'm good."

"Just so you know, sir, the offer stands. Whenever. Whatever."

Eric met her dark eyes, an inward gulp cutting off his breath at the unexpected come-on. "I'll keep that in mind," he said to be polite. "Thanks, but my wife and I have worked through everything that's come up so far."

"You had time to *talk*, sir?"

The crude laugh in her voice rocketed his blood pressure, but he felt no need to explain or defend his relationship with the woman he had loved all his adult life. "That will be all, Private Watts. Good night." He hadn't noticed that she'd come halfway across the floor and now stood at the foot of his bunk. He watched her walk to the door, conscious that there was a sway in her movements that hadn't been there before.

Angel turned her head at the door, still keeping her glances shifting from his face to the bunk. "Any time, Major Wasserman. At your service."

Eric turned his head to stare at the computer screen and waited for the door to close. Before he did anything, a notice appeared in the lower right corner. Without thinking, he clicked the oblong bubble, and Steve Langdon's e-mail opened.

From: S. A. Langdon,   Sent: Tue 10/26 09:00
Vice President, International Mutual
To: Wasserboy
Cc:
Subject: Sylviana—at her best
Attachment: JPG (247KB)

Hey, Buddy. Congratulations. You didn't have the guts to tell me yourself, but I thought you had a right to know what sort of woman you married.

Eric hit the Delete icon, emptied the folder, and shut down. He unfolded the two pages of his wife's first letter she'd written since getting home and read through what she had said about her daughters and what she was doing, and he noticed a few changes in what she was willing to share with him. *We're fine. We're doing fine.*

When he couldn't sleep that night, he stared at his watch, with no need now to calculate back ten hours. 1700 hours. 5:00 PM. Another day over. Another meal cooked, homework done. No e-mails for awhile—except from Steve. Eric clenched his eyes shut. Steve Langdon had his e-mail address. No warning, but there was no doubt in his mind who had given that information to his former best friend. Not a battle he wanted to fight, that night or in the near future. Eva's loyalty to her father was a bigger issue than he could tackle long distance. He'd have to live with it for now. *Bright side, Wasserman. While Steve's after you, he'll have less time for your wife.* How much wishful thinking he was doing, he had a good idea.

From: S. A. Langdon,   Sent: Tue 10/26 09:03
Vice President, International Mutual
To: Wasserboy
Cc:
Subject:

Just in case you deleted the last message, I've posted that and more on my Facebook page and sent a notice to your unit's page so all your buddies on base can share the fun.

"Clee, come in here. Any chance you can help me out with this?"

"What is it, sir? I don't understand."

"This guy is Sylviana's ex-husband."

"Ugly."

"Can you do anything to block that notice?"

"Too late for that, but I can remove the link."

Eric watched her work through the admin back of the Web page he'd asked her to set up for friends and family to have daily access to information about his unit.

"How did that guy get in?"

"I gave the information to Sylviana. Somehow he got it. How did he do this?"

"It's easy, Major. Once you're recognized . . . He must have used someone's identity."

"Yeah, I guess." Eric shook his head, a cold smirk on his lips. "Can you block him?"

"Sure, but that means blocking whoever gave him access. Your wife, sir, or one of the girls?"

"One of the girls is my bet."

"Could be hard to explain, sir." His second in command turned on her heel and just as quickly turned back. "You know, sir, there's no one in our unit who'd give this guy a look-in if he's out to mess you up."

"He is. Worse, he's out to mess up my wife. I can handle whatever he wants to dish out to me."

"Sure. I'll do all I can to help, sir."

From: EDD Wasserman   Sent: Wed 10/27 10:23
To: Sylviana Innocenti
Cc:
Subject: RE: Hi, it's me again.

I know you're still sleeping, Sylviana. Just want you to have something to keep you company for the rest of your week. We're fine, baby. We're doing okay. Eric xxx

Sylviana set the iron down on its holder and shook out the dress she was going to wear to the second-grade class' Halloween play. Enid was leaping from one room to the next, dressed in her costume, with Eva tromping from her room to the kitchen.

"Do I have to go, Mom? It's Friday night."

"Yes. Enid is in the play. We're in the audience. That's the deal."

"Is Dad coming?"

"I don't know. Enid told him the date. Grandma and Grandpa will be there."

"It's no fun without Dad. He always takes us for ice cream after."

"I'll take you—or Grandpa will."

"It's. Not. The. Same."

Sylviana covered her eyes for a moment. "This is not my fault. Your father has only ever been around for you when there was something in it for him." As soon as the words had escaped, her tears came. Although it was as true as anything she could have said about her ex-husband, she had broken her number one rule about their divorce. "I'm sorry, Eva. I shouldn't have said that."

Enid stood in the wide doorway to the living room.

"Your father did his best."

"Not for you, Mommy. That's why you have a new husband."

"Yes, Enid."

"And he's not here either."

"No, he's not," Sylviana agreed, and she sat on a breakfast bar stool, covering her eyes, letting the dress she'd ironed start to wrinkle on her lap.

"We could call him, Mommy. I want to talk to Eric too."

"Why, sweetie?"

"Because. I want to show him my costume."

"We can't do that."

"Yes. We. Can." Eva's tone was resigned. She was living with techno-morons. Without a word, she sat at the computer and opened the e-mail program. "Here's a message from Daddy."

"Don't open that."

"I know. It's private." She sent her message to Eric.

"Wait. What time is it there?"

"You said ten hours ahead."

"He'll be asleep. Sorry, Enid. We can try when—"

"He's answered." Eva opened another program, and three windows popped onto the screen. "I'll close this one," the twelve-year-old said. "I hate looking at myself when I'm talking."

"What is this?" Sylviana stared at the screen, watching Eric rub his eyes. "We woke him up." He was wearing a T-shirt, boxers, his watch. *War zone.*

"Hi," he said into the screen of his laptop, looking at Eva before he raised his eyes to see Sylviana standing across the room. "What's up?"

"Enid. She wanted you to see her costume."

"Hi, Eric," the seven-year-old said, leaping at the screen. "I'm a zombie."

"You could have fooled me, Enid. You look like an angel."

"Mommy hasn't finished my makeup. I get to say four lines in the play. My teacher wrote it, and Grandpa promised he'd make a video, but his camcorder never works. We saw you and Mommy get married. That was nice. I want to go to Italy too."

"Hush up, Enid. Let me talk," Eva interrupted.

"Are you going to the play, Eva?"

"I don't have a choice."

"It'll be good practice, Eva," Eric said, glancing in Sylviana's direction.

"For what?"

"For becoming a gracious young lady."

"I'm only twelve."

"That's why it's good to practice. Well ahead of time. Takes a lot of skill—ask your mom."

"All those little kids are silly."

"Just like you, four, five years ago."

"Yeah, I guess," Eva conceded. Eric grinned at her for a moment, then caught a glimpse of Sylviana moving away. "Is it hot there?"

"You could bake a cake in the shade some days. Nights are cold—cold enough to make ice cubes." He dropped his gaze when Sylviana covered her lips; a second later he grinned straight at her.

"Can we come to visit you?" Enid begged.

The question caught him, threw him off balance, but he said, "I don't think so, Enid, but I'll see what I can do about coming to visit you."

"Mom wants to talk to you too," Eva said, gesturing for Enid to follow her out of the room.

Chapter Fifteen

Sylviana came toward the counter, into range, looking around the screen and avoiding the camera. "I miss you."

"What's wrong, baby?"

"I just miss you. I'm not handling this very well. I'm all out of sorts and can't seem to shake the jet lag, or something. Are you sleeping any better?"

"A bit. Thanks to the T-shirt."

"Eric?"

"What, baby?"

"Has . . . Have you gotten anything from Steven?"

"Yes. Came yesterday."

"Oh." She turned her face away and fixed her gaze on the dark window looking into the garden.

"I deleted the file, never saw what he sent." Eric studied her profile, but the light in the kitchen was behind her. "You don't have to worry about him, Sylviana."

"Can you show me your room?"

Eric turned the Webcam away and swept the space—as he had told her, it was spartan, except for the photos he had put on his desk.

"It's not so bad."

"It's not Florence, baby, and you're not here."

"Can we come to visit you?" she asked, sounding almost exactly like Enid.

"This is not a good place for you or the girls. I'll be getting my leave assignment in a few months. I'll let you know when—could be sooner than I said."

"How much sooner?"

"A few weeks."

"So, not before Christmas."

"No, baby. Some of my people haven't been home for Christmas since they were assigned."

"Neither have you."

"Nope. The military hasn't changed, Sylviana. The next time I see you, I'll take you and the girls to Disneyland or wherever you want."

"I do love you, Eric."

"I know. I do know that. I love you, Sylviana Innocenti."

"Wasserman."

"Hmm?"

"I changed my name legally to Wasserman."

He was stunned. Happily stunned. "I thought that would be too complicated, with the girls, school, your work."

"I didn't want to accommodate anyone or stay stuck in the past. Besides, now there'll be only two names above the doorbell."

"Langdon and Wasserman." Eric laughed. "That *is* funny."

"I guess it is." Sylviana smiled. "It is very funny." After a moment, she asked, "What will you be doing today?"

"We're going out into the backwater to support a clinic. For women and children."

"Any orphans I should know about?"

"Too many. Way too many. Until last week, this was a war zone."

"You didn't tell me that, Eric."

"Unless I'm Stateside, Sylviana, I am in or near a war zone. Don't worry about it."

"How can I not worry?"

"I've been doing this for as long as you've known me—give or take a few months. I know my job."

"But—"

"Hush. For me this is routine. No more dangerous than driving on the 280. A lot fewer unpredictable crazies to deal with. You can't change anything by worrying, and I take good care of myself and my people. Just do the same for yourself and your daughters so I don't have to worry about you."

"You haven't driven the 280 in fifteen years." When he stopped laughing, she said, "I'm okay."

"So am I."

The one question that had been drilling a hole into her confidence stuck in her throat. "Are you having any trouble shaving?" she said instead. *Twenty women and one with—don't go there.*

"Does it show?" He rubbed a hand over his chin. "My hand isn't as steady as yours. Blade's a bit dull by now."

"Are you still using that same razor, Eric?"

"Can't seem to part with it."

"I feel the same about your T-shirt. I see you every time I feel it against my skin."

"I wish I was that shirt."

Sylviana bowed her head for a moment. "Thank you for the pictures of the base but especially of you, sweetheart. I know we can't talk like this every night, but it's important to know I can if I have to. I was so horrible to Eva, but she set up this call without my even asking."

"Tell her thanks from me. Talking and seeing you is important to me too. There are a few weird things going on here."

"Like what?"

"Like all of a sudden, I'm not just a CO but a man."

"That doesn't surprise me," Sylviana said, studying his face. Right in the middle of her chest, she felt a kick so hard that she was knocked back fifteen years to the night of Aggy's party, watching him walk out the door of the apartment, never turning his head once to see her pressing her fingers to her mouth to contain the fear that she wasn't going to see him again, wondering what she had said wrong. *I always say the wrong thing. I talk too much.* "I saw that the first time I met you, remember?" She leaned closer to the screen. *Please, let me get this right, just once.* "You know what I'm thinking about right now?"

"What's that, Sylviana?"

"I'm sure you'll figure it out, Major. But just to help you out a bit—you're so good with ice."

"Is that good or bad?" The burning he felt at his jugular had nothing to do with incendiary devices and everything to do with their wedding night, a bottle of prosecco, and ice-chilled kisses.

"What do you think, Frosty? I'm going to invest in a frozen meat locker of ice cubes."

"Might last a week."

"We'll replenish as we go along."

"Arrange a daily delivery, Sylviana. It'll take me at least a month to get over the heat in this place."

From: snarextrom   Sent: Mon 11/22 16:18
To: EDD Wasserman
Cc:
Subject: It's just me, Eva

Hi. I'll bet anything you can't believe I'm sending you an e-mail. Well, I am. I know you're not as bad as Mom with this stuff, but I'll write so you can understand. You know. In English. I know it's not fair, but I don't want you to tell Mom I've written, okay? If that's okay with you—it's nothing bad, I promise—let me know. Eva Langdon

He didn't recognize *snarextrom* and was heading for the Delete button when he saw the subject line. No attachments took him out of the sniper's alley enough to open the message. Eric was pretty certain Eva was on the other end of the message, not her father playing another of his tricks—one too many of those had gotten through his blocked-sender's filter since Steve's first assault around Halloween. Replying was just as risky, but he gave her the benefit of doubt this time.

From: EDD Wasserman   Sent: Tue 11/23 05:32
To: snarextrom
Cc:
Subject: RE: It's just me, Eva.

You're right, I can't believe it. What can I do for you?
EDD

From: snarextrom   Sent: Tue 11/23 17:34
To: EDD Wasserman
Cc:
Subject: RE: RE: It's just me, Eva

I'm supposed to be doing my homework, but Mom's on the phone with Grandma, and Enid is practicing her part in the Thanksgiving play—I don't have to go this time because it's during school.

Unless Steve was a lot smarter than anyone gave him credit for, or Eva was a lot more communicative with her father than any other twelve-year-old he'd known in his life, Eric thought it was a stretch that she'd tell Steve about not wanting to go to her little sister's school play. Too much ammunition, like handing over a loaded gun when you know you're the target. He'd handed over a few guns to this guy himself. By now, he was more cautious than the twenty-two-year-old pump-jockey GI he had been.

If you had a friend, your best friend, someone you could talk to, and one day, your friend stopped talking to you and being your friend, wouldn't even come to the phone when you called, what would you think?

She didn't sign off, just left the question for him to decipher. He had ten hours to figure out what she needed to know. He also had a mission that was going to take every one of those hours and more. He figured Eva wouldn't be asking if she didn't want his help. He figured she'd rather go to her sister's school play than ask him anything. He figured he had a chance to break through to her—and an even better chance to crash and burn.

"Let's go," he ordered his eight-man patrol, taking point for the first leg into the scrubs the combat unit had nicknamed East LA. "Keep sharp, Cooper. Pair of walkers two o'clock."

"Got 'em."

While he ordered his group forward, flushing out the locals and their cattle for escort through the desert to the NPO camp,

keeping one eye on his men and the other on the wasteland for
combatants, in his head he heard his wife's worried voice. The
patrol was within sight of the camp. The cattle were moving like
camels, swaying from side to side. The women and children
walked ahead of him, between the patrol and the herd. "Trombone." Wasserman watched his men throw themselves to the
dirt, dragging the locals down too. He watched their faces, shouting, arms waving. *Down. Get down.* But, for him, the ground just
rocked.

On the stove, the water boiled for the second time, but, hard as
she looked up and down the block, there was no sign of Steven's
car. *Damn him. Damn him.* He knew they were going to her
brother's straight after dinner to spend the Thanksgiving weekend. He knew she didn't like taking the Muni and BART so
late. He knew she'd have the dinner ready five minutes after the
girls came through the door from their afternoon with him—a
concession for the girls' sakes because she didn't want them at
his house on Thanksgiving. He knew the last BART train going
that far out was too late to ask either her sister-in-law or brother
to collect them. *I should have told him no to the afternoon with
the girls.*

She didn't say no because Steven had been decent about the
long holiday weekend. She didn't say no because he had let up
on his threats to sue for custody. She didn't say no because that
word, more than any other, brought on the fights that drove Eva
into screaming fits and turned Enid's fairy-dust sprinkling into
puppy-eyed misery. She didn't say no because she wanted to get
away to her big happy family and have all the time she wanted
to show them Eric's quarters, let them talk to him on the computer, let her papa tell his son-in-law all about her naughty tricks
as a girl. She should have said no.

And for some reason, she sobbed, pressed her forehead to the
glass, and let the whole weight of happiness and misery crush
her.

Steven Langdon chose that moment to honk the horn of his
expensive car and wave through the windshield, grinning as if
he'd just conquered the world.

Sylviana scraped the wetness from her eyes and met her daughters at the door, hushed their excited chatter, and shut the door in her ex-husband's face. For good measure, she slapped the security chain into place and ignored the ringing doorbell and the hammering.

"You'll have to do without pasta. We don't have time. Eva, get that ciabata. We'll have Sloppy Giulio's instead."

"What's that?"

"Use your imagination."

"Hey, have you had an e-mail or anything from Eric?"

"Not today. He doesn't usually—What are you doing?"

"I just want to check my e-mails."

"No. Absolutely not. Sit down and eat. We have to get going."

The phone rang, and Enid launched herself toward the hallway. Sylviana caught her in flight and set her back in her seat. "It's just your father. Eat. Brush your teeth. I packed everything you need so we can go."

"But, Mom, I really want to check my e-mails. I have to," Eva whined.

"No. Tomorrow. Uncle Jerry has e-mail." The phone didn't stop ringing. The bell didn't stop buzzing. She screamed at the door. "Go away, or I'll call the police!"

Steven raised his fist and hit the beveled glass panel, putting his cell phone where she could see it. "You see this? You see this? This means you're done. This means Eva is coming to live with me, just like she wants. This time, I'm not taking no for an answer. You got that? I'm not taking no ever again."

"Mom—"

"Eat your food, and get a move on."

"We can go out through the alley, Mommy."

Sylviana just sobbed.

In two hours, Jerry Innocenti was waiting at the BART station at the end of the line for his hysterical baby sister. All he knew was that the three of them had escaped through the basement, broken out of the backyard, and run down the back alleys for six blocks to catch a bus. When they got back to the ranch-style bungalow, Papa was pacing the terrace entry, and their mother was clapping her hands to her face in the kitchen window.

"This isn't right. This isn't right." Sylviana's mother paced in front of the kitchen counter of her son's house, waving away her grandchildren and scolding her daughter.

"Momma, it's okay. I just lost it. I don't know what happened. I just couldn't take another second of it."

"What does Eric say?"

"I haven't told him."

"Why not? This has been going on for weeks, getting worse every day."

"What can Eric do, Momma? He's so far away, and he's got his own problems."

"Don't tell me he doesn't want to know. He's your husband. He's a good man. He'll do something. He'll want to do something."

"Momma, I know that, but there's nothing he can do from half a world away, is there? I'm going to have to get a court order. I didn't want to do that, but Steven's gone too far this time. Way, way too far."

"That terrible man. He's terrorizing his own children. He's terrorizing us all."

"I'll talk to my lawyer. She'll know what to do."

"And Eric. You must talk to Eric."

"I will, Momma. Tomorrow. He's sound asleep right now." *0835 hours*. Thanksgiving morning in east Africa. He was at his desk or walking the perimeter or having a coffee with Cleonina; breakfast was two hours in the past for him. He had eaten a stack of pancakes with maple syrup, if he was lucky, scrambled eggs, tomato juice, hash browns, sausage—and he'd still be hungry.

From: snarextrom	Sent: Wed 10/24 21:49
To: EDD Wasserman	
Cc:	
Subject: Me again, Eva.	

Just so you know. It doesn't matter about my friend anymore. I'm going to go live with my dad and change schools. That will fix things.

Breakfast at the younger Innocenti household began with the five children mixing up a banana pancake recipe with their grandmother, squirting the batter onto the griddle on the range, and watching the bubbles form around the edges, then flipping the pock-marked disks. Enid was relegated to holding the serving platter ready for the table. Eva disappeared as soon as the meal was over and she had no more responsibilities for clearing the table or putting dishes in the sink.

"Mom. Come here."

"What's wrong? Why are you on the computer at this time of the morning? It's a holiday. You can talk to your friends tomorrow or Saturday—"

"There's something wrong with this."

Sylviana peered at the list of e-mail messages. *Mail delivery failed: returning message to sender.* "What does that mean?"

"It's a mistake. It must be. I . . . Oh, never mind. I must have typed it wrong."

"Whose address is that?"

"No one special. Just . . . you know, a friend."

"We're here for family today, Eva. Get off that computer, and play with your cousins," Momma Innocenti said.

Sylviana rolled her eyes at her mother and went back to the kitchen with her sister-in-law to stuff the turkey. She didn't say a word about Eva's "boyfriend" or the anger that spit between the two of them if she even hinted she knew her daughter had a crush on the ninth-grade band member.

"This is important." Eva studied the message and the e-mail address. She hadn't made any mistakes and sent it again. Within a few minutes, she gasped when *Mail delivery failed: returning message to sender* came back. "What's wrong?" she whispered to herself, closing her mail service and typing the address of the combat support unit's fan page. *Oops, this is embarrassing. We can't find the page you want. Try typing the address again, or there may be a problem with the server.*

Eva cleared the history and closed the browser program. She joined her cousins on the patio, took the Ping-Pong paddle from Enid, and sent the white missile straight at her eldest cousin's shoulder. The fourteen-year-old grabbed the ball out of the air and tossed it back at her. "Try that again, Evie Peevie, and you'll get one in the eye."

"Josh, don't talk like that to anyone," his dad said, folding the daily down just enough to see what was happening, flipping it up again, and snapping it straight. "You'd think they'd get along—hardly see each other from one year to the next. Hey, Sylviana, when are we going to meet this new husband of yours? Must be past supper time wherever he is. Time for turkey sandwiches and leftover fruit salad, right?"

"We told him we'd put a call through around noon, Jerry. Eva knows what to do. Eric won't be expecting anything until then—less likely to be interrupted by his job."

"Won't interrupt the game either," Papa Innocenti offered.

"No, Papa. The game doesn't get interrupted for anything. Eric knows that, everybody knows that. Even *I* know that," Sylviana said, sighing at the normalcy, the quiet, grumpy family holiday. *I wish he could be here.* After a while, she put her arm over her eyes. *He is. He knows everything about what we're doing today, but it's not the same. . . . Happiness. Remember happiness.* She sent him a happy thought and a kiss.

Momma held her schooner of sherry in her hand, pretending an interest in every word her granddaughter said to explain everything she was doing to make the electronic voice connection halfway around the world. Josh hurried Eva, from his greater knowledge and vast, first-year-in-high-school experience. Seventh grade or not, she knew what she was doing and batted his hand away every time his fingers crept onto the keyboard.

Uncle Jerry patted his son on the shoulder, winked, and sent the teenager to the back of the family group. He wrapped his arm around his baby sister's shoulders. "I can't say this is the least conventional Thanksgiving we've ever had, but it's the first one we've had with a computer the center of attention."

Oops, this is embarrassing. We can't connect your video call to the contact you have selected. Try typing the address again, select another contact, or there may be a problem with the server.

"Mom, I don't know what's wrong."

"Let me try, Evie Peevie."

"Don't call me that. Mom, I did everything right. Something's wrong."

"Haven't you done this before?" Josh was edging forward, pushing her aside.

"Yes. Of. Course." Eva didn't say, *You dumb boy. Just because you're fourteen doesn't mean you know everything.* She didn't say, *All fourteen-year-old boys are so dumb.* "Most of the time we use Mom's address."

"Try that, Eva," her mother said, scooting the twelve-year-old over on the chair. "That always works." *2217 hours. He'll be wondering what's the holdup.*

"That isn't working either," Eva screamed at the monitor.

"Sweetie, calm down, it's just a technical problem."

"You don't understand. It's been happening all day. All day, Mommy."

"He's in a desert, Eva. There's bound to be—" Sylviana caught her breath and turned toward her mother, that terrible weight over her head. *Misery.* "Momma, I'd know. I'd know." *How can I? I'm not home. They can't call me if I'm not home. Maybe they did. Maybe he's been hurt . . . or dead . . . for hours . . . since last night. Somewhere. Alone.* "Momma!"

"Papa, you and Jerry do something. The turkey will be ready in forty-five minutes. I want a word with that young man before we sit down and give thanks."

Chapter Sixteen

Don't blame Daddy!"

Sylviana hadn't meant for Eva to hear her. She hadn't meant to blame anyone out loud. Eva's grandmother got up from the edge of the bed in the guestroom and walked the twelve-year-old down the corridor to the family room. Papa, Jerry, and Josh were making changes to the computer, trying this and fiddling with that. Papa oversaw, looking at his watch every few minutes. Eva's grandmother sat her down on the chair next to Josh and told them to work it out between them. "I want to talk to my son-in-law. Today."

"Momma, that may—"

"Don't say anything, Jerry Innocenti. Not until you are one hundred percent positive. Two hundred percent."

"How is she?" Papa whispered.

"Bad. Get in touch with someone, Papa. Pretty quick."

"I felt something. Last night. You know?" Sylviana had said to her mother. "But I thought it was because Steven was playing his games again. I thought it was just that."

"It could be. You don't know."

"Then all this." She wiped her face hard. "Eva's been sending him e-mails. Did you know?"

"How would I know that, Sylviana?"

"Why would she do that? She won't tell me what she's written."

"Maybe it's innocent. Maybe it's a good thing."

"I don't think so. And Steven's been doing the same thing. They've done something."

"You don't know that either. Papa says there's nothing on the news, even international. Maybe it is just technical or whatever it is they're doing out there. You said yourself, it's desert. Primitive."

"It's a war zone, Momma. He's always in a war zone."

"Even so," her mother began, but she didn't have any other words of comfort to offer.

Ice. Ice cubes. The prosecco bottles were dry. Major Wasserman lifted his arm over his head, squeezed the switch on the side of his watch, and focused on the green display. *1512 hours.* Didn't make any sense. His mouth was dry, the wine gone. He'd reached into the mini-fridge, worked an ice cube free, popped it into his mouth. Kissed his wife's shoulder. She'd detonated like a firecracker. The ice tray was empty by 0600. Those two hours were not *Yeah, I guess.* He swung his legs off the bunk, then swirled like a top and almost lost his lunch. *What lunch?* He rubbed his right ear to get the fizzing sound out. *1517.* He couldn't remember the video call. And he wasn't wearing his socks. Or a T-shirt. Or shorts. Pajama bottoms? Green. "Okay." He blew out the word with a "phew" at the end. He wasn't in his quarters. No desk. No laptop. "Okay." He wasn't in a tent or a cavern, no hole in the ground somewhere in the desert. He rubbed his hands over his face. *Need a shave.* He let what he couldn't see inform him. He could smell. *Yeah, that's canvas. Musty. Government-issue.* The other, stronger smell was him. Sweat. Dried. "Okay." He puffed out a breath, rubbed his forehead. *That's blood.* Quick assessment. Nothing to worry about. Last thing he remembered was . . . "Trombone."

"Where do you think you're going, Major?"

"Phone my wife. Where's Clee?"

"Right here, sir. We've done that," the lieutenant said, on her feet at attention. "No answer at that number, Major."

"She's with her brother's family today. How long?"

"How long what, sir?"

"How long have I been out?"

"Since yesterday. Took a while for the patrol to radio back. And the chopper—"

"What about the escort?" He stuffed his arms into his jacket, saw the damage, and shrugged it off. "Can't wear this when I talk to my family. Anyone hurt?"

"No, sir. They were on the deck as soon as you gave them the warning. Do you remember what happened?"

"Pretty much."

"Strange one, Major. I don't remember 'trombone' being on the alarm list, but it worked. No civilians hurt either." His second in command followed him to his quarters. "We've been silent since the attack, Major. Nothing in or out."

"Open up, Clee. People will want to talk to their folks today." He wiped his hand over his cheeks in front of the mirror, felt the bandage at the back of his head. The medic stood in the doorway. "Good job, Feltzer."

"Sir, you need to be checked out. X–rays and a regular medical."

"Later. You see a shirt anywhere around here I can wear? Have to meet my in-laws face-to-face right now. They're not going to be too happy."

"Why's that, sir?"

"Interrupting the football game. Least I can do is look less like a bum, right?"

While he waited for the screen to light up, he buttoned the shirt, tucked in the tails, ran a comb through his hair as far as the bandage, and rubbed his right ear. As soon as his laptop was up and online, notices flashed at him, filling the window. "Sylviana is not going to be happy," he laughed, double-clicking on the last one to open, and hit Yes. The first face he saw was a kid he didn't recognize and Eva's back as she ran from a room he'd never seen before.

"Hi."

"Hi." The boy turned his face away. "Grandma, Grandpa. Come quick, it's him."

"Who are you?"

"Josh. Eva's here somewhere. Where have you been?"

"Long story, Josh. Sylviana around?"

"Hello, Eric," Momma said, "We've been worried about you."

"Sorry about that, Mrs. Innocenti. Communications problem. Security. Nothing out of the ordinary. Sorry to interrupt the game. Sylviana around?"

"Hey, *paisano!* We thought you were lost out in the desert or something."

"Nothing like that, Mr. Innocenti. I'll explain later." The room filled with more kids and two more adults, all asking questions of one another, staring at him. He looked over their heads and watched Sylviana at the door of the room. "Come closer, baby." Everyone else within the range of the Webcam moved out. Josh gave up his chair and held it for his aunt, who sat down and dropped her head onto her arms with a sob. "Do I look that bad?" Eric murmured.

"Where have you been? Don't you ever do that to me again." She dragged her fingers over her eyes, unable to keep the tears and the grins from spoiling her composure.

"If I could promise that, I would."

"I know. I know. What happened?"

"On patrol. Routine. We were ambushed. It could have been worse, baby. A lot worse."

"I don't want to hear *that*, you know. We've been so worried, Eric. Eva said e-mails and the unit's Web page have been down since last night."

"Just a precaution, in case it's bigger than a local thing." He tapped on the Webcam casing. "Come on, let me look at you."

"I'm a mess."

"You look good to me, Sylviana. You always look good to me."

"How good?"

"No way, Innocenti. I'm not going there. Have you had your turkey?"

"No. No one felt like eating. Josh and Eva have been working on getting through to you since noon. Eva sent you an e-mail last night too. It bounced back."

"Is she there?"

"She was. I think she went outside."

"Bring her in, okay? I want to talk to her."

When his stepdaughter was persuaded to come into his view, her mother was scowling at her and grinding out whispered threats.

"Hi, Eva."

"It's my fault, I know."

"How do you figure that?" Just like her mother, she wasn't looking into the camera lens so he could read her eyes. "I was just going to say thanks."

"What for?"

"Eva, for heaven's sake, can't you be even the tiniest bit polite? After all this?" Sylviana asked.

"What for?" her stepfather echoed. "I'll tell you, Eva. If not for you, a lot of people would have gotten hurt yesterday. I was thinking about friends who stop talking, you know? And when it hit me what that was all about, I said it out loud, right there in the desert. My patrol thought I'd raised the alarm, so everyone took cover, and nobody got hurt."

"Wow."

"Yeah, wow. So, some friends are smarter than others."

"Yeah?" Eva glanced over her shoulder at her family and leaned closer to the screen, looking straight into his eyes.

"When things change, some friends take a while longer to get used to the difference. If it's worth anything, hang tight."

"Okay . . ." she said, with a question in her olive-eyed frown.

"About the rest, not going to happen. Is that clear?"

"Maybe."

Eric lifted his gaze to take in the rest of the family group. "I'll be there to visit you all a few days after Easter. I'll give you the dates when they've been firmed up. Okay, Sylviana?" When she nodded, he gave her a wink. "Gotta get some fuel. You know how it is with me and chow."

"I know, sweetheart. I'm still working on the meat locker."

"Good thing. We'll talk around Christmas. Okay with you?"

"Okay with me, Frosty."

Eva read the whole story of the ambush on the fan page, but neither her mother nor Enid had a chance once she had read the alarm call her stepfather had given. No way did she want her mother to know that she had asked that jerk, Major Eric Wasserman, anything about fourteen-year-old boys who were just too dumb to understand anything about how a seventh grader might feel about someone so nice. Keeping that a secret also allowed her to keep a few other secrets about how her dad was making a fool of himself and getting a lot of people mad at him when he commented on the fan page about jerks and pump-jockeys who couldn't keep their hands off other people's families.

She wanted to tell the other families whose sons and brothers hadn't been hurt because their CO had said "Trombone" that she didn't agree with her dad, but she wasn't ready to crash and burn that happy family dream. Instead, she sent that jerk, Major Wasserman, a message.

From: snarextrom	Sent: Fri 12/03 17:47
To: EDD	
Cc:	
Subject: Trombone	

It's two weeks to Christmas holidays. I've been hanging tight, like you said. Nothing happening. There's a school dance. Can I ask?

From: EDD Wasserman	Sent: Sat 12/04 05:38
To: snarextrom	
Cc:	
Subject: RE: Trombones	

If you don't ask, you won't know. Question is: are you ready to know?

Sylviana had no energy to put into a long battle with her ex-husband about harassment. She was having enough trouble keeping the girls happy and not letting her new husband know too much about how angry and combative they tended to be at the end of the weekends Steven had them. He cancelled their scheduled weekend for the tenth of December because the Municipal Mutual International's Christmas party was a conflict. He knew months before but cancelled four days short of the weekend, rescheduling for the seventeenth.

"How could you do this to me?" Eva demanded of her mother.

"Eva, what's wrong?"

"You must hate me. I can't believe you would tell Daddy it's okay. How could you?"

"Sweetie—"

"You've ruined everything. It's always the same. You think

you know everything but you don't. I wish— No, I don't. I'm going to live with Daddy. That's better than this. Anything. Is. Better. Than. This."

The door of Eva's bedroom slammed so hard in the frame that chips of paint fell off. Sylviana listened at the door, raised her hand but couldn't force herself to knock when she heard the gasping sobs. Instead, she started the Wednesday night supper routine, boiled the water for pasta, reheated the sauce from their Monday night meal, sliced sourdough bread and chopped green beans for the salad. When she called Enid and Eva from their rooms, she met pure hatred and puppy-eyed misery. "I can't do this."

"It's way too late for that, Mother." Eva grabbed her plate and stuffed her mouth full of penne. "Daddy will never let me stay home now. You've ruined my life."

"I'll talk to him. We'll work something out."

"Don't you get it? Daddy will never, ever let me go to the dance."

"What dance?"

Eva's mouth was overflowing with sauce. Her eyes were overflowing with tears, but she refused to look at her mother. Great inflamed blotches broke onto her cheeks. She neither chewed nor swallowed. She stared through the back window of the kitchen into the drizzling darkness.

"What do you want me to do, Eva?"

Through clenched teeth, her daughter said, "Eric knows."

Sylviana's eyes shot wide open. After a few seconds she looked at Enid, but the seven-year-old was as dumbstruck as her mother. "Eric knows what exactly?"

"Everything. He's smarter than you. He's smarter than Daddy." The shriek of self-condemnation that followed this declaration trailed behind the almost-teenage girl all the way back to her bedroom, where she filled the flat with wails and a tantrum of growls and flying objects.

"Gosh," Enid said.

"I'll say." Sylviana stirred her fork around the penne and mushroom sauce on her plate, spearing a few noodles and letting them drop off the tines. "I guess I need to talk to your father. And Eric."

"Yeah, I guess, Mommy."

The latter task was the more pleasant and definitely the priority. It was too early to make a video call, and she couldn't do that without Eva's help, anyway. She didn't even know which program she had to open to send him a notice that she was waiting on the other end of the link, half a world and too many time zones away. Enid sat between her knees, on the edge of the kitchen chair. Every time something in Eva's room hit the door or the wall, they cringed together. The *To* field filled itself as soon as she typed the first capital *E*. Sylviana rested her chin on Enid's head when they tabbed to the *Subject* line.

"What about 'Eva's School Dance,' Mommy? He'll know what you mean then."

"Okay. Go ahead, sweetie." She watched with embarrassed awe as her baby girl's little fingers whizzed over the keyboard. She gave her a hug. "You're pretty smart, you know."

"I know, Mommy. So are you. What do you want to ask Eric?"

"Tough one. How about 'What can you tell me about Eva's school dance?' No, wait. That sounds like I'm spying." *Be honest.* "Okay, don't listen, Enid, just type."

From: Sylviana   Sent: Wed 12/15 18:57
To: EDD
Cc:
Subject: Eva's School Dance

Steven cancelled last weekend, and tonight I told him he could have the girls this weekend instead. Eva is crying her eyes out because she had planned to go to a school dance on Friday—I didn't know anything about this—but she's told me that you do. Any suggestions on how I can fix this?

"That's good, Mommy. I think you're smart."

"You're the smart one, sweetie."

Sylviana picked up a few paint chips from the floor of the hallway on her way to Eva's room. Eva's tantrum had run through half a shelf of books and all the soft toys on her bed. It had run through the twelve-year-old and left her lying on her stomach with her head hanging off the side of the bed farthest from the door. "I've sent a message to Eric, but if you want to tell me about it, we'll get this straightened out with your father tonight."

"What did that jerk say?"

"*Eric* doesn't wake up until you've gone to bed. What does your stepfather know that I need to know to get your father to do what you want?"

"I was going to tell you tonight, but that's all changed. I can't go now."

"Of course you can go. If you want to go, Eva, you. Will. Go."

"You can't make Daddy do anything."

"I can try."

"Eric doesn't know much, and I don't want to tell you," Eva said. "I want to go to the dance."

"Okay. That's good enough for me. Don't call your stepfather a jerk. His name is Eric, and he doesn't deserve any disrespect from you." She *didn't* say, *Save that for your father.*

Five phone calls to Steven's answering machine came to nothing. On Friday afternoon Sylvia phoned his office. His secretary said her ex-husband was in a meeting and couldn't be contacted. "Then I'll leave a message." The secretary gave a verbal shrug, and Sylviana took a breath, exhaled, and said, "Please tell Mr. Langdon that Eva will not be going with him tonight but Enid will. I will bring Eva over on Saturday morning." The secretary repeated the message word for flat word as though she had been bored beyond endurance listening to her employer's ex-wife's voice. "It is very important that he gets this message before he leaves the office."

"What was your name again?"

Papa Innocenti arrived at the apartment on Hill Street at 1800 hours. Eva kissed her mother and waved good-bye to her little sister before she opened the door to put hand on the railing, taking no chances while she was wearing nylons and pumps. Grandma made her stop there to take a picture—to send to Eric. Although he had been offered the honor of driving his daughter to her first dance, Steven hadn't responded to any messages.

Momma Innocenti went into the apartment to have ice cream with the rest of "her girls" left at home on Friday night. Enid copied the picture of her sister from her grandmother's digital camera and attached it to *RE: Eva's School Dance* with a short message: *Thanks, EDD. Love, Enid.*

Along with that message and the attachment, Major Wasserman received notice from his wife's ex-husband that he was named as co-defendant in a suit for alienation of affection and sole custody of his children. For the first time in sixteen years, Eric laughed out loud at the tantrum underlying the abuse aimed at him. *Dead in the water and knows it.* He reread all the messages in the string titled *Eva's School Dance* and changed his desktop photo to the pretty, scared little girl about to meet a nice trombone player in the school gymnasium.

He sent a message back: *My pleasure, Enid. Your grandpa knows he has to stick around to the last dance, right?*

Sylviana replied: *Are you kidding, Frosty? He's going to hold her hand the whole time.*

Good. That's what I'd do. He knew Steven hadn't stepped up. *Gotta get on the job, baby. Nothing special today. Let me know how it goes at the dance.* He signed off and shut down, his focus in another time zone on a twelve-year-old in a pink dress and her first pair of nylons. *If that jerk—* Of course, he himself had once been *that jerk,* maybe not at fourteen, but not so long afterward. Well, not anymore. The combat support unit CO straightened his shoulders, took himself off the rack, and did his job.

Enid waited at the living room window, dancing from one foot to the other, then ran to the bathroom and ran back. Every car that slowed to turn the corner at the top of the hill received her scrutiny until it rolled past the parking space in front of the apartment. At seven, she returned to the kitchen, where her mother and grandmother were preparing a meal for themselves. "Did he get your message, Mommy?"

"I talked to his secretary. She promised, Enid. Maybe the meeting ran late."

"May I have a cookie?"

"Wait for a while, just in case."

The seven-year-old wandered down the long hallway, opened her suitcase, and checked that she had packed her favorite books. Satisfied she was ready, she stood at the window for another fifteen minutes until a car drifted on the slant into the parking space and her father left it there, with the lights on.

"He's here, Mommy."

Sylviana's spine slumped in protest, but she got up from the table and followed Enid to the door. She checked his profile for a moment before she opened the door, detecting all the signs that meant another Friday night knock-down drag-out.

"Yeah, I know, I'm late" was his only greeting.

"I didn't say anything."

"You don't have to. Are they ready?" Enid was standing beside her mother with her pink and lavender bag hanging from her hand.

"Of course she is. Have a good weekend, sweetie."

"What a minute. Where's Eva?"

"Steven, I've left you messages since Wednesday evening and again today with your secretary."

"Where is she? I'm not going without her—you know that."

"She won't be back for hours."

"What? You rearranged *my* time with my children and didn't tell me?"

"I left you several messages."

"But you didn't make sure I knew, did you? What if I had something special planned? What if I was going to take them to Disneyland this weekend?"

"Are you, Daddy?"

"Not now, Enid. Not since your mother messed up. Again."

Sylviana clenched her fingers but let the moment of murder pass while she took a breath and thought.

"Nothing to say, Sylviana? How do you get away with being so stupid and still hold down a job? I've let you off the hook every time. Every time. This is it."

"Eva had something she wanted to do tonight. I left six messages, all with the same information. I will bring Eva to your house tomorrow morning. Enid is coming with you now."

"Where is Eva?"

"She went to a school dance."

"And you didn't think that was important enough for me to know?"

"Eric knew," Enid said. "He knew before anyone."

"What? What? How could you do this to me? You let that scumbag make decisions for my daughter and don't tell me anything?"

"I told you. I left messages on your home phone and your cell and with your secretary. It's not my business to make sure you take responsibility for listening to your messages, Steven. What if I had to tell you that something had happened? Something terrible?"

"Lame excuse, Sylviana. You'd have made sure I knew. You'd have come to the house or my office. But no, just my daughter's first dance, and you let that second-rate rookie hick make decisions about my children. The judge is going to love this."

"Eric is—"

"I don't want to hear anything about that jerk. You hear me? Nothing." He turned and was down the front steps before Sylviana knew what he was doing.

"Steven, what about Enid? She's been waiting for you."

"Forget it. See you in court, Sylviana."

"Daddy!" But the little girl's cry was drowned out by the roar of his revved engine and the scream of tires as he whipped back into the street and shot down to the corner.

"Sweetie, I'm so sorry. I'm so sorry."

Enid reached out and pushed the door closed. "Now I'll be home when Eva gets back from the dance."

Chapter Seventeen

The woman in the seat next to him during the leg of his flight from Paris was on her feet again the moment the captain announced the imminent landing at SFO. The only way for her to get by him and his long legs was for Eric to stand in the aisle, blocking the cabin crew's carts as they collected the remainders of the meal. The woman apologized, he said, "No problem," and he sat down for the time she was in the restroom. When she returned, her makeup was refreshed, and she had doused herself with perfume. The man next to the window pushed into the aisle before she sat down and came back two minutes later with specks of toothpaste at the corners of his mouth. The American Army major rubbed the back of his head, still conscious of the ridge of flesh sewn together over the grenade injury, dropped his body into the seat, and pulled his legs in from the aisle when the steward reminded him to.

Thirty minutes later Eric Wasserman was directed to the immigration line designated for military personnel, welcomed home by J. Hernandez, and walked through customs, his duffle bag on his back. He caught the first shuttle into the city and sat at the back with the bag wedged between his knees—everything he owned and a few things he'd brought for the girls. Nothing for Sylviana except himself. While he watched the sun dip behind San Bruno Mountain, he wondered if that was a mistake. *Too late, Wasserman. You're history.*

Hill Street was the last stop on the shuttle's route through town, and he moved up toward the driver when the only other traveler alighted on Webster and Vallejo. The driver looked at him and smiled. "Home on leave, soldier?"

"That's right."

"Someone waitin' for you?"

"Wife and daughters."

"Golden." After a few sharp corners and steep climbs, the shuttle pulled up in front of the set of apartments he recognized from the photo of Eva on her first date. Even if he'd been her biological father, he couldn't have felt any more proud, or terrified, when that photo appeared in his e-mail. "Here you are, soldier. Looks like they've pulled out all the stops to welcome you home."

"Looks that way," he said, as he dragged the bag from the seat and pressed a few bills into the driver's open palm.

"Have a good one. And thanks." The driver touched his forehead in a casual salute and drove up to the corner, tooting his horn.

Eric turned to face the front of the building, shaking his head at the balloons and crepe-paper streamers taped to the banister and window casements. In the top flat, a couple peered down at him, and he touched his beret to acknowledge their wave before he took the few steps to the stairs leading up to the front door and the banner that read: *Welcome home, Eric.* He read the names over the doorbell and allowed himself a quick smile. He didn't have to see Eva's face to know something was wrong, but when she refused to open the door, he choked on the sniper shot and forced his hand to open from the fist that wanted to smash through the glass panel.

"Mom, you have to come to the door. Now." Eva darted out of sight, into the room he knew would be the kitchen. "There's a delivery guy at the door."

"Eva, don't interrupt when I'm talking to your mother."

"Mom, you have to sign something. You gotta go." She dragged on her mother's arm until they were in the hallway, then pushed her forward and dragged Enid back with her to the kitchen.

The door was closed and the chain in place. All she saw was a dark shape. Sylviana opened the door a crack until she saw Eric's bowed head. The chain tightened, snagged, but when she ripped it from its holder, she was in his arms and kissing him. He scooped her up and carried her into the hallway, still locked in the kiss he'd been waiting 184 days to feel again.

"I'm so glad you're here," she said against his mouth, locking her arms around his neck.

This time Eric felt the impact before the ground under his feet had a chance to rock him.

"You were never any good at anticipating enemy action, Wasserboy." Steven Langdon stood in the doorway of Sylviana's kitchen.

"You're right, Steve. Could be because I had trouble recognizing who my friends were." He lowered his wife's legs, and, when her feet touched the floor, he loosened his arm from around her waist, taking her hand, offering the other to her ex-husband.

Steven sneered at the hand held out to him and put his arms around his daughters' shoulders. "Guess I'll take the girls with me tonight. Give you two some privacy to get down to business."

"Steven!"

"Cut the pretense, Syl. We all know what you see in this guy. Get your coats, girls."

"I can't, Daddy," Enid said. "Mommy's taking me to school early for my drama group."

"Don't worry, I'll get you there."

"I've got too much homework, Daddy."

"Eva, just bring your books."

"But I need the computer. All my work's on it. Enid and I can come tomorrow night, Daddy."

"Forget it. I was just trying to give your mother some time to be alone with her new boyfriend, but you're both too selfish."

"Hold on, Steve. I'm the one who's upset their routine. Eva and Enid have good reasons for wanting to be home on a school night. If you've got a problem with me being here, I'm ready to hear it, but leave the girls out of it."

"Oh, yeah. The diplomat. Not good enough you steal my wife and break up my family—now you want to drive a wedge between me and my girls. I'll tell you what you are, Wasserboy."

"Any chance of a coffee, baby?" Eric murmured against Sylviana's temple.

"Sure, Frosty. Americano okay?"

"Anything you have to offer," he said with a grin.

"You think you can order my wife around? You want to know what we were doing five minutes ago? Huh? I told you what to expect from her—"

"Eva, will you and Enid help your mom with that coffee?"

"I'll help," Enid said, tugging on Eva's hand. Eva glanced at her father.

"You can't tell my daughters what to do," Steven hissed, lurching forward. "Eva, stay where you are. This jerk is nothing. He has no right to bully you."

"Daddy, I have homework. In the kitchen." She followed her younger sister.

"You scumbag."

"Come on, Steve. I've been their stepdad for six months. You can't have thought nothing would change. What are you doing here, anyway?" It was 1830. A week night. No reason for Langdon to be at the flat. He had alternate weekends, no school nights. Eric took off his beret and folded it into his side pocket.

"This is *my* family, *my* home."

"Your daughters but not your home. Sylviana is my wife. Eva and Enid are my stepchildren. Go home. It's not even your weekend."

"You're keeping track? What are you, some kind of control-freak?"

"You blindsided me once. That's not going to happen again. Anything you say or do to hurt me or Sylviana is bound to blow up in your face."

"You can't throw me out."

"I'm not lifting a finger. You're going to leave before you show your daughters what a fool you are." As he walked past Steven Langdon, he unbuttoned his fatigue jacket and found an apron on the back of the door. He knew the kitchen, had seen it from every angle over the months since Eva's school dance.

"If you want dinner, you'll have to be on KP for a while," Sylviana said, avoiding her ex-husband's glare as she tied the apron behind Eric's back, surrendering to the urge to lean against him.

"What's first, babe?"

"Potatoes."

Before he reached the sink, Steven rolled up his sleeves. "Where's this poor guy's coffee, Sylvi? I thought that's what he told you to do. Not much of a servant, are you?"

Eva and Enid stood on the other side of the kitchen, silhouetted by the big window. Sylviana counted, held back her fury, keeping quiet, being still.

"The cups are in the top cabinet, Dad," Eva said. "Eric knows where they are."

Taking the cue, her stepfather pulled the cabinet open, offering his once best friend a mug. "Sylviana's Americano is legendary, Steve. Have some."

"You hick. You think I don't know how she makes coffee? Or anything else she likes? You think because you've—"

"I made *this* pot, Eric," Enid bragged, climbing onto the stool beside him.

"Well, let's just see how much you've learned," Eric said, taking a swallow and savoring the taste. "You've got competition, baby."

"You think you can come in here and bust up my family with your hokey, small-town clichés? You are dead wrong, you stupid hick."

"Go home, Steven." Sylviana stepped closer to Eric, and Enid stared at her father. For a while, Eva poured her attention into the computer screen, covering her ears.

"I'm not leaving my kids here with this scumbag. What kind of father do you think I am? Who knows what this dumb cluck will do? Did you think I'd just walk away and let you have my kids, jerk?"

Eva's scream pierced through the kitchen like a Fury as she flew from her chair. "Why are you doing this to me? I have homework and you. Are. Ruining. It."

"Eva, darling. It's not me. I'm doing all I can to protect you."

"No. You. Are. Not. You're mad at Mom. You're mad at us. I can't stand it. I hate you all." Her body hit the kitchen's swinging door so hard, it hit the wall and whipped back into Steven's face.

"You see what you've done, Syl? You've turned my own daughter against me. I'll see you in court. Both of you." When he slammed the front door, the building shook, and the three people remaining in the kitchen were silent.

Enid released her grip on her stepfather's hand, dropping onto the stool seat again. "Eva was sure mad at Daddy." She picked up the potato peeler and worked a bit of peel free. "She's mad at him all the time."

"Is she, sweetie?"

Enid nodded and finished the potato Eric had started.

"I'll talk to her," Sylvania said.

The kitchen door whispered behind her for a few moments. Eric relieved Enid of KP, asking her to top up his coffee.

"Daddy's like this all the time. He doesn't like you."

"Doesn't surprise me, Enid."

"I do. I like you, Eric."

"Thanks. I like you too. And your sister."

"Eva's just scared."

"Of what?"

"That you and Mommy will have another baby, and you won't want us anymore."

"Are you worried about that, Enid?"

"Yeah, I guess."

Eric couldn't repress his smile.

"Grandma and Grandpa love us, but they're too old."

"I don't think they'd agree with you there, but you've got nothing to worry about. Are we done here?"

Enid nodded, dropping the last potato into the pot. "Time for a powwow, Enid." And he led the little girl from the room.

Sylviana stood at the door of Eva's room, knocking once in a while, asking to be allowed to enter.

Eric glanced at Enid. "Mind if I speak to her, baby?"

"She's not talking to me, so best of luck."

Eric meditated for a moment, took a breath, and grinned at Enid. "All right?"

"Okay."

"Eva, I'd like to tell you a story if you'll hear me out. A long story. May I come in?"

"I still have homework to do."

"Five minutes. Ten, tops." Eric wrapped his big hand around the doorknob and pushed the door open so that the light from the hallway made a bright patch across the floor, illuminating the twelve-year-old's legs. Enid went to her mother. Eric stepped into the oblong of light, his tall frame silhouetted so that Eva couldn't see his expression if she had looked in his direction. "When I first met your mom, the first time I set eyes on her, I was in love. Like a ton of bricks had fallen on me. Couldn't eat. Couldn't sleep. Couldn't think. One day, your dad told me he felt the same and was going to marry her. Your dad saved my life once on a battlefield. He was my best friend, and for years I told myself I'd done the right thing when I walked away—the right thing for your dad and your mom—but, for me, it was the biggest mistake of my life and the dumbest thing I'd ever done.

"I still loved your mom, and that didn't change. Your dad told me what a great life he had with her, and I knew it could have been my life. After a while, I couldn't take it, so I stopped listening, and I never accepted any of his invitations to visit because I was afraid your mom would find out how much I loved her. I couldn't do that to your dad. So I made myself disappear. I didn't want to know anything about you or Enid or your mom, but your dad kept me in the loop. Just about the time your parents separated, I lost touch completely and forgot as much as I could, but your mom found me. So here I am. A dumb hick, still mad crazy in love with your mom and happy about the chance to be a friend to you and your sister.

"I used to think, if I'd stuck around, your mom and I would have been the happy couple with two kids—beautiful, smart kids—but they wouldn't have been you and Enid. If your mom and I ever do have kids, I know you two will be great sisters to them. I'm not asking you to choose between me and your dad. I can't ever be a replacement, but I'm here, and I love you all. Call me whatever you want, I'll still be that guy married to your mom."

Eva hadn't moved or even lifted her head. Eric slid his hands into the pockets of his desert fatigues and stared at the floor.

"Is dinner ready?"

"It'll be ready faster if you pitch in."

"I don't peel potatoes." Eva set her feet on the floor. When she walked past him, she caught Enid's hand and dragged her to the kitchen.

"That was good, Frosty. You did real good," Sylviana said in admiration.

"It's what I'd want to hear."

Sylviana stopped in the hallway to stare at him. "I was mad crazy for you too, you know. How come you didn't know that?"

"I told you I wasn't too smart."

"You've wised up a bit since then. Maybe you were right, Eric. Maybe we were meant for each other but not then."

Mrs. Sylviana Langdon
81 Hill Street
San Francisco

April 6

Dear Mrs. Langdon:

Pursuant to a request from our client, Mr. Steven Langdon, we are writing to inform you of our client's request that the arrangements for the shared custody of the minor children, Eva Langdon and Enid Langdon, be adjusted to a more equitable schedule.

Our client has suggested an alternating two-week period in which each of you will have sole care of and responsibility for the above-named children. This arrangement will benefit the children by giving them an equal amount of time with their father, which, as you must realize, is important for children of their age.

We look forward to your positive response to this proposal through your legal representative.

Sylviana left the remainder of the letter unread, sliding it across the table while she drank her coffee. "You know, we've been married six months and three days. He hasn't let up even one week."

"He doesn't like to lose," Eric said, reading through the letter and the cover letter from Sylviana's lawyer. "I'm no lawyer, but this sounds like bad news for the girls."

"Isn't there something in international law we could use?" After a moment, she said, "This is totally bogus, Eric. As soon as he gets a judge to agree, he'll beg off. He'll disrupt their lives, school activities, mess with their heads and their health, and go back to every other weekends, when he feels like it. Then he'll say I'm making it difficult, and they'll be in the middle of a tug-of-war, no love involved. He doesn't want them. He just wants to mess me up and make me the bad guy."

"I think Eva and Enid are smart enough to know the game."

"He's hurting them, not me. I know what he's like. They still believe—"

Eric reached across the table and clasped her fingers. "What do you want me to do, Sylviana, now that I'm here?"

"What I really want, I wouldn't ask you to do, although you could probably make it look like an assassination by a known terrorist. Any other suggestions?"

"Anything we do will drag the girls into another mess. We need a family conference."

"With Steve?"

"He's not part of *my* family." Half his leave was gone, eroded away by the incendiaries Steve Langdon kept hurling at them. Eric figured the former war hero was locked down—no negotiation, no diplomacy, no making him see he was losing. The Army major wondered if Steve had ever wanted what he was throwing away in his effort to outgun the people closest to him. *It's all about being top dog.* A moment later he realized who, in Steve Langdon's book, was the dog to bring down. That afternoon, he met Enid at the school gate, and they waited for Eva at the bus stop.

Eva stood at the back door of the bus, stepped onto the sidewalk, and turned in the other direction, waving good-bye to Trombone.

"Where are you going, Evie?" Enid trotted alongside.

"Why are you here? It's so embarrassing. I'm not a baby, you know."

"That pack looks heavy, even for a big girl." Eric lifted it off her back and slung one strap over his shoulder, already carrying Enid's pink fake-fur bunny backpack.

"You're just trying to make me like you better than my dad. I have a dad. I don't need you." She walked as fast as she could toward the corner, but, before she slammed the door of the flat, she growled, "All my friends think you're special. My. Stepdad. But you're just the jerk who married my mom."

Enid clasped his long fingers. "She already does, you know, like you better than Daddy. That makes it real hard."

"I know, Enid. That's why I wanted to talk to the both of you."

"Talk to me, Double-D. I can make Evie listen."

Eric put the backpacks on the porch and sat down on the steps. Enid sat on the wall beside him. "I know you're having a tough time, and I don't want to make it any tougher. Your dad is mad at me, and he's hurting you and your mom to get at me."

"Because Mommy loves you."

"Something like that."

"Mommy loves you more than Daddy."

"How do you feel about that?"

"Kinda sad. And sorry. It's nicer to have parents who love each other. Do you love us, Double-D.?"

"I do."

"Then, it's okay. Can we have ice cream before Mommy gets home?"

"No, miss. Your mother would take my head off."

"That's what I figured."

"Why'd you ask, Enid?"

"Always worth a try," she giggled, all that fairy dust and sparkle shining in her eyes.

The same insignia as his regiment tie and the badge on his beret was on the cover of the brown leather album Eric had left on the kitchen counter. Eva had emerged from her room, and the kitchen was empty, but the Chianti was ready for her mother's return from work. She went straight to the fridge and poured a glass of juice. The album was open to a page with a photograph of a baby in a hospital cradle. Her name and date of birth were written under the picture. Eva flipped through the pages like a wind storm and shoved the album away, spilling the juice over the counter. She snatched the glass, grabbing for a towel, and mopped up the juice before it ran over onto the floor. None of the liquid had touched the album, but she was more careful when she closed the cover. Eva took the album with her to the living room, where her mother's new husband was helping Enid with her homework.

"What is this? Where'd you get this?"

"Your dad sent those to me over the years. Have you looked at them?"

"Yeah. So what?"

"So I've watched you and Enid grow up—until about three years ago. Now I know why he sent them, but what's important is that I've known enough about you to care what happens to you since you were babies. I'm not trying to take over from your father, Eva. I can never do that, and I'd never expect you to let me. But you can depend on me to be as good a stepdad as I can."

"I don't want a stepdad."

"I'm sorry, Eva."

"I want a real dad. Like all my friends have. They're sorry for me. I hate it. Their dads come to school. Their dads show up when it counts. Their dads are always, always there when they need them. I. Want. That."

"Eva."

She turned her back on him, shoving the album onto the arm of the sofa.

"Eva, I promise, to the best of my ability, I will do anything within my power to be as close to a real dad to you and Enid as I can."

"You won't be here either."

"I'll make sure you know I want to be."

"Prove it." She jerked her head up with a sniff and stalked from the room. Enid dragged the album into her lap and peeked under the cover. Eric opened the front and found the first page with her baby picture on it.

When Sylviana came through the door, Eric met her in the hallway. *Fatigues, T-shirt, and socks.* When she'd left him to catch her bus, he had still been in bed, flat on his back, just a corner of the sheet over him for modesty and all that male energy in his eyes, watching her dress. "I could get used to this," she said as she surrendered to his hands on her hips and let him take over the coming-home-from-work routine so all she had to do was loosen her grip on her bag, unbutton her jacket, and be led into the kitchen. "I'm already used to this," she sighed and wished she could take it back the second she saw the doubt flicker in his eyes. "I'm so happy, Eric."

"Stay there, baby," he said, taking her back into his arms, lifting her to sit on the counter, wedging his hips between her knees. "Good day?" She nodded, shrugged, filling her senses with his sparkle. "I could get used to this, waiting for you to get home just so I can take care of you."

"How was your day, Eric?"

"Long. Thinking about you."

"Boring, huh?"

"Not in my head, Sylviana." He slid his hands around her waist and tugged her closer.

"I could definitely get used to this," Sylviana whispered when his mouth covered hers.

"Oh, yuck. Is that all you guys ever do or think about?"

"Eva, you should knock." Sylviana pulled her skirt down. Eric grinned.

"This is the kitchen, Mom. I have homework."

"Should we go to our room?" Eric asked, a laugh beneath his contrition.

"That's worse. I'm almost thirteen, remember. I know all about that stuff. Besides, you promised to help me with my project."

"Did I?" He gazed into Sylviana's eyes. "Okay, but first I. Want. To. Kiss. Your. Mom."

"Five minutes. That's all."

"Yes, miss," he agreed with a lazy salute, and he led Sylviana to their bedroom.

"What's going on between you two? She's almost tolerant."

"We had a slam-dunk talk. If I hold up my end of the deal, she'll let me stay."

"What deal? You don't have to take that from her, Eric. She's a kid."

He was already peeling away her layers of silk and lace, settling his agitation and finding his way. Somewhere in the flat, the phone rang, and the neighbor above came home from work.

Sylviana closed her arms around her husband's neck, getting used to another home-from-work routine.

At Eva's insistence, Eric was in his dress uniform, all metals and insignia in place, hat square on his head, when the taxi arrived to take them to the band's Spring Concert. To her friends, he was introduced as R.D. Sylviana thought it was short for Eric Daniel David because Enid called him Double-D. Eric understood and acted in accordance with his newly won title.

When the concert came to an end, Papa Innocenti offered to take them all for an ice cream in his rattling sedan.

"Best gelato in town, Eric," Papa assured him as they tumbled out of the car into the parking lot. "Don't ever think you can cheat these girls by taking them anyplace newfangled."

"No, sir."

"Daddy did once," Eva told her stepdad, "but after that, he let Grandpa have it his way."

In the parlor, Papa sent the women to a booth, then led his son-in-law to the counter and the minefield of flavors waiting to test his powers of mediation and deployment. "You won't go wrong with chocolate, but they're fickle as all get-out, my boy. Think it through."

The four women heard Eric's short laugh and smiled at one another, watching him prepare to do battle with the wall menu. Every once in a while Papa winked at them but gave nothing away. The two men returned to the table empty-handed to frowns that lifted into a collective grin when the ice cream jockey brought a rack of waffle cones and an assortment of tubs. Six flavors. All favorites.

Eva said, "Gosh."

Eric started to scoop, youngest first.

"I thought this is where you'd be," Steven said, scraping a chair up to the end of the table. "Initiation rite, eh, Pop?"

"Nothing changes, Steven. How are you?"

"Good as can be expected. Great concert, Eva. Sorry I was late."

"S'okay, Dad. You didn't miss much." Eva accepted the cone of mint chocolate chip and mocha.

"They've swallowed you whole, eh, Er?"

"Looks that way. What can we do for you?"

"I'm here just like the rest of the clan. Family ritual. Every school event, guaranteed to find the Innocentis right here after."

"No issues with that for me," Eric said, finishing Sylviana's cone with a scoop of spumoni on top of pistachio. He made eye contact with his mother-in-law and dug into the mocha and caramel. When it came to Papa, he went for vanilla. "The rest is mine."

"No way," came a chorus of female voices, followed by hands laying claim to half-empty tubs.

"Didn't take you long to know the score in this group. Easy pickings for a boondocks hick like you."

Papa shifted in his seat, but Eric filled the last waffle cone with the dregs and met his wife's eyes when he swept his tongue around the lip.

"Give Syl a break, jerk. This is a family joint—save it for the alley."

Papa shifted again. Sylviana held her breath, and her mother fussed with napkins around the girls' chins. Eric took a bite of the half scoop of pistachio, watching Sylviana, deciphering what he had to do from the distress in her pretty eyes.

"Is that what it is, buddy? You like that kind of thing? You'll sure get plenty of that, but don't think you've got an exclusive," Steven goaded.

"Like you said, Steve, this is a family place. Take it outside."

"You're on, Wasserboy, you two-faced sniper." His chair thumped the floor as he slammed the flat of his hand onto Eric's chest. "Outside, pump-jockey."

"Finish this for me, baby."

"Daddy, don't."

"Hey. None of that in here." The ice cream jockey waved his hands over the counter.

Before Eric followed his ex-Army buddy to the parking lot, he took off his tie and was rolling up his sleeves as he walked into the fog, ducking when Steve swung at him.

"You think you can come back after all this time and take what's mine?"

"I don't want to hurt you, Langdon."

"You? Hurt me? You don't have it in you, Wasserboy. You never did. One big duck-and-dive rookie. Never taken a bullet for a buddy, have you?"

Out of the corner of his eye, Eric saw the girls pressing their hands to the plate-glass window. "I don't want this, Steve. Neither do you."

Langdon taunted him with another swing. "That's you all over, Wasserboy. Back off."

"Not this time, Langdon." Eric dove, caught the insurance company vice president around the waist, and slammed him against the wall.

"Call the police, Papa," Momma screeched.

"You want me to do that, Mr. Innocenti?" the jockey called.

"One time, Steve, one time, I let you win."

"*Let* me win? You never had a chance. I did you a favor, squadie jerk. She was way out of your league, and she'll soon get tired of all your hokey whining." Langdon swung again, catching Eric in the side.

The soldier hissed, grabbed his opponent's arm, and twisted him around to face the wall, holding his jaw against the pink concrete. "You knew how I felt about Sylviana."

"Yeah. Moon-dog, puppy-love stuff right out of the comic pages. Laughed our heads off when you ran, tail between your legs."

"You knew, and you lied to me." His voice was a ragged hiss as he strained to hold back his rage and keep Steve Langdon pinned to the ice cream parlor wall.

"You made it easy, dumb cluck. You wouldn't have had a clue how to handle a woman like her. I did you a favor."

"You lied to me. You knew I loved her, and you lied. Why? You had no reason. You weren't interested—not until you knew how I felt."

"Get off me, Wasserboy."

"I want to know why you did that. What had I ever done to you that you'd want to ambush me like that?"

"You really want to know? Let me go, and I'll tell you."

Eric stepped back, releasing his grip a muscle at a time. Langdon turned around, rubbed the side of his jaw, and grinned at his two little girls. "Just like now, Er. You make it easy. Sure. I knew you had it bad for Sylvi. Just like all the rest of the jokers. But none of you had the guts to take me on. One puff, and you were gone."

"I thought you loved her."

"What's not to love? Looks good walking into a room on your arm. Not bright enough to get in the way."

"Get out of here, Steve."

"I'm not going anywhere. You're the runner, pump-jockey."

"Not now. I should have knocked you out of the ball park then."

"You don't have that kind of backbone, Wasserboy. Not then. Not now."

The first blow sent Steve Langdon back against the wall. "That's for Sylviana." The second blow doubled Langdon over. "That's for lying to me." Eric shook his fingers, then flexed his fist. "Come around again, and I'll put you in the hospital."

"I'm going to sue you right back to rookie. Dishonorable discharge. Stripped down and spit out. Kiss your pension goodbye, rookie. Sylviana won't give you the time of day when you're on the street, begging like the rest of the losers."

"Game over, Langdon. You lose."

Eric kept his head down when he walked back into the ice cream parlor. He figured real dads didn't punch out little girls' fathers. He figured he'd lost the title he'd held so briefly the moment he let Steve Langdon make him forget his training. He figured he was out of that job before he'd even finished the first event.

The girls were silent and wide-eyed on the journey home. Once there, Sylviana patted a damp cloth on his knuckles. Papa made a pot of coffee while Momma got the girls ready for bed.

"I'm sorry, baby."

"He had it coming," she murmured, but she was thinking about the lawyers' fees and claims for damages.

"I couldn't walk away."

"I know."

"Not again. I'm not backing off, Sylviana. Never again."

"I came to say good night, Double-D." Enid bounced into the kitchen in her bunny slippers.

"No, you didn't. I did." Eva stood in front of him. Eric lifted his eyes to meet hers. "Thanks for the ice cream."

"You're welcome, Eva. I'm sorry about tonight. I shouldn't have hit your dad."

"That's okay, Eric. He asked for it."

Eric. He covered his eyes and dropped his head.

"Real dads go crazy sometimes."

Major Wasserman watched his stepdaughter walk out of the kitchen hand in hand with her younger sister.

"Are you sure you're all right, Frosty?" Sylviana ducked her head to look up into his glistening blue eyes, surprised to see that magic-place, world-of-wonder smile jump out of his soul.

"Nothing a meat locker of ice won't fix, ma'am."